"Violent, c

"Yet it is a tale power of hope. *L* fight to expel evil — white, black and red — battle hatred with faith and truth. This is an exciting book!"

The Sunday Advance (Elizabeth City, NC)

"Levin makes a place for God in modern fiction without sacrificing action, suspense or believability."

"In *Devil's Gut,* he has brought back the hero, and her name is Kate, Charity, Lucy. His women erase the damsel in distress stereotypes and infuse the novel with strength, born of faith and nurtured through love and hardship. This book teaches you more about good and evil than you could learn from going to church for a month of Sundays."

Herald Journal (Spartanburg, SC)
A New York Times Company

"A fantastic story!"

"I read it straight through one evening, even missing one of my favorite basketball teams on TV. One does not forget its impact on putting the book down, and I kept thinking over and over again — what an absolutely spellbinding movie this story would make."

Dr. Wendell Hawley, Senior Vice President
Tyndale House Publishers

You've heard from the reviewers.
Now turn the page to hear
what *readers* have to say. . . .

DEVIL'S GUT

A NOVEL OF GOOD & EVIL

Ron Levin

The characters and events in this book are fictitious. Any similarity to real persons, living or dead, is purely coincidental and not intended by the author.

Devil's Gut

Library of Congress Catalog Card Number 95-095337

First Printing: March 1996

Published by My Father's Business, Inc.
(A 501 (c) (3) Registered Ministry
4303 Old Greenville Highway
Liberty, SC 29657
864-646-6425

PRINTED IN THE UNITED STATES OF AMERICA
Faith Printing, Taylors, SC 29687

ISBN 0-9640720-1-7

For my loving and faithful daughter,
Gretchen, who always loved for
Daddy to tell her a good story.

The author also wishes to acknowledge and
thank the faithful remnant who,
with their prayers, support and love,
helped to make the writing of this book possible.
May God bless you all. . . .

To my nephew, Robin,
with love,

Row

Official Commemorative Marker of the North Carolina Historical Society Erected May 12, 1928

Two miles north of this spot in May of 1863, the Yankee gunboat, *Dauntless*, with a company of militia on board, sailed up the Roanoke River, attacked and sank a barge laden with molasses destined for the Confederate soldiers. The gunboat then proceeded to bombard the town of Williston, at which time a small contingent of Confederate troops under the command of Colonel James Josiah Reardon returned fire to protect the citizenry. The ensuing battle was fierce and bloody, but through their remarkable valor, the Confederate soldiers forced the Yankee gunboat to retreat downriver, thus sparing the town. In honor of their gallantry and to honor those who made the supreme sacrifice, at war's end, the city fathers voted to change the name of the town to Sweetwater.

Foreword

Summer comes to Sweetwater not as a hot season but a harsh sentence pronounced upon the people. A sledgehammer pounding field hands into the land like fence posts. By August, the Roanoke river, in a final act of surrender to summer, grows sullen and dark. Where it meets the swamp, the fingers of water embrace the wilderness, and their clasp forms an impenetrable green tangle of woodbine, honeysuckle, poison ivy and crossvine. Here under towering gum, juniper and cypress roam black bear, some 500 pounds and faster on their feet than a man wants to think about. Come autumn, wildcats mate with bloodcurdling shrieks that sound like a child's screams when waking from a nightmare.

In the river's depths swim gar as big around as a man's leg. Water snakes skim the surface and will attack a man for no apparent reason and bite until they are exhausted. Hawks patrol the skies while great herons dip and wheel, spire and steeple against the relentless sun. Whitetail, grey fox, possum and coon abound, sharing their home with cottonmouth, copperhead and rattlesnake. Some even swear cold sober they once heard the bellow of a bull gator after sundown, but no one had ever seen it, or if he had, come back to tell about it.

The first loggers who came to eastern North Carolina in search of rich timberlands left the main body of the river and explored a tributary called Dark Creek in Martin County. It snaked its way up and back in a labyrinth of vine-choked channels and cutbacks leading them to the remote heart of a great wilderness swamp. They called it as they found it.

Devil's Gut.

These were hard men. Splintery, like rough sawn lumber. They worked and fought and drank and cursed the heat, the yellow flies and mosquitoes and ultimately, each other. Over time, their numbers dwindled through malaria, quicksand, snake bite and something else called swamp fever that made them feel as though something in the Gut were drawing their very lives out of them, breath by breath.

Every so often, a hunter would go into the Gut and not come home by dark, and his family would report him missing. The townspeople would try to get up a search party, but suddenly men discovered they had a lot of things to do more important than to go looking for some fool who more'n likely got drunk and lost his way in the Gut.

After everyone knew he would not be coming back, the men would cluster in front of little stores stooped and bent on broken bricks, and sitting there on drink crates and busted cane chairs, chewing and smoking in the dusk, the whine of mosquitoes in their ears, they would turn and say to one another, *God only knows what happened to him.*

Then as dusk turned to dark and the sky gave up a crop of stars, something foul would creep out of the Gut, steal across the rows of freshly plowed earth, enter their presence and suck the spit plumb out of them, leaving their mouths filled with sand. The men would clasp the faded, worn knees of their overalls and stare down at their dirt-daubed shoes, tasting fear like barbed wire on their tongue as the old words came churning up again from somewhere deep within . . .

God only knows. . . .

1

12:22 AM, Wednesday, August 1, 1945 . . .

Randall Chestnut hadn't been on the ward more than five minutes when he found Miz Bertie. Her usual spotless, starched white uniform was splattered with blood, her body lying there all twisted around like a wet towel wrung out hard. Her eyes stared up at the ceiling, and Randall didn't waste time trying to get a pulse—that woman's heart would never hit another lick. The more he looked at her, the more he felt like the chicken-fried steak he'd had for dinner was going to come back up. He squeezed his eyes shut and clenched his jaws until his stomach quit churning.

Randall had to admit there was no love lost between him and Miz Bertie. In fact, hardly a day went by when he didn't wish she might break a leg or get sick—anything to keep her out of work and give him a break. But not that woman. She hadn't missed a shift since the day he'd come to work at Dorothea Dix, next month would be two years. He remembered because it was the same time his baby brother had been killed in the Pacific on one of those islands whose name he never could get right. Randall had also tried to enlist right after Pearl Harbor but was turned down because of his hearing. When he was in the third grade, somebody had tossed a firecracker at him that had exploded about a foot from his left ear. Anyway, with Germany having surrendered back in May, the papers were saying it wouldn't be long before we'd have to invade Japan to finish them off. Course, the way Randall saw life, everybody had to fight somebody, and with him it was Miz Bertie—up until now.

From the day he'd come on the ward, it seemed like she had made up her mind there wasn't one thing about him she liked. And she let him know it every chance she got.

Chestnut, toilet's stopped up again in main lavatory. . . . Chestnut, Lee Earl and that new boy are fighting, go break it up. . . . Chestnut, Elrod is walking around naked, get his robe back on. . . . Chestnut, Buddy Boy is taking a dump in the day room, clean it up and hose him down. I mean, right now!

An hour earlier, when Randall had started to leave the house for work, the battery in his Chevy was dead. By the time he managed to wake up his cousin and borrow his truck, it was almost twelve fifteen before he signed in. He hadn't been too worried because this had happened before, and anyway, he knew Miz Bertie could run the ward all by her lonesome if she had to. Maybe even the whole hospital. She was as tall as he was, five-eleven and had arms the size of his, and he'd seen her stand up to the worst kind of crazies and never bat an eye. That woman hadn't known what *flinch* meant.

When he first walked into the nurse's station to find her missing, Randall had checked the notepad she always kept on the desk. That was the one thing she never forgot to do. Even if it was no more than going to the bathroom, she'd write it down in that ledger along with the time. He scanned the last entry:

12:02 AM, August 1. Gone to check on BB and find out why he's yelling and won't go to sleep. Maybe his straps are too tight.

Randall had dashed down the long, dimly lit corridor to BB's room. The door was wide open, and inside he saw the straps had been pulled out of their bed mounts. The six by nine room was empty except for Miz Bertie's body lying there on the green tile floor. He ducked out into the long corridor and at a glance saw the huge steel bar was in place over the outside door to the recreational area. On a hunch he ran to the bathroom. There, a good six feet above the high block walls of the showers, the heavy iron ceiling grate had been ripped from its hinges, the glass shattered, pieces of it now crunching under his feet. How he did it, Randall didn't know, but none of that mattered now.

BB had flat cleared out. That boy was gone.

Randall swore under his breath, realizing it was all going to come down on him. Maybe if the trackers and their dogs could pick up his scent and bring him back before he hurt anybody else, it might not be too bad. Randall had seen BB in action only once, but that once had been enough. He went about 270, was built like a gorilla, only lots taller, and he had stood off four attendants at once, slinging them off like a bear would a bunch of hunting dogs that had made the mistake of getting in too close.

She said he'd been yelling. That was to get her in there to get the door open. He was probably already out of his straps waiting. BB had to have been planning this for a long time. And they said he was crazy, thought Randall. That's when it hit him. What if he'd gotten to work on time? *He* would have been the one to go check on BB, and now he'd be the one lying there on the floor instead of Miz Bertie. A shudder ran through him.

Whatever happened, he figured it was probably going to cost him his job. He cursed softly, lit up a cigarette, hunkered down on the green tile floor and started blowing smoke rings. Much as he didn't want to, he knew he had to call Doctor Maynard and tell him the bad news. The only good part was that Randall was glad he was *inside* the hospital, and BB was *outside.* He couldn't figure out why they hadn't gone ahead and given him one of those operations like they did with the other crazies. It didn't make sense to him, but that wasn't none of his never mind. Finally, Randall managed to blow a perfect ring and that calmed him down. He picked up the phone.

The receiver on the other end rang three times before Elliot Maynard, Medical Director for Dorothea Dix picked it up. He lived in a cottage barely a hundred yards away, and the instant he awoke, he knew he would have a hangover in the morning. He shouldn't have let that fast-talking pharmaceutical salesman take him to dinner. Of course, he'd only had two glasses of the burgundy. Well, maybe more. He wasn't sure. Oh, Elliot, he thought. This is not good. This is not good at all.

"Yes, what is it?" Maynard lived in constant fear of the after midnight calls. They were always bad news, and that was the one thing he did not need any more of around here.

"Doctor Maynard, this here is Chestnut. On D-3? It's about BB."

"Yes, what about him?" Maynard's stomach began to twitch. Dear God, not a problem, please. That was the last thing he needed a week before the trustees met to review the new budget.

"He's gone."

"Gone? What do you mean gone? Gone where? He can't have gone anywhere. He's secured in his bed." *Silence.* "Well, isn't he?"

"No sir. I mean I guess he was until Miz Bertie checked on him."

"I don't understand. You mean something happened? She undid him? It's against the rules after lights out. Chestnut, weren't you with her? And why are *you* calling me instead of Miss Croft? Is something the matter with her?" Before Randall could get a word out, Maynard began again. "Wait a minute, Chestnut. Why haven't you sounded the alarm?" Some of these people down here, thought Maynard, were a different species. Sometimes, he wondered if they had the right ones locked up.

"Cuz I thought you'd want to come down here first to have a look see. I remember the last time the alarm went off—them people from *The News and Observer* was all over this place, taking pictures, asking questions and all, and I remembered how upset you got over that."

"Yes, yes . . . all right, Chestnut, can you be more specific about what has happened?" He fumbled for a cigarette, squeezing the pack until he realized it was empty, then cursed and wadded it up, throwing it at the wastebasket. It bounced off the rim, and Maynard interpreted that as a bad omen.

"Do what?"

"Can you be . . . Chestnut, I want you to tell me in plain words what happened."

"Well, you know . . . Miz Bertie. . . . ?"

Dear God, thought Maynard. They had the infuriating habit of turning every sentence into a question. He knew he should have stayed at Mass General. Raleigh might have been the state capital, but it was a million miles from what he had known in

Boston. *Boston.* He tasted the word on his lips. Civilization. He would keep his voice calm. Remember, Elliot, he told himself. These people spook like horses in a thunderstorm. "Yes, Chestnut. What *about* Miss Croft?"

"She uh . . . well, just between you and me, she used to love to take that headknocker of hers and use it on BB cuz of that time when he wet on her new uniform the day the staff had their pictures taken. And with her being right handed, it all kind of makes sense. Leastways, to me it does."

As he half listened to Chestnut, struggling to make sense of his jumbled narrative, Maynard kept tugging at the warped drawer of his night table, giving one final jerk. It came all the way out and landed on his instep. He started to grind his teeth, then spied the opened carton in the back and pulled it out. Empty. He could actually feel the pressure growing in his arteries. His head began to pound. "For God's sakes, man, *what* makes sense? She's not hurt, is she?"

Silence.

"Chestnut? Is she hurt badly? She's not—" he paused, swallowed, then managed to get the word out of his mouth. "Dead?"

"Yessir, she surely is. And BB took something off her before he left, but knowing Miz Bertie, I bet she put up a good fight." Randall had to give her that much. For all her faults, she'd had real grit.

Maynard wasn't hearing any of this. He kept hearing the word *dead* echo over and over in his ears. This could spell the end of his career. He'd be lucky to get fill-in work in a charity clinic.

"Chestnut?" This was met by a long silence, and not being able to deal with this any longer, Elliot Maynard screamed into the mouthpiece.

"Chestnut!"

The sound of his voice reverberated in the small bedroom. Maynard paused. He took a long, slow breath through his mouth, letting it out slowly and reminded himself that doctors—especially psychiatrists—who are in control of their emotions, do not yell at their staff. If the word got out, he'd be gone in a heartbeat. He listened and thought he heard Chestnut crying. Keeping his voice calm and level, he spoke slowly and deliberately as though conversing with a very small child.

"Chestnut. It's all right. I'm sorry I yelled at you. Now try to be calm and tell me exactly what was it BB took that was so important. Would you do that for me, Chestnut . . . please?"

Randall sniffled once or twice, then cleared his throat.

"Yes sir, doctor. BB . . . uh, he took Miz Bertie's right arm."

2

4:17 AM, Wednesday, the first . . .

BB heard the dogs. They were far away. Their barking told him they had treed her arm that he had thrown high up into the branches of a huge water oak. It had fallen down twice, but the third time it caught. He knew it would fool the dogs and slow them up. He stopped and tasted the thick, wet air.

water
find a fast running branch
soon

He was sloshing through the swampy land and knew there had to be a creek close by. Suddenly he stopped, listening to the baying of the hounds. It had changed. It was louder and higher. They had picked up his scent again even though he had back tracked his trail from the oak.

momma they smell bb
coming to get me and lock me up
hurt me more

Within minutes, he found the creek, plunged in up to his middle, and followed it for a hundred yards or so until he saw what he needed. A large low-lying branch. First he dunked himself under the water and came up with handfuls of mud that he smeared over his entire body. Then he grabbed the branch and with barely a grunt, swung himself up and began to snake his body along the branch that bent under his weight, but did not break. Within seconds, he had clambered up the trunk and hidden himself in the heavy foliage. It was still dark, but he knew dawn was coming, and the light would let the bad men see him.

He clung to the limb, his body molding to its shape. The leaves were wet, still dripping from a brief shower that had fallen during the night. He watched and waited. He heard the dogs come to the edge of the creek upstream. Their baying changed again. He heard them splashing in the creek. Then he heard the voices of the men.

badmen angry

The men and dogs began tracking along both edges of the creek, following it upstream, trying to pick up the scent. Now they came back working downstream. He heard them cross over to his side, the men trying to keep up with the dogs who were thrashing through the thick underbrush. He could smell them now. He could see the picture in his head just like she had said.

them doctors and all say you aint smart baby but I know you are

you see things just like the pictures in this here magazine dont you baby

The dogs came to the base of the large gum and began to mill around, sniffing the earth at the creek's edge in an attempt to pick up the scent while lapping water. There were three men. One was the tracker who handled the dogs. His name was Clete. The other two were from the state. They wore khakis and cradled twelve gauge pumps in their arms.

"Clete, I hate to say it, but them dogs done lost it for sure," said the larger of the two men in khakis. His name was Thurman, and this was the morning he was supposed to have gone fishing if some crazy hadn't broken out of Dix. He was breathing heavily as he hunkered down to light up a cigarette.

"Aw right, dogs!" yelled Clete. Y'all hush now!" The pair of bloodhounds came to him and lay down, panting heavily, watching him for a release. "I know for a fact he went into this creek. And the dogs know it, too. The only question is did he go upstream or double back." He bit a chew off a plug of tobacco and after a brief moment spat near one of the dogs, then laughed. "Shoot, Bo, you done lost that man for sure, ain't you, boy? And what about you, Big Pup? You ain't much better." Before he spoke, the dogs had been looking at him wonderingly, their tails moving slowly. As he spoke to them, they whined eagerly, their tails now wagging furiously. They wanted to pick up the chase. Minutes earlier, the scent of the prey had been rich and full in their nostrils, and suddenly it was gone.

From his perch, BB could not see down through the leaves, but the smells and sounds made a picture . . .

the man smell
the smoke
the tobacco juice
the dogs

"Well, what do y'all want to do?" said the smaller of the two state men. His name was Tom.

"I think we ought to give it up," said Thurman. He was thinking if they left now, he would stay up and go fishing like he'd planned.

Clete felt a few drops of water falling from the leaves overhead, glanced up absently, then shifted his bulk and spat again. "Whatever y'all want to do is all right by me. Whoever this guy is, he may be a crazy from Dix, but I'll tell you this—he's some kinda smart. He must of put something up in that tree to throw Bo and Big Pup off the scent. Otherwise, we'd a had him for sure. I'd give a week's pay to know what it was. Them two was barking like they'd treed a boar coon."

Thurman took one last drag on his cigarette, then thumped it into the creek. He stood up and yawned. "Yeah, well . . . I reckon we done lost him. Way I figure it, he could be anywhere by now." He looked up toward the east. "It's gonna be light in about a half hour. I say we go on back, notify the uniform boys, and they can do what they want. Me, I gotta get rid of some of this coffee before I drown." He went over to the edge of the bank and relieved himself. BB's nose twitched. He picked up the sour smell from his perch 30 feet above.

Within a minute, the men and the dogs had left the area and started working their way back to the dirt road about a mile away where they had parked their truck. BB waited. The dogs barked excitedly when they flushed a rabbit, a man hollered angrily, and they were quiet. Soon BB heard the sound of the truck, the engine coughing as it finally started. From his perch, he could see the rim of the sun coming right up out of the ground. When he could no longer hear the truck, he came down slowly from the tree. Watching everything. Hearing everything.

light comin
soon

He kneeled down and drank from the creek's edge, tasting the water, swirling it around in his mouth then swallowing it.

bb hungry
eat now

It was light enough to see the holes along the bank where turtles had laid their eggs. He dug and after two tries was successful, his hand emerging filled with the small, cream colored eggs, and he broke open the shells and sucked out the contents. He tried two more holes but something had been there before him. He looked further along the bank and found what he wanted, a rotting stump. With one blow of his fist, he shattered it, knowing the cream colored, oblong eggs of a black snake would be inside. He devoured these as he had the turtle eggs.

bb feel good

He knew he had to go home to Momma, except he knew she wasn't there anymore. But he knew that was where he belonged. It would be better there than in the doctor place with the bright lights and all those noises.

go safe place
yes momma
the place bad men called devils gut

3

8:52 PM, Friday, the third . . .

Curt Ragg leaned back in the swivel chair, heard the thunder and knew the bottom was going to fall out any minute. Ordinarily, he didn't like storms much, but the way things were going lately, he didn't care if it came down a frog strangler. He finally had Standing Bear where he wanted him, and he could pretty much do with him as he pleased. There wasn't anyone who would go his bail. Then eventually . . . well, thought Ragg— the way the world is these days, it's awful dangerous out there, and accidents do happen.

He ran his finger down his cheek touching the small scar, remembering the time she had cut him. Bear's mother, Naomi. It had been a long time ago. . . . Ragg had been on the force just a year, but he could remember every single detail, starting with her scent that drove him wild. He had gone over there to serve a warrant on her husband, Tom Running Elk, for being in a fight and sending a man to the hospital. It was after ten on a summer evening. She had come to the door in a thin cotton shift hanging down in front and told him Tom was not home but out in the Gut working his trapline. Ragg never heard a word of what she said because a switch clicked on inside his head. Sometimes, he would come across a woman that he had to have right then and there, and she had been one of them, and he told her if she didn't give him what he wanted, he'd put her man on the chain gang and make sure he stayed there.

She still said no, but that made him want her all the more. Problem was, she didn't want *him* and said so, cursing him, but he hit her once, then dragged her into the bedroom, ripping off her shift. Then she screamed, and for a second, Ragg thought he heard someone in the house and glanced over his shoulder. While his back was turned, she had come up with a blade, and as he turned around, she sliced his cheek. He knocked her back on the bed with his fist, took away the knife and had his way with her, even though she fought him the whole time. He liked it when they fought. It made it better.

When he finished, he noticed her staring over his shoulder, and he glanced around just in time to see the small boy standing there in the hall, watching, clutching his teddy in one hand, the tears streaming down his cheeks. She jerked herself out from under Ragg's sweating body and went to her son, telling him that it was nothing but a bad dream. It was all right.

Ragg wasn't really worried about her pressing charges or anything like that. Who would take the word of a squaw against a policeman. He'd clamped her jaw between his thumb and forefinger, squeezed real hard and told her that her husband might just have an accident if word of this ever got out. And she knew the white eyes meant it.

Ten years had passed, then one night as Ragg was leaving to go to work, he heard a whoop, and saw Running Elk come charging out of the dark with a tomahawk in his hand, yelling like crazy. The policeman knew that after all these years, she had finally told him, and he drew his revolver and shot his attacker point blank dead center. There was a coroner's inquest and a hearing, and the judge said it was a clear case of self-defense by a peace officer against a crazy, drunken Indian. The town agreed, glad to wash their hands of it, and that was it. Ragg never saw her after that. Then, about five years later, Bear had gone away to the Marines and wound up overseas. She'd started hitting the sauce real heavy by then, until one night while she was walking down the Atlantic Coast Line tracks, dead drunk in a pouring down rain, the twelve-eighteen hit her, dragging her 82 feet. Ragg hadn't shed any tears over that. Life goes on.

Most of the time when Ragg made women do things like that, he could scare them into keeping their mouth shut. He had a favorite line he liked to use . . . *well, now darlin,' whose word they gonna take, yours or a police officer? . . . You don't want the whole town to know what happened, do you? And what about if your husband finds out? Huh?* It always worked.

Course there was that little kid who came in the police station to use the bathroom one night in early June just after the scout meeting had let out. Ragg hadn't done anything like that before—well, maybe a time or two—but it wasn't like he was gonna hurt the boy or nothing. Sometimes when he got like that, he couldn't help himself. That night he hadn't gotten farther than asking the boy if he could touch him, and the kid had backed off in the corner by the urinal, his lower lip trembling, the tears starting to come. Ragg told him he wasn't going to bother him none, then pointed his finger at him and said if he ever talked about this, he'd hunt him down and cut that little pecker of his slam off, and the boy had flown out of there with his fly still unbuttoned. Ragg hadn't seen him around again and didn't think he would. Anyway, kids knew better than to talk about anything like that. They weren't dummies.

He pulled a fresh King Edward from his pocket, ripped off the cellophane, licked it, then rolled it around in his mouth. He lit it, took one good puff and leaned back in the chair to enjoy a good smoke, when the phone rang.

"Police department, Ragg speaking."

"Officer Ragg, this is Dr. Elliot Maynard."

Him again. The nuthouse doctor from up at Dix. He'd already called once before wanting to know had BB showed up in Sweetwater, and Ragg had told him no, he hadn't, and as far as he was concerned, he didn't think he ever would.

"Doc, first off, what makes you think BB would come back here? How's he even gonna find his way? Boy can't read a lick. Another thing, doc. It's a good 100 miles from Sweetwater to Raleigh, and BB's walking. Ain't no way that boy could make it here in three days."

Maynard tried to explain. "Please understand, Chief Ragg. BB is a rather extraordinary person. Though he has a low IQ, he has an almost animal-like sense of direction, time and place, his stamina is amazingly high, and something inside him will lead him back to where his memory tells him he needs to be, and right now, we think that's Sweetwater. It's the same instinct migratory water fowl have that allows them to return to the same place year after year."

Migratory water fowl, thought Ragg, and stifled his impulse to laugh, thinking the doc was the one they ought to have locked up. "You mean, because his momma came from here and all that. Shoot, doc, she's dead. Don't BB know that?"

"Yes, he knows it, but not in the same way we do. *Dead* to him means something different from what it does to us. His ability for speech is rather limited. I'm sure you know that he actually lived in the swamp for nearly a year as a 13 year old on his own and apparently survived quite well. In fact, when he was admitted here for the first time, the record states he was more like a wild animal. Nonverbal . . . almost completely uncommunicative."

Uncomm . . . Ragg tried to form the word on his lips silently and say it the same way the doctor had rolled it off his tongue. "Yeah, well everybody around here knows that. BB never had a lick of sense from the day he was born."

"Well, as you and I understand intelligence, I would say you're right, except that for BB, his mind works in a different way than ours." Maynard paused, wondering why in God's name he was telling all this to a hick police chief. Then he remembered the paper he wanted to present at the society's meeting in late October, and like it or not, he needed this man's help to get his prize patient back.

Maynard knew he had gone out on a limb by using an experimental drug that his former colleague had come up with at the Boston labs. It was a substance strictly forbidden without government approval, but it took those morons in Washington forever to approve something, especially with the war on, and time was the one thing he didn't have. He didn't think his dosages were too high, but of course, there was no way of telling, since there was nothing in the literature yet. In any event, Maynard had been certain his presentation would be the hit of the seminar and his ticket out of Dix to someplace else. *Anyplace* else.

"Well, we'll keep an eye out for him, and I'll let you know if I hear anything." The chair squeaked as Ragg shifted his bulk. "Say, he ain't gone and done something bad again, has he?"

"No, no," said Maynard. "Of course not." He had managed to keep the circumstances of Croft's death out of the newspapers, and since she had no close relatives and only an aunt living in Arizona, he had ordered a closed casket funeral and told the mortician he wanted him to embalm her personally; and furthermore, if word of this leaked out, she was the last body the man would ever get from Dix. That was all it had taken.

"However, I should add this is a man with whom you need to exercise extreme caution. During his stay with us, we found him to be very clever about locks and restraining devices. Anything that prohibits his freedom of movement."

"Uh, huh," said Ragg, as he puffed out a small cloud of blue smoke. "Yeah, well, I sure appreciate the advice, Doctor, and we'll be on the lookout. Thanks for calling."

"You have my number, don't you? It's very important to me."

"Got it right here." Ragg had no idea what he'd done with the number. He had his job to do and the doc had his. It was that simple. He hung up and sat there thinking that maybe BB was more important than the doc had let on, and if he *was* to find him and bring him back, this might be just the thing he needed to convince Herb Johnson and the town council that he deserved the raise they'd been promising him. They expected a grown man to live on $24 a week, and if it weren't for knocking down a bootlegger now and then, he would have long since starved to death.

"Hey, Ragg! How about some supper?"

Ragg realized his prisoner had not eaten yet, but maybe it'd do him good to wait. Like it or not, the Indian was going to have to play by Ragg's rules. He went back and stood in front of the cell.

"Well now, if you was to be polite and call me *Chief* Ragg, I might think about getting you something to eat. Tonto!"

Bear looked at him with a baleful glare, then suddenly smiled.

"I'll call you whatever you want. You want me to call you Chief, I'll call you Chief, but just because I do, it doesn't *make* you any more than what you are."

"It may not," said Ragg, "but it sure makes me feel good." He laughed. "All right, hold your horses, and I'll have Ben bring you a plate." As he got back to his desk, the phone rang.

"Police department, Chief—"

Before he could get his name out, the voice on the other end squawked in his ear. He'd know it anywhere. Maggie Wilson.

"All right, now. Whoa, Maggie. Tell me that again." He listened, the cigar clamped tightly between his lips, his eyes widening all the while. "Okay, okay, I'll be right there," he said. "Don't y'all do nothing stupid. Just stay put." He hung up and grabbed the mike.

"Eldon, this is Ragg. Eldon, do you read me?"

"Yeah, Chief, what's up?"

"Maggie Wilson called from over at the cafe. Something over there I need to check out. You come on back in and keep an eye on things. Oh, and pick up a plate for Tonto. I'll see you when I get back. Ten four."

As he grabbed his hat and started for the car, he thought that Maggie was acting a little crazy like maybe she'd had too much to drink, which happened just about every night ever since her husband Jake had run off with a young waitress. He sauntered outside, heard the thunder again, this time louder. He pulled out into the street in the black '40 Ford, turned on the flasher and left a streak of rubber all the way past the firehouse and up to the Sinclair station. As he sped by the movie theater, the kids out in front sitting on car hoods whipped their heads around and gawked, a couple of them whistling through their teeth, one hollerin' out, "Go get 'em, Chief."

A peal of thunder shook the town, and the first large drops of rain splattered on his windshield. You're exactly right, Ragg thought, smiling to himself. In the town of Sweetwater, I'm the one that gets 'em.

4

9:12 PM, Friday, the third . . .

Maggie had just finished ringing up the last customer who had hurried out to his car to avoid getting caught in the storm, when she heard the noise from back in the kitchen. At the same instant, the first clap of thunder hit, rattling the large plate glass windows, and because of that she wasn't sure just what it was she had heard, but there was something going on back there that wasn't right. One thing for sure, it was going to storm within seconds, and just as she hung up on Ragg, the lights went out. The man from the power company had been telling her for weeks not to worry—they were fixing to replace the transformer on the pole outside. Yeah, like she was fixing to be a movie star. *Men.* They would tell you anything. She made a face then sipped at her Jim Beam and coffee.

Ragg was no better'n the rest. She had known him since the third grade. He'd grown up the meanest boy in school from the meanest part of town, out there at Doodle Hill with the rest of the white trash. Course for a boy growing up with a last name like his, Maggie figured there was no way he could have grown up *except* mean. She remembered how the other boys had teased him about it, *Curt's on the rag, Curt's on the rag*—kids were like that— then he'd get whipped by the principal, a man who could be counted on to blister your butt good and give you ten more licks if you said a word back. Girls got whacked on the hand with a ruler. Then, when Ragg got home, he'd gotten a second beating from his father. J.D. Ragg loved beating on anyone and anything he could get his hands on, including his wife, four kids, two dogs and a mule.

The rain was falling in earnest when she saw the police car pull up to the door. She watched as he opened the door, then seeing her lights were out, reached back in for a flashlight. He dashed into the cafe, removing his cap and shaking off the water. A thick candle sat on top of a saucer near the register, its flame giving enough light so they could see each other's faces.

"Evenin', Miss Maggie."

She hated being called that, and he knew it, and she hated the way he looked at her, and he knew that, too. Ragg deftly lifted a King Edward out of the open box lying next to the register and rolled it around in his fingers. As he started to reach in his pocket, she said, "It's on the house."

"So what is it this time, Maggie? One of your niggers get drunk and do a little fancy carvin'?"

She shook her head with a quick motion, staring down into the cup.

"Woman, you look like the devil's got hold of you. So just calm down and tell me what's going on back there. Okay?"

"I'm not sure, Ragg. My last customer had just left, and I heard this noise coming from the kitchen. It sounded like Jasper yelling, he's my cook, but I can't be sure because right then it thundered, the lights went out, and that's when I called you cuz I was scared half to death. Still am."

"Jasper, huh? Is he the one that went up to New York, then came back?"

She nodded.

"He ever give you any trouble before? Tell me the truth now, Maggie. See, I don't wanta go back there in the dark and get stuck with a butcher knife. They don't pay me that much. The other thing . . . you can't see Jasper in the dark, and that gives him an advantage. I bet you never thought about that, did you?" Ragg smiled. Maggie thought to herself that he was the only man she knew who could actually smile crooked.

"No, Jasper's the best cook I ever had, and he doesn't ever give me any trouble, least not since he got saved." Maggie reached for her pack of Luckies, drew one out and managed to get it into her mouth. Her hand was trembling as she held the zippo, but she got it lit. She watched Ragg watching her with his raised eyebrows and that crooked smile.

"All right. Let me go back in there and find out what all is going on. Anybody else with him?"

"Well, Violet is . . . *was*. Shoot, Ragg, I don't know. Maybe she's already gone home. Sometimes she leaves early and doesn't tell me."

"Violet?"

"My dishwasher and cleaning woman."

"She that fancy lookin' high yella I've seen around here mopping floors?"

Maggie nodded, drawing deeply on the cigarette, then picked a shred of tobacco from her tongue. The thunder struck again, rattling the windows, and at the sound, Maggie jerked, knocking her coffee cup to the floor where it shattered, one jagged piece striking her ankle. She yelled and jumped, then got another cup and somehow managed to fill it with coffee, her hands shaking.

"Okay, let's just settle down now, Maggie. Pour yourself another shot of whatever you got stashed under the counter there and take a load off, okay? Old Ragg's gonna go back in there and see what's what." He walked toward the rear of the restaurant, the flashlight splashing a circle of light on the walls and ceiling in an eerie pattern. When he got to the swinging door that entered the kitchen, he shined the light through the small grease-stained window, but he couldn't see anything. He cracked the door a few inches.

"Jasper, you in there? This here is the po-leese. You know me, boy. Chief Ragg. Now if you're in there, you say something."

Boom!

The thunder was so close, Ragg could feel the floor shake under his feet. "All right, now," he said. "Whoever you are, I'm coming on in, so don't try nothing or you'll be awful sorry in the morning."

Maggie watched him almost slide through the two doors

like a snake slipping into the water pretty as you please. When the door closed behind him, she reached for the half pint of Jim Beam, which sat right where he said it was, and poured herself a good shot in the cup, her gaze fixed on the two swinging doors.

Crack!

The lightning sounded as though it had struck right out in the alley that ran beside the building. Her mind was a blackboard and the devil was scratching his fingernails down it. Oh, Jesus forgive me, she said to herself, but I gotta have another one. This time she took a healthy swig of the Beam straight from the bottle.

Inside the kitchen, the light bounced off the big aluminum pots and pans hanging overhead, but other than that, the darkness swallowed the narrow beam of light.

"Jasper? Violet? All right, y'all. Don't be playing games with me, you hear? This is the police so y'all come on out. I'm not gonna arrest you or anything like that. Y'all hear me?"

Ragg edged around the end of a counter, feeling his way with one foot at a time, and that's when he bumped into the body. He slowly traversed the light up the stained white apron until it shone upon the man's head, lying at a sharp right angle to his body. Broken just like you'd snap a pole bean. He bent over and saw that Jasper's eyes were wide open and staring off into the darkness, a look of complete astonishment on his face.

Ragg tightened his grip on the Smith.

"Hey, now, whoever you are, you come on out and show yourself, and I'll go easy on you. I promise. You hear me?" The rain drilled on the tin roof overhead, and he heard the thunder again.

He kept moving slowly down the aisle between the two counters, and he heard the moan just as he was about to step on her. The light fell on her eyes which were staring straight up at him, the whites like cotton bolls. It was Violet. Her dress had been all but torn from her, the handle of the butcher knife sticking out of her stomach, the blood already a dark pool on the concrete floor. Her bare right shoulder appeared to have been— Ragg couldn't tell what. He leaned over to bring the flashlight closer, and that's when he saw the toothmarks. He let out a sound-less whistle. Whoever it was had actually bitten her. Just then, her eyelids fluttered, and she moaned again. He started to prop her up, when he heard a slight noise near the back of the kitchen and glancing up, noticed that the door to the walk-in cooler was half open. Ragg moved closer, cocking the .38. It had to be him. BB. He'd come back just like the doc said he would. There wasn't anybody else who would do something like this. Ragg took a deep breath and let it out slowly.

"Now BB, you've been a bad boy, son, and you know it. But that's all right, cuz the doctors up there at the hospital, they're not gonna punish you for this, you know—hurt you or anything. They just want you to come on back cuz they got a brand-new room all fixed up so they can look after you real good, okay?"

The policeman moved into the doorway of the cooler and played his light on the hams and sides of beef hanging from the hooks. He could see that one of the hams had a big chunk bitten out of it. Not sliced. *Bitten.* For an instant, he thought he saw something mov-ing between the shadows of the huge slabs of meat, and as he raised the light in one hand, the gun in the other, the thunder came again in a deafening boom that shook the floor under his feet, and the power suddenly came back on, the one large naked light bulb right next to his face blinding him momentarily.

At that very instant, a gigantic figure came charging out from the meats, a presence so fearsome and quick that Ragg watched it as though it were all happening in slow motion, just like in the movies except this was happening to *him,* and before he could catch his breath, the man ran right over him, slamming him to the floor as though he were a broom handle. But in the fraction of a second before he fell, Ragg's eyes managed to focus briefly on the face that loomed before him, the blood-smeared mouth gaping wide like an open wound, the teeth large, crooked and yellowish. He heard his gun go off, a distant scream, a siren, what seemed like a band playing, and then all the sounds run-ning together.

After that . . . nothing.

5

9:22 PM, Friday, the third . . .

Eldon Carver played a hunch.

Ordinarily, it wasn't like him to do that, but when he returned to the jail and saw that everything was okay, something told him he ought to go check on Ragg. He told Ben to stay there, that he was going over to Maggie's just in case Chief needed some backup. A minute later, he gunned the Ford up the back alley near the ice plant and noticed the storm had gone as quickly as it had come, the rain now barely a drizzle. When he turned the sharp corner with tires squealing, he spotted the huge figure running down the alley. The man stood stock-still for a second, blinded by the car's headlights, and before Eldon could stop, the Ford skidded on the wet asphalt and hit BB a glancing blow that knocked him down to the pavement.

Eldon sat there behind the wheel for a moment, shaking and not knowing whether he was more excited than afraid, or both. He collected his wits then scrambled out of the Ford with his gun drawn. The man lay there motionless except for the rise and fall of his chest. He was the biggest man Eldon had ever seen. Anyone else, thought the policeman, it would have killed him. The man's wrists were thick as small tree limbs, and Eldon barely managed to get the cuffs on. He heard a door open and looked behind him to see Ragg standing there, touching the back of his head gingerly.

"Godamighty, Chief," said Eldon. "You all right?"

"Yeah, I'm just bleeding a little, but it's nothing like what's in there." He jerked his thumb in the direction of the kitchen. "It's a good thing you came along when you did." Ragg came over to stare down at BB. "Did you run him down on purpose? Not that it makes much difference."

"Naw, I wouldn't do that, Chief. I came around the corner, my lights caught him, and he froze, just like a deer. I put on brakes, but the car skidded and down he went. Shoot, I thought I'd killed him. Hey, who is this guy, anyway?"

Ragg explained briefly while Eldon listened, his mouth half open. They both looked down at the prostrate figure and were silent for a moment. Ragg felt the top of his head again and winced. He'd have to let Doc Reardon patch him up.

"Okay, let's get him into the car and I'll follow you back down to the station."

"Need some help?" Ragg turned to see the town's ambulance driver, Whit Sewell.

"Yeah. Hey, how'd you get here?"

"I called him, that's how," said Maggie, who came out the back kitchen door and stood there, swaying slightly, her speech slurred, the half pint of Beam in her hand, not caring whether they saw it or not. "When the lights came on, the jukebox started playing, and Whit pulled up in front, his siren goin' full blast — hey, I thought the world was coming to an end, know what I mean?" She took a swig and offered it to the men. They shook their heads, exchanging smiles. "Well, I lost me a good cook, that's for sure, and maybe even Violet, too. Lordy, Lordy!" She finished the bottle then tossed it in the trash can.

Whit had already carried out Jasper and Violet from the kitchen and gotten them into his ambulance. The two policeman thanked him, said good night to Maggie, who stood there waving after them when they pulled out, and ten minutes later, they had BB in the over-sized holding cell across from Bear.

"Eldon, I'm going over to let the doc take a look at my head."

"Sure, Chief," said the younger man. "You go ahead, and don't you worry none. I'll keep an eye on things."

"Yeah, you do that. I'll probably go straight home from the doc's, but don't take any chances with that guy, and if you have any problem, call me, you hear?"

Eldon nodded and Ragg left. As he drove the few blocks to
the doctor's house, Ragg chewed his lower lip for a moment,
not feeling entirely happy with the way things had worked out.
Carver would wind up getting a good share of the credit, but at
least people would know it was him, Ragg, who had the guts to
go in there after BB. Two minutes later, he was knocking on the
door of Doctor Jesse Reardon, whose office and home were on
North Reynolds Avenue. Lucy answered the door, not at all
surprised that someone would come at night for help. In this
town, they came at all hours.

Ragg said, "Gal, go tell the doc I'm here."

Lucy pressed her lips together, arched her eyebrows and
folded her arms. "Chief Ragg, for your information, there is no
gal and no *doc* who live in this house. There is a Nurse Melton
and a Doctor Reardon, and you are speaking to Nurse Melton.
Now, if you will please wait one moment, I will notify the doctor you are here. Thank you, sir."

She spun around with a crisp rustle of her starched cotton
uniform and walked into the book-filled study. "Doctor, it's the
chief of police. He needs to see you."

Her employer looked up from the large leather chair where
he had been reading and noted that the corners of her mouth
were turned down ever so slightly, the eyes tightening. Jesse
Reardon knew there was no love lost between the colored community of Sweetwater and the chief of police. In under a minute,
having donned his white coat and with his usual efficient, well
controlled movements, he was examining Ragg.

"Does it hurt when I press here?"

"Naw."

"Here?"

"Uh uh."

"You're not seeing things fuzzy or wavy?"

"No sir."

"No ringing in your ears?"

The chief shook his head.

"Now . . . keep your eyes on my finger as I move it from side to side. Okay. Now, up and down . . . uh huh. Okay, that's good. Well, I don't see any evidence of concussion or anything serious. I think you're going to live."

Ragg let out a sigh of relief. He wanted to light up a cigar, but thought better of it.

"Okay now, I'll just put a little of this on it—it's gonna sting a little. You don't need a head wrap or anything like that, but I'm going to put on a gauze pack just to be sure."

"So, Doc," Ragg was saying. "What is it with someone like BB? I mean, what's really wrong with him?" He had already filled Reardon in on the earlier events of the evening.

"Oh, I don't think anybody knows for sure. There just hasn't been enough work done on that kind of thing."

"What kind of thing?" asked Ragg, his eyes narrowing.

"Well, in BB's case, a psychiatrist would say he's a chronic psychopath." He saw the puzzled look on the policeman's face. "That's a person who has no sense of right or wrong. They basically do what they feel like doing, and if they have to hurt someone in the process, it appears to be of no consequence. In fact, they may even enjoy it, like a child enjoys playing."

"But why does he bite people . . . and do what he did? Shoot, Doc, he didn't even know them two niggers."

Jesse flinched slightly at the sound of the word. He had never liked it, even as a young man, having been taught better by his mother. He reached for the peroxide.

"What makes *any* of us the way we are?" He looked to see if his jab had registered with the chief but seeing no evidence of this, began to apply a bandage. "Well, whereas if someone does or says something *we* don't like, we might hold back our anger, yell at the dog, punch a hole in the wall, things like that. BB reacts differently. If you do something he doesn't like, or keep him from doing something he wants to do, he'll bite you or try to hit you or snatch something away from you. Two year olds do it all the time, but they grow out of it, and BB didn't. The big difference here is that we're not talking about a two year old. The man has super-human strength, and when he wants something, he is not going to stop until he gets it. I would classify him as an extremely dangerous human being."

"It's like maybe his wires got crossed, huh?" Ragg touched his finger to his head to feel the bandage. Reardon pushed it away with a frown. "Try not to move—I'm almost through."

"Sorry," said Ragg, "but okay—so what makes him so strong and so fast?"

"Nature's gift of compensation. If she cheats you with one thing, she generally makes up for it on another. And even though he has a low IQ, he's smart enough to cope. But more like an animal . . . say a ferret or a boar coon who's been hunted so many times, he knows how to survive."

Reardon paused. "Cunning," he said. "That's the word I wanted. BB is very, very cunning, and you mustn't ever sell him short. To do so, I think, would be a big mistake." Jesse finished, pulled off his gloves with a smack and tossed them into the sink.

"Well, Doc, what do I owe you?"

Jesse waved his hand with a smile. "Always glad to help out a public servant."

"Well, thanks, Doc." Ragg saw Lucy out of the corner of his eye standing in the entry way to the study. "*Doctor*."

Jesse took note of this but gave no sign that he did, and saw the policeman out the door. He returned to the welcome solitude of his study, knowing it would be only seconds before Lucy was in the treatment room cleaning up the mess and returning everything to its former neat, antiseptic state. He walked to the oak cabinet, removed the bottle and carefully measured out the one ounce of Jack Daniels that he allowed himself every night. Straight. No ice. One ounce. No more. No less.

Settling into his chair, he turned back to the article by his friend, Blalock. Good for you, Al, he thought. He'd have to write him over the weekend. Jesse had been a resident at Johns Hopkins when Al had come along as an intern, and Jesse had always thought that the young physician was one of the brightest men he had ever met, and the news of his progress made him feel good. Jesse had been invited to stay on to replace the Chief of Surgery at Hopkins, but his father had been taken ill, and he had made the decision to come back to Sweetwater with Alice, his bride of two years, to take over the practice. A year later his father had died of a heart attack. Jesse had lost his mother when he was twelve.

Alice gave birth to Stephen, but she experienced an extremely difficult delivery, and he had thought it better they not try for another child. They had a happy life together, the three of them. Then it hit Jesse . . . it would be seven years ago next week that his wife awoke one morning, screaming in pain, saying her head was about to split open, and she was seeing double. She had never had a headache before in her life. Jesse x-rayed her head and felt his throat tighten when a faint shadow the size of an orange showed up on the film. He drove her up to Duke Hospital that very afternoon, and the next morning, the neurosurgeon opened up her skull and took a section for a biopsy. When the lab report arrived later that day, the answer was written all over the surgeon's face. Jesse knew the tumor was malignant. He took Alice home, and she lasted four months, the last week or so filled with violent screaming and seizures so severe that the morphine hardly made a difference. On a Sunday morning just before dawn, she had died in his arms.

Then it was the two of them, father and son. On Stephen's eighteenth birthday in 1942, he dropped out of college to join the Air Corps and a year later, he was a copilot flying bombing raids over Germany. Jesse remembered the day he got the telegram about Stephen's missing in action, and his hopes were kept alive for a week or more. Then three days after the biggest snowfall Sweetwater had ever had, he received the final news. His son would not be coming back. Nor would there be any body. Jesse had walked outside, the telegram in his hand, immune to the bitter cold, knowing only that his heart had turned into something resembling the grey, icy slush lying on the ground.

He blocked the images in his head and glanced around the study, looking at other images: the familiar photographs, momentos and news clippings. Soon after Alice's death, Lucy, who had both been maid and cook, tried to help him keep up with things, but then to his great surprise, one morning showed up for work carrying two small, battered suitcases, a hat box and a tiny radio.

"Doctor Reardon," she said, speaking very properly as she had been taught by her mother, a schoolteacher. "There is no way you can keep up with your patients, the house, and your flowers and everything else that is going on. Your bedroom is a mess. I leave the kitchen tidy, and by morning, there are dirty dishes everywhere. Your study is a mess, and the examining room is on its way toward *becoming* a mess. There is a slew of *National Geographic's* and *Reader's Digests* lying all over the floor of your bedroom, some of them dating back to the Lord only knows when. Now, Doctor Reardon, let me say this the best way I know how. Either I move in and work full time, or I'll have to seek employment elsewhere."

"Well," he said, not knowing how to follow that up and focused on the woman who stood there with a somewhat defiant look on her face. He collected himself and said the word again. "Well. I suppose we'll just have to turn the garage into an apartment, won't we?" Jesse had always warmed to people like her, for his mother had had that same quality.

"Yes, we will, Doctor," came the crisp response accompanied by that triumphant smile of hers. And that was it. Lucy cooked, cleaned, shopped, ran errands and in general, helped him concentrate all his energies on the practice. He had trained her patiently and carefully, until he knew she was the equal of any nurse who had gone through school.

He thought about BB again and shook his head slowly. He had not told Ragg that after each encounter BB had with authority, the anger would surface again, each time worse than before, and through some strange trick of the blood chemistry, each episode enhanced his strength and the blind fury of his rages. Jesse was relieved to know they had him safely locked up in a cell, and by tomorrow he'd be on his way back to Dix where he belonged. Jesse had been selected to serve on the public health team that evaluated the youth for admission. He remembered the child's mother, Mary Lou something . . . yes—Rainey, that was it. She had been a prostitute, selling her services to all kinds of men, anyone who had the money, and her son, already brain damaged through a congenital defect, was sometimes chained out in the back in a small shed while his mother entertained her customers.

Due to an overactive pituitary gland, by the time the boy was 13, he stood six feet and weighed 190 pounds, all of it hard muscle. There was no more tying him down with a chain, and one night he burst into his mother's bedroom and saw her lying underneath a man and screaming. He snatched the hapless customer from the bed and heaved him through the bedroom window. Jesse remembered because he had put nearly two hundred stitches in the man's face and arms, and it had taken until three in the morning.

The man never filed charges, but after that, there were other incidents. Jesse would read about them in the papers or someone would tell him. BB would be hospitalized, turned loose, incarcerated, turned loose, sent to a work farm, turned loose, sent to prison where he would always be confined to solitary, and then again released. During one of these stays, Jesse couldn't remember which, BB's mother contracted syphilis, had been forced to work in a laundry to sustain herself, and one day swallowed the contents of a bottle of lye and went screaming through the plant shouting, "Lord, I wanted an angel, but You gave me a devil!" Within seconds, she fell to the floor, the deadly green froth boiling out of her mouth. The authorities had done the only thing they could do and sent BB to Dix where he belonged.

Jesse took another sip. Tonight, he would go to bed earlier than usual. It had been a long, grueling day, and the visit by Ragg had not been the best way to cap an evening. It had touched a raw nerve within him, making Jesse feel strangely uncomfortable—as though his home had been invaded by an alien presence.

Another sip. The day's images softened. Became blurry. Melted into one huge collage in his head. He walked over to the mantle, picked up his wife's picture, kissed it and said, "I love you, dear," then did the same with Stephen's photo, his son having just earned his wings at flight school, standing there with a huge smile, one arm around a friend, the other hand giving the thumbs up sign.

The physician stepped back, let out a sigh, drained the glass, rinsed it out carefully in the sink, then brushed his teeth, prayed and was asleep before his head hit the pillow.

6

10:20 PM, Friday, the third . . .

After Ragg exited through the door on his way to Doctor Reardon's, Eldon stood there for a moment, waved after the car, then walked back inside. The earlier excitement had vanished, and he actually felt a little depressed. Not knowing what else to do, he poured himself a cup of fresh coffee from the pot that Ben had made before leaving, then he walked back to the cell block and stared down at his new prisoner. BB was still lying in the same position they had left him after they had dragged him in there by his ankles, the effort requiring all their strength.

"I heard Ragg call him BB," said Bear. "I remember hearing something about him before I enlisted. What happened?"

Eldon had all but forgotten the Indian was there.

"What happened is, ol' Eldon here knocked this boy into the middle of next week. The rest of it ain't none of your business, Bear."

The phone rang, and Eldon left the block and walked to the front office to answer it. "Sweetwater Police Department. Eldon speaking."

"Eldon who?"

"This here is Officer Eldon Carver. Can I help you?"

"I certainly hope so. I'm Dr. Elliot Maynard. Is Chief Ragg there?"

Eldon didn't know any Doctor Maynard, but he knew enough to be nice. After all, the man was a doctor, and he just might be somebody important. "No sir, he ain't. He went to the doctor's to get his head patched up. Cause of him falling down in the cafe."

"Falling down? I hope he's not hurt badly."

"No, just a head bump. Chief went over there to check out a report of possible trouble, and it turned out that somebody named BB was hiding out in the meat cooler."

"BB?" came the excited voice. "BB? You've found him?"

"Sure did. As a matter of fact, we got him back there in our cell right now, handcuffed, and I'm keeping an eye on him." Eldon added, "I'm the one who ran him down with the patrol car."

"Ran him down?" Maynard drew in his breath sharply. "I don't understand."

Eldon briefly explained what BB had done. The news of the murder threw Maynard off, but maybe with luck, it wouldn't find its way into *The News and Observer*. The war still dominated the newspapers.

"Well," said Maynard, relaxing a little. "That certainly was fast thinking, officer. Oh, excuse me. You don't know who I am, do you?"

"No sir, I surely don't."

The physician filled him in quickly, then said, "Officer Carver, all this is very interesting, but now, I'd like you to do one thing for me. This man could provide us with some very important answers about his kind of problem, so it's important that you make sure he's not bleeding anywhere. If so, he needs medical attention right away. First thing I need you to do is check his eyes to make sure his pupils aren't dilated."

"Dilated. . . ." Eldon let the word hang.

"Yes. You know, big. If they're big, that means he could be in serious medical trouble."

"Now wait a minute, I don't know anything about stuff like that. I'm a police officer, and I ain't about to play nursemaid to that . . . thing in there."

"Officer," said Maynard, mustering up his sternest voice. "If something should happen to that man, *you* will the one held responsible. There will be an official hearing, and you will have to come up to Raleigh and testify before a panel. You don't want that, do you?"

"Well, no," said Eldon, feeling a little sheepish. Wouldn't that be just his luck? To capture BB, then get in trouble over it. "All right, Doctor. I'll go check on him, and if he looks bad, I'll get Doctor Reardon in here to see him."

"Oh, and one other thing. Make sure his handcuffs are not too tight. With those big wrists of his, the cuffs could cut off his circulation and cause a problem. I've seen that happen before. Now you help me, officer, and I'll send an official letter of commendation to go in your file."

"Oh, well, thank you a lot, Doctor. You can count on me." Eldon said good-bye, hung up and grabbed the cell keys off the desk. A letter of commendation in my file. Well, lah-de-dah, Officer Carver. First, you run down BB, and that will be all over town by morning, starting at the coffee shop. And next, maybe an official letter of commendation. Eldon's sagging spirits were lifted by this news, and he started to whistle.

While Carver had been on the phone, Bear stood there, his hands draped through the bars, musing over the events of the past several days. He had been driving his '37 Ford that was close to going to the junkyard, when Ragg pulled him over, walked up behind the car, and Bear had heard the sound of the nightstick breaking glass. Ragg told him his taillight was out and he had to get it fixed now, or else he couldn't drive the car home. It was a cheap cornball trick, and both of them knew it. Bear's first instinct was to flatten the man with one judo punch, but he managed to hold his temper in check.

Instead, Bear told Ragg he'd be glad to get it fixed in the morning, but there was nobody open at this time of night who could fix it. Ragg asked him if he was arguing with the law. Bear said no sir, officer, he wasn't. Ragg said he *was* arguing with the law, and he was going to take him in, and if he resisted arrest, that would just make it worse. Bear cursed him in Cherokee, calling him a name he had heard his grandfather use, but only for the worst people in the tribe. It meant something like "You were hatched in a steaming pile of fresh horse manure."

Bear knew it didn't matter. Ragg would have eventually gotten him for something. It seemed that the white eyes had had it in for him for as long as he could remember, even when he was a kid. When his father had been killed, he was barely 12, but he had wanted to go after the policeman and kill him. His mother had taken him by the shoulders and shaken him hard, screaming, telling him, "No, no, there's nothing you can do. Don't you understand? You're just a Cherokee boy, and he'll kill you, too, and nobody will say a word!"

It never got any better, and he couldn't wait to get out of Sweetwater, even though it meant leaving his mother alone. In June of '41, he'd forged his mother's signature and joined the Marines even though he was a month away from being 17. He was 21 now, but an old 21, having already seen more killing than most people see in a lifetime. While overseas, he had not known about her drinking or any of what was going on. He wrote once a week and sent money every month, but she never wrote back. It was while he was recovering from the shrapnel he took on Guadalcanal that she was hit by the train, and by the time he got the news two weeks later, she was already lying cold in the ground.

Once home with his two Purple Hearts and Silver Star, there had been a brief write-up in the paper, but after that, nothing. He stuck out in the town like a cornstalk in a field of cotton, and he knew it. Most of the townspeople regarded him as being somewhere between white trash and colored people, if that. He also knew that Ragg was determined to run him out of Sweetwater or send him up for a long stretch. He was also savvy enough to know that for an Indian to go up against a white eyes and a lawman at that, it was a losing proposition.

Carver hung up the phone and sauntered back down the corridor with the key ring in his hand.

"All right, now, " said Eldon. "Let's just take a look at Mister BB here and see what's going on." He opened the door and entered the cell, and remembering what the chief had said, he unsnapped the holster catch on his revolver. It's a good thing the doctor had called, thought Eldon. He certainly didn't want BB dying on him, and then he'd have to go up to Raleigh for some kind of investigation. This job was the best he'd ever had, and it sure beat plowing a mule or picking cotton, both of which he'd had enough of, growing up the son of a sharecropper. Ragg had told him that if he kept his nose clean, he had a real future in police work.

"Hey, BB! You awake?" He nudged the man's huge thigh with his shoe, and seeing no response, kicked him lightly.

"Hey, boy! What's the matter with you? Get up." He kicked him again, only harder.

BB lay there immobile. The stench of his body fluids rose strong in Eldon's nose. "Well, Mister BB, I believe it's your bath time, big'un." He went back to the end of the hall, filled up a galvanized mop bucket with cold water, came back and sloshed it onto the prostrate form. Still no response.

"Hey, boy, get on your feet, and I mean now!" he yelled.

Nothing.

Eldon started to get worried. He didn't like doing this, but he knew he'd have to get close enough to check his eyes like Dr. Maynard asked him to. This was important stuff. He reached for the keys to the cuffs.

"I'd be careful if I was you," said Bear, his voice quiet and even.

"Do what, Indian?" Eldon sneered at his other house guest.

"You heard me. That man is dangerous. People like that— my father knew some in the tribe—the Cherokee believed they were possessed by demons and had powers we don't even know about."

"Oh, yeah. You mean like evil spirits and all that stuff?" Eldon chuckled. "Hey, don't you worry none, slick. I can look after myself."

Bear was going to say something else but thought better of it. He turned and sat back down on the bunk.

soon

Eldon rolled back the eyelids, and the pupils looked all right to him. The man was still out like a light. Anybody could see that. Now, the cuffs. The doctor was right. They were too tight and had started to cut into the fleshy part of the underside of the wrist. As he inserted the small key into the lock on the left cuff, the man's smell assaulted his nostrils, and he tried to hold his breath, feeling his stomach churn slightly. He turned the key.

now

As the ratchet came loose with a sharp, distinct click, everything changed permanently in the world of Officer Eldon Carver. His hand made a reflexive move toward the holster, but it was too late. Another hand, this one twice as large and ten times as strong, whipped around his leg before he even saw it happen, and he was lifted off the floor of the cell, spun in a huge arc, his head and body grazing whatever it raked against until bits and pieces of flesh and then bone began to break off and stick to the walls and bars and ceiling, all the while BB making a sound that was halfway between a cry and hysterical laughter.

Bear watched in horror from his cell, not able to move. He had known carnage in the war. He had seen men ripped apart by mortar shells and grenades. He had watched their heads burst open like a ripe canteloupe. He had seen one man crawling around on his stumps looking for his legs that had been blown out from under him. But never before had he witnessed anything like this. Then it was over. Carver, or what was left of him, lay on the cell floor resembling more a stuffed doll that a child had ripped apart than what had once been a man.

BB unlocked the other cuff, dropped them on the floor, then walked through the open door and over to Bear's cell, peering at him through the bars. BB grabbed them with his giant hands, shaking them violently, and for a moment, Bear wondered if they would hold. Then the man stopped, stepped back and looked through the bars at Bear, making a grunting sound.

no bad man

Bear met the glance of BB squarely, their eyes locked on each other. Then BB turned away and walked up the corridor into the office. He picked up the huge metal desk, chairs, filing cabinets and whatever else was in the room and tossed them around as though they were playing blocks, turning everything upside down. Bear could only see partly from where he stood, but from the noise, he could imagine what was going on. Then he heard the door slam, the sound echoing in the cell block. Finally—silence.

BB turned north and ran down the dark reaches of Reynolds Avenue, loping along in a gait that was half-man half-animal, like a great ape would run, his long arms swinging by his side. Something within him steered him, told him, turned him in the right direction, just as a gull that had strayed too far inland would pick up the faint scent of the sea. Between streetlights, his form cast a long shadow, and at one house a dog saw him and ran out to investigate, barking furiously. When it got within a few yards or so, it sniffed, then whimpered and tucking its tail between its legs, ran under the porch where it let out a long mournful howl.

Within minutes, BB had left the tar and gravel street for a dirt road that ran by a field of tobacco and then he was swallowed up by the trees and underbrush that led into Devil's Gut. Less than five minutes had passed since he left the jail. No one had seen him but the one dog.

safe soon
bad men not find BB
BB want hurt bad men

Where the tar and gravel of Reynolds ends and the dirt road begins, stands a century-old, two-story house that had once upon a time been white but now badly needed a coat of paint, the roof missing some shingles. As BB ran by, the woman named Charity Whitley Trace stirred in her bed in the back room on the second floor, the same bed she had been birthed in during the Battle of Gettysburg, then awoke, the dream images still fresh and vivid in her mind. She had seen a vision of . . . something, she wasn't sure, but she knew it was not of this world. She got out of bed, turned on a small light and in spite of the pain, kneeled on her arthritic knees, the words tumbling forth from her mouth. . . .

Dear Lord, I know there are evil demons in the night running loose, and I know they mean to do us harm, Lord, and I pray You will protect me, Lord, and especially protect my little friend, Joshua, and his mother, Deborah, and Lord, I pray You will reveal Yourself to Joshua when the time is right. O, thank You, Lord. Amen.

When she finished, she climbed back into the big four-poster bed, clasped the gold cross that hung around her neck that had been worn by her mother and *her* mother before her, closed her eyes, her lips relaxing into a gentle smile.

Charity slept like an angel.

7

5:40 AM, Saturday, the fourth . . .

Edgar Davis, the milkman from Meadowlands Dairy, came by the old Whitley place as he did every morning at this time. He looked forward to this part of his run not only because it meant he was through for the day, but more importantly, because Charity would be out in her garden singing hymns. In the silence of the early morning, her silvery voice would carry all the way to the street, and he loved to sit there on the running board of the truck, have himself a smoke and listen. Most of the hymns he remembered from when he was a little boy, though ever since his momma passed, going to church didn't seem the same. But listening to Charity sing for those few minutes made Edgar feel like God was back in his life sure enough.

Charity had been outside for a good 20 minutes before the milkman arrived. As usual, she'd awakened promptly at four-thirty, prayed, enjoyed a cup of coffee, some streak o' lean and a biscuit, then put on her bonnet and gloves. Once outside, she noticed that her petunias looked a little peaked from the heat, but she reckoned they'd get through till Labor Day. She had some mother-in-law tongue set out in pots on the porch, and they were doing fair but not as good as last summer. Her roses were always lovely—the prettiest in town, everyone said—and she attributed that to the fact that over the years, she had learned just what they liked. Charity knew you could fool some plants, but not roses. If they weren't happy, they'd let a body know about it right quick like. In the garden, there were field peas ready for another picking. And in about six weeks, she'd dig the sweet potatoes and store them in the cellar that Caleb had made for her. Just as Edgar drove up, she burst into the second chorus, the notes trilling from her throat . . .

Have we trials and temptations?
Is there trouble anywhere?
We should never be—

That's when she saw it.

It was standing at the end of the row of peas looking at her. A crow or raven—she didn't know which—but the bird was as big as she was. It cocked its head and fixed its gaze upon her with a malevolent stare from blood red eyes. Then it picked up one long, bony leg and made a move toward her. She knew exactly what it was and who had sent it. There was no question about that. Charity clutched her cross, closed her eyes and began to pray silently, forming the words on her lips without realizing what she was saying, and suddenly she felt her body quiver and tremble with the presence of the Holy Spirit, and her unwavering voice shattered the stillness of the garden.

"Get on out of here, you beast of Satan. God the Father commands that you be gone!"

So saying, she raised her hoe and began to advance toward the end of the row, and in that instant, the bird vanished. Edgar heard all this, stood up on his running board, craning his neck to see what was going on. He saw Charity brandishing her hoe at someone or something, and since he didn't see anybody else but her, Edgar decided he didn't want to wait around to see any more. He cranked the Dodge and spun his tires in the dirt until he got onto the hard surface. Charity heard the sound of the engine and the tires, and knew he had been out there listening. She also knew that soon the word would be all over town, but she didn't care. The Lord had sent the Holy Ghost to help her, and if other folks didn't believe that, it was their loss, that's all there was to it. Anyway, she didn't have time to worry her head about what folks thought. She had a garden to hoe.

Behind the house in a hollow next to the weeping willow lay a small cottage, and in the tiny back bedroom, Deborah Grayson had been lying awake in her bed, knowing she had to get up and prepare for the trip. Hearing Charity's voice in the distance, she raised herself up on one elbow and peered through the screen to see what was going on. But the branches of the willow were so thick with leaves, she could barely see the figure of her landlady. No telling what Charity was doing, thought Deborah with a smile, then reluctantly put her feet on the floor. The job offer was in Rocky Mount, 48 miles away, and the only time the man had agreed to see her was today. Her bus left at 7:20 and this left her just enough time to dress, get Joshua up, set out his breakfast, then walk down to the bus station.

She had laid out her clothes the night before, choosing her best dress, though nothing flashy. Looking at her image in the small mirror as she put on her makeup, she looked at the snapshot of Martin and her taken on their honeymoon. The memories began to loom up before her, and she squeezed her eyes shut, but it didn't help . . . the call had come on that cold, grey afternoon back in March . . .

"Mrs. Grayson, this here is Bobbie Lee Haynesworth, I'm the sheriff up here in Gates County. Uh, ma'am, is your husband Martin Grayson? Well, I hate to have to tell you like this, but he's been in a serious accident and. . . ."

She hadn't heard the rest, having collapsed on the floor with the phone still clutched in her hand. Martin had been driving back from Norfolk, a freezing rain had started and the roads turned deadly. The driver of a truckload of pipe lost control, skidded into Martin's lane, hitting him head on. All the rest was something she didn't ever want to think about again. After the funeral, there had been nowhere else for her to go, so she decided she would stay here at least until school was over. Now, what insurance money there was had all but run out, and it was get a job or go back and move in with her mother, and that was out of the question.

Oh, Martin, she thought, and touched his face with her finger. She had still been living at home with her mother in Winchester, Virginia, and had just turned 18. One afternoon in late June, walking home from her job at the cannery, she got caught in a drenching thunderstorm, and that's when Martin had stopped and offered her a ride. She had never gotten into a car with a man before, certainly not a man she didn't know, but there was something about the way he looked and spoke that let her know it was all right. By the time he got her home, 20 minutes later, both of them were crazy about one another.

All Deborah had known growing up was a drunken father who'd come home and want to argue with her mother, the words eventually turning to blows. She would lie in her bed trembling, hearing everything, and wondering when it would end. Finally, her father left and took up with a younger woman who also liked to drink, and that's when her mother had started yelling at her, saying she could do nothing right and she'd come to no good and if she, Deborah, had been nicer to her father, he wouldn't have left. *Nicer*, thought Deborah. She remembered how her father had always looked at her with those hot eyes, his tongue touching his upper lip, and even though he had never laid a hand on her, she knew he had wanted to.

Then Martin had come along, and not two weeks later, there he was in the living room, waiting quietly while she packed her one suitcase, all the while her mother standing in the doorway of her bedroom and screaming at her, "You marry that man, and you'll be the sorriest woman on the face of the earth, you hear me, girl? He'll cheat on you just like your daddy did me, and run off and leave you, and you'll be back here on my doorstep crying for me to take you in. You mark my words!"

Deborah *had* marked them, but she had never been back. Never written. Never called. After getting married, they had stayed in a tiny garage apartment in Norfolk where Martin's job was. Joshua had been born, and the next ten years were happy ones for them. Then the firm sold the bushel basket company they had in Sweetwater and made Martin part of the deal. In January they had moved here, and things couldn't have been better for them—until that day in March.

With his death, Deborah and Joshua had to move out of the duplex they were in, and she was grateful that Charity had rented the cottage to them for eight dollars a month. The one thing she didn't like, though, was that Charity seemed to spend a lot of time with Joshua, talking to him about God. *Too* much time.

For herself, God hadn't mattered to Deborah in a long time. Her mother had been Pentecostal and had dragged her to church, and after her father left, the two of them would sit there on Sunday mornings while the preacher ranted and raved for two or three hours, and then again that evening, and when revival came, it was four and five hours a night, seven nights a week for two or three weeks. They'd get home near midnight, even when she had to get up the next morning to go to school, and she had grown to dislike church, then hate it. And finally, with Martin's death, to hate God as well.

She had once asked Martin if he believed in God, and he'd told her that he believed in being good to people, and if that's what God was all about, then yeah, he believed in God, but he wasn't going to go to church because look what it had done for her mother and her father, and if that's what church did to you, he didn't want any part of it. Deborah never brought it up again.

But she kept wrestling with the question of Martin's death. He was such a good and kind man, and God knew that, so why did he have to die for no reason at all? If there was a God—and she wasn't convinced of that, but *if* there was—she was angry with Him, and she really didn't care if He knew it. How could God hurt them like this? She and Joshua never did anything to hurt *Him*, at least, she didn't *think* they did.

The difficult part came when Joshua would ask her questions about God, the usual questions that kids did, to which she had one stock answer. "I don't know. Why don't you ask God. Maybe *He* knows the answer." Hearing this, Joshua would turn his face into one big squint and say, "Aw Mom, you know people can't talk to God." And she would shrug her shoulders, saying, "Well, then, what good is any of it? Besides, your mother has more important things to do than worry about God." Somehow, she would always manage to sidestep the issue by changing the topic, but she knew this didn't satisfy him. The truth was, if *she* didn't know who God was, how could she tell her son.

Deborah finished with her rouge and powder, did her eyes, then put on just enough lipstick to give her some color. She looked one last time, gave her hair a toss, then went in to wake her son. Buddy was asleep curled up in the small of Joshua's back, and as she entered the room, he looked up and wagged his tail but didn't bark. She had gotten the dog a month after Martin's death. Joshua had been waking up crying in the middle of the night, but once she got him Buddy, and they started sleeping together, the crying stopped. The dog was about six months old now, and he and Joshua were hardly ever separated. She looked at the peaceful expression on her son's face, that wore the trace of a smile even in sleep, the soft brown hair with a slight wave in it, just like his father. Feeling something tighten within her breast, she bent down to kiss his cheek, and when she did, he opened his eyes. They were the warmest, brownest eyes she had ever seen and absolutely huge. Oh, how she loved her son. He was all she had now.

"Honey, you have to get up now. This is the day Mother has to go interview for my new job."

"Mom . . . where are you going?" The words came out in a yawn.

"Remember, we talked about this. I have to go to Rocky Mount for a job interview at that furniture store. Mr. Clippard, the owner, is expecting me, and if I get the job, we'll be moving there very soon."

"But Mom," said Joshua, now raised up on one elbow. "I like it here in Sweetwater. I'm really starting to make some good friends and I'm going to be a Boy Scout on my next birthday. When school let out, I went to one of the meetings with Jimmy Woolard, and I met Standing Bear who teaches them all kinds of stuff about the woods and everything. Mom, he's a real Indian and he was a Marine and won a purple heart and a shooting star. . . ."

"Silver star."

"Yeah, silver star, and he's. . . . "

She shushed him with her finger.

"I know, honey. But we may have to do this because . . . well, we just may have to, that's all. I can't find a job here that pays enough. Rocky Mount's a lot larger, and things will be better there, you'll see. Anyway, you're real good at making friends just like your father was, and I'll bet we won't be there a week before you'll have a whole *new* bunch of friends to play with. Now please get up, Joshua. Your cereal is already on the table, and I've sliced up a banana, okay? I'm going over to have a quick word with Charity before I leave."

The boy nodded slowly, got out of bed and plodded to the tiny bathroom. Deborah waited until she heard the tinkle of water in the toilet, then walked outside and across the stone path to the back door of the huge, old house. Before she had time to knock, she heard the voice.

"Oh, come on in, girl, but be quick and don't let the flies in. I vow, they must smell this stuff from a block away."

Deborah opened the screen door, closing it quickly behind her.

"Well, you're up mighty early." Then before Deborah could respond, Charity said, "Oh, I remember now. Today's the day you're going for that job interview, isn't it? Here, let me pour you a cup of coffee, and you just sit down right here and have one of my buttermilk biscuits. They're fresh out of the oven. Besides, if you're going to be interviewed, girl, you need to eat. Caleb always said, you can't have gumption unless you get your groceries."

Deborah knew better than to say no. As she sipped at the coffee and munched on the biscuit, she knew she had to bring up a topic that was unpleasant, but better now than later.

"Charity, I want to talk to you about Joshua."

"Oh, isn't he just wonderful! Truly, God has blessed you beyond measure. Here, try these plum preserves." The older woman opened the jar with a deft move and set it in front of Deborah who had learned that Charity had a way of taking command of every situation, but in a nice way. And she wanted everybody to call her Charity: not Miss Charity or Mrs. Trace—just Charity.

"Thank you. Well, what I wanted to say was . . . I think maybe you shouldn't be talking so much with Joshua about. . . . "

Charity spun around from the stove and finished the sentence for her. "About God?"

Before Deborah could respond, Charity came over to the table, sat down and put her hand on the younger woman's arm.

"Deborah! Child, look at me." Her voice was stern.

Deborah met her steely glance.

"You don't like God very much, do you?"

The younger woman's eyes widened, as she peered over her coffee cup at Charity. She started to deny it, but couldn't find the strength.

"How do you know that? I mean . . . is it that easy to see?"

"For me it is." Charity let out her breath in a sigh, then got up and fetched the percolator from the stove. She filled both their cups and sat down.

"Girl, when you've lived as long as I have, there isn't much about people you *don't* know. And remember, my husband, Caleb, was a minister, and when you're a minister's wife, you learn mighty quick who likes God and who doesn't. Truth to tell, some of those who sing the loudest like Him the least. But you already know that, don't you?"

Deborah nodded. "Charity, it isn't so much that I don't *like* God. It's just that, well, I'm. . . ."

"Angry with Him?"

Deborah felt her face flush and looked down into her coffee. "Yes, I *am* angry with God. I truly am." She punctuated this with a determined nod.

"Because of Martin?"

"Yes." She put down the last half of the biscuit. Her appetite had vanished.

"You think God took Martin to punish you and Joshua?"

"Well, it sure wasn't to help us, was it? I mean, if that's His way to love people, then I don't need any more of that. I had enough when I was growing up."

Charity put her hand over Deborah's. The younger woman looked at the pale blue veins against the white skin, as fine as silk. Charity's palm was warm, its touch seeming to calm her.

"Girl, it's not given to us to know what God means to accomplish when He does things in our lives. It's beyond us. We just have to trust and obey . . . and have faith, and I can tell you, after 82 years of living, to keep on doing those three things is mighty hard." She paused and sipped from the china cup. "I know. You see, I loved my Caleb like you loved your Martin, and one minute he was here, and the next he was gone. He. . . ."

"Mom, you're gonna be late for your bus!" Joshua burst into the kitchen with Buddy at his heels. She glanced at her watch, the one Martin had given her, and said, "Oh, my gosh. Thanks, honey. I'd lost all track of time."

Charity started to offer to drive her, then remembered the battery in her ancient Chevy was dead, she hadn't driven it in so long.

"No, no," said Deborah. "There's enough time if I walk fast. Besides, it's still cool yet, and I need the exercise. Joshua, be sure to let Charity know if you go off anywhere. I should be home by five." She bent down to hug and kiss her son then vanished through the door.

"Well," said Charity, when the front door had closed. "Did you have your breakfast yet?"

Joshua shook his head. He didn't want to tell her about the cereal still sitting on the table getting soggy, even though he'd gulped down two slices of the banana.

"Well, seems to me like one of my ham biscuits might be just the ticket. What do you think? Maybe even a treat for Buddy, too."

Joshua's eyes widened in anticipation, and he nodded vigorously, his face one huge grin.

"Now today, I'm going to tell you about a man named Jacob and how he wrestled with God."

"Wrestled! Honest, Charity?" The boy's face turned into a squint. "Boy, he must have been been brave to do that. Uh, Charity. Who won?"

"Who won?" The woman broke into laughter. "Great day in the morning, child, you always want to know everything, don't you? Well, it was a tie, but only because God let Jacob get the upper hand. But God could have won in a heartbeat if He'd wanted to."

She laughed again and bent down to give him a fierce hug. He was the son that she and Caleb would have loved to have had, but the Lord had decided to bless them in other ways. Thus all the years Caleb had been alive, they had "adopted" young people and taken on their raising as part of their ministry. Joshua watched her as she bent over the stove. He liked Charity's hugs, and he liked the way she smelled of flour and sugar and raisins and apples, and he liked her stories, and he didn't want to leave Sweetwater, and maybe he could ask God to do something about it, but he didn't have any idea how to go about it.

"Charity?"

"Yes, Joshua."

"Can you . . . well . . . do you talk to God?"

"Why do you ask?"

"Because all the kids at school say you talk to Him all the time. And some of the teachers say it, too."

"Well, boy, I reckon I do."

"Is it hard?"

"To talk to God? Nope . . . easy as rolling out dough. In fact, if you like, I could teach you how."

"You could? Well . . . when? Charity, when?" She noticed his voice was just starting to break like they all did at that age.

"Soon," she said, "but first, you go straight into that bath-room and do a proper wash up and don't just run water in the sink either."

"How did you know I was going to do that?" asked the boy.

"Because I'm Charity Whitley Trace, that's why. I was born knowing things, and when I die and get to meet God, I'll know all there is to know, and anyway, whatever I didn't get to know on earth wasn't worth knowing in the first place. Now get on in there, before I change my mind and feed this to the chickens. Go on now, young'un. Skedaddle!"

Joshua skedaddled.

8

7:18 AM, Saturday, the fourth . . .

The bull alligator had lived in the Gut for seven years. When it was just two years old and barely four feet long, a man named Zeno Gilman had paid a dollar for it down at White Lake and had brought it home with him. He figured he could make money by charging people to see it, and on Saturday afternoons, a small crowd of people would gather, and he would toss a small rabbit into the boarded wire enclosure he had built, first making sure he had collected a dime from everyone.

The gator would lie there eyeing the frightened animal with half-lidded eyes, as though it had scant interest in it, and suddenly the rabbit would disappear into those jaws so fast a body could scarcely see it happen. At first, people found this entertaining, but gradually the novelty wore off. Then, too, the alligator was growing fast, had lost its fear of the man and had started to snap at him without provocation, and that was it. Gilman decided its days were over, but before he could get around to killing it, the alligator came up with a solution of its own.

With the cunning born into it millions of years ago, it dug out from under the fenced enclosure one September morning and made straight for the swamp where it took up residence in Dark Creek. When the temperature dropped in late October, it built a hibernation mound and its heart rate dropped from 28 to five which allowed it to enter a state of torpor and thereby endure the winter. In early spring, it emerged and went on an eating spree. Over time, it had become a very skillful predator, and since it had no natural enemies except man, it fed voraciously and grew to be an unusual size. Its diet consisted of squirrels, raccoons, snakes, beavers, deer, bear cubs who hadn't learned better and an occasional cow who wandered off into the swamp. These hapless victims would approach the water to drink without the fear and caution that nature and parental training might otherwise have given them since gators were largely unknown this far north. Whatever it caught between its jaws, the killing strategy was always the same. It would dive below the surface, rolling over and over with the animal clamped tightly in its jaws until its prey's lungs had filled with water, then devour it at leisure.

The alligator had one other delicacy it enjoyed above all, and that was man. It had killed only two men in the time it had been here, but had developed a special taste for the flesh of the two-legged creature. It was not afraid of the man thing, for in the confrontations it had experienced, it had found the standing animal to be easy prey. From one such encounter, it carried a 30-06 slug in the thick part of its tail, having received this from a hunter, who while wading in the shallows, was attacked by the gator and panicked, managing to get off a quick shot. His last.

Now at nine years old and in its prime, the alligator measured 12 feet from snout to tail and weighed just under a quarter of a ton. Its 26-inch jaws had a crushing power that could snap a thigh bone as easily as a child could bite a peppermint stick in two. It could out-maneuver almost anything that lived in the water other than the elusive otters, and on land, propelled by its short but powerful legs, it could outrun a man for up to 20 feet.

The alligator ordinarily hunted by night, and during the day dozed in the shallow water. Completely submerged now save for its nostrils, it had come near the bank, and though not really hungry, its eyes focused on the fat grey squirrel that climbed down the trunk of the live oak and approached the edge of the water. The more it watched, the primeval urge of the predator would not be denied.

The squirrel knew its way around the swamp after two years, had learned to be wary of its enemies and was always on the lookout for potential danger. It also knew the most dangerous place of all was at the water's edge where 40 pound snapping turtles lurked. It had seen one of these grab the leg of a playmate and drag it down into the depths there to be drowned, then leisurely devoured.

The squirrel had learned that this time of day was best, and it would inch cautiously through the thickest part of the under-brush. It knew that owls came out only after dark, and foxes and ferrets it could smell long before they got close. Worst of all were the larger snakes, for they were hard to see and struck so fast no animal could escape their fangs. For this reason, the squirrel took a few small furtive steps, then paused, its ears cocked for the slightest sound. Now it moved closer to the edge near a large mound of moss and rotting vegetation, scanned the area one last time, then bent its head to drink.

In a move so fast the squirrel did not see it until it was too late, BB's hand shot out of the rotting mound of leaves and gripped the back of the animal's neck with fingers of iron, snap-ping the spine with a crunch. The alligator had been no more than six feet away ready to spring out of the water when this happened, and now angry that it had been cheated of its prey, decided it would take the man-thing instead. With a huge splash, its giant, fearsome body left the water in an explosive charge, rushing at BB, the cavernous jaws open wide, ready to seize the man-thing and drag it into the deepest part of the creek.

As fast as it was, BB's reflexes were a split second faster, and he rolled to one side just before the jaws snapped shut with a loud *kerchunk*. As he did, he scrambled back a couple of yards, dropping the squirrel and glancing around, reached down and seized a large limb that had fallen from a tree. It was eight inches in diameter and six feet long, so large an ordinary man could not have wielded it, but BB handled it as though it were a baseball bat.

The gator pressed the attack, making straight for BB, hiss-ing loudly with its jaws open, sure of the kill. BB waited until the last second, then jumped high in the air and upon landing, brought the limb down on its head with all the force he could muster. The gator had never experienced this kind of behavior before from the man-thing, and before it could recover, BB hit it a second time on the bony ridge just above the eyes, then jabbed it in the side using the branch like a battering ram.

Neither BB nor the alligator moved. They were no more than six feet apart, neither afraid of the other. The alligator was not hurt and prepared to charge again when BB bowed his head down, bared his teeth and let out a yell that echoed across the swamp. Then jabbing the limb at the alligator's head, making sure he remained out of lunging distance of the jaws, he began to advance upon the animal. The alligator hesitated. The man-things had done nothing like this before. This one was different, and it did not look like or smell like the others. Perhaps it was best to leave it alone. Slowly, it gave ground, its huge bulk sliding back into the water. There would be other times.

BB went to the water's edge, his teeth still clenched, roaring in a final act of defiance. The only emotion he had experienced was anger that the alligator had tried to hurt him and rob him of his meal. Finally, satisfied it was gone, BB found a sharp rock, skinned the squirrel and devoured it, all but the feet, the head, the skin and the tail, which he buried in the damp earth. When he finished, he approached the water again, sniffed, scanned the surface warily, then bent to wash his face and hands.

Finally, he drank, not as a man would, cupping his hands, but as an animal, lapping it silently, all the while his eyes peeled for the creature. When he had drunk his fill, he stood up and belched loudly. He dropped the thin light blue cotton trousers issued to him at Dix, squatted and emptied his bowels, then dug a hole and buried the steaming feces as he had the squirrel's remains. A swarm of mosquitoes hovered about him, but he paid them no attention. He scanned the surface of the creek again, but the gator was nowhere to be seen. He looked up into the towering cypress, smelled the air and let out a sound that was half yell, half roar. The swamp birds grew quiet, and he could hear the echo coming back at him. He liked to hear the sound of his voice.

good eat
find more food
momma bb safe now
bb home mommmmmm-a-a-a-a-a

9

8:12 AM, Saturday, the fourth . . .

"Ben! Now you listen to me real good, you hear?"

Ragg fixed his baleful stare on the jailhouse janitor, who stood there mop in one hand, bucket in the other. Ben knew better than to interrupt or even blink. Both men were sweating heavily since they had spent the last 30 minutes trying to put the office back together, with only limited success. The phone was still not working from having been pulled out of the wall, but somebody was there working on it. Homer Biggs, the coroner, had already come with his assistant and removed the mutilated body of Carver though there wasn't much of a body to speak of. Homer said it was more like what you'd have left over after a hog killing, and Ragg had told him he didn't want to hear about it.

"Ben, I want every tiny little bit of Eldon picked up out of that cell, the walls, the bars, the floor and whatever else you can find. Scrub it down with that bristle brush we got, and if that don't do the trick, use a wire brush, and don't ask me where to find one either. Boy, you pick this cell clean as a chicken, take that mattress and burn it, and then you wash the whole place down with Lysol from top to bottom, and when I come back in here, I don't want to be able to smell nothing but Lysol from one end to the other. You hear me, boy?"

"Yessuh, Chief." Ben hit the floor running. He had been the first one to find Eldon when he had come in that morning and had run out of the jail screaming at the top of his voice and had run right into Ragg, almost knocking him down. Recalling this seemed to put the chief of police into a worse mood than before, and he wheeled to look at Bear hunkered down on the floor, his back against the wall.

"Hey!"

The Indian looked up to see Ragg standing there, his hands clenched into fists that were shaking. He was looking directly at Bear.

"You saw all this, and I want to know what happened here!"

Ragg couldn't finish. He didn't really want to know anyway. He chewed on his upper lip for a moment then said in a hoarse voice, "I'm gonna find this BB guy. Whatever it takes, I'll find him, and when I get through with him, I swear to God there ain't gonna be enough left of him to make a can of dog food."

He glanced at Bear as though looking for affirmation. Bear met his gaze calmly and gave an almost imperceptible nod of his head. There was a time to say nothing, and this was it. For a long time, he had not been able to sleep after what he had witnessed, the stench rolling over him as though he were standing downwind from a slaughterhouse. Finally, he had sat on the floor cross-legged, his back against the wall, closed his eyes and began to chant as his father had taught him to do and sank into a peaceful trance.

Ragg turned on his heel, walked up the corridor and through the door into the office. He sat down amidst a sea of papers, folders, files, pencils, and everything else that had been lying on his desk and the shelves. The repairman held out the phone and said, "It's working now, if you want to use it." Ragg grunted and snatched the phone from his hands, jiggled the hook, then jammed a fresh cigar into his mouth.

"Grace, get me Oliver Hagy. No, honey, I *don't* know the number. Lookit, sweetie, you're the operator and I'm the chief of police, you got that? Well, keep trying to get him and call me when you do."

Ragg was sitting on the edge of the desk chewing on his cigar. He had called and asked the remaining member of the force to come in, and Parker Peele was on his way. He threw a backward glance toward the cell block and saw Ben cleaning away for all he was worth. From where he was sitting, Ragg couldn't see Bear. The Indian must be on his bunk. The policeman remained there a moment longer, while gradually the outline of a plan began to form in his mind.

He wasn't crazy about it, but it was all he had at the moment. One thing for sure—the longer he waited, the worse it would get, and once the state boys got involved, that'd be all she wrote. The one thing that was on his side was that none of the suit and tie boys wanted to go knocking around in the Gut, and certainly not looking for BB. He picked up the key ring and went back to the cell, unlocked the door, then motioned for Bear to come out to the front and join him. There was only one chair with all four legs still attached. Ragg jerked his thumb, as a sign that Bear should take it, then he resumed his perch on the end of his desk.

"Coffee's over there," he barked, the words sounding more like an order than an invitation. Bear shrugged, went over to the pot and poured a cup, then came back and sat down. Each man eyed the other. They were almost the same height, just under six feet. Ragg was thirty-seven, Bear twenty-one. The police chief had hard, flat eyes the color of muddy water that narrowed into slits when he became angry and he wore his thinning sandy hair in a crew cut. The skin on his face seemed to be stretched tightly over the bones and was slightly pitted from a case of severe acne in his teens. And of course, there was the scar. By contrast, Bear's skin was the color of tan saddle leather, his face devoid of any beard. He wore his black hair short as he had in the Corps, and his eyes were large and dark, set deep within their sockets.

"Now listen, Bear. I know there's bad blood between you and me, and I know you don't like me cause I killed your father, but I had no choice, and a jury said so. I reckon if you had a chance and thought you could get away with it, you'd probably kill me right now, wouldn't you?"

Bear sat there sipping his coffee, his face a mask.

"Okay, I didn't expect an answer. But listen here, Bear. We need to put all this behind us cause I got something I need to talk to you about. You were a witness last night. You saw what BB did to Eldon. Now that boy wasn't no Dick Tracy, but he never hurt nobody much and was on his way to becoming a right fair policeman. And now he's just spare parts, and all because them clowns up at Dix didn't do their job." He paused and went over to get more coffee, but the pot was empty. He came back and sat down again, this time clasping his hands in front of him as though he were going to pray.

"Let me give it to you straight up, boy. I know all about you. I know how you grew up with your daddy hunting and trapping in the Gut from the time you were seven years old. You know every square foot of that place, where to step, what to look out for, where to hide, and you're probably the only person in Martin County who could go in there, find BB and bring him out alive. I'll make you a deal. You do that for me, I'll let you go."

Bear looked down into the coffee cup. He was wondering what his father might have done.

"It's not that easy," he said.

Ragg was instantly wary. "What do you mean?" His eyes narrowed, the thin lips forming a scowl.

"Ragg, I didn't have a busted taillight, and you know it. I'm in here for no reason at all. Now it's on my record. You're going to have to wipe all that out and clean my slate before I do anything."

"Hey, you ain't hearing me good. I'm giving you a chance to walk out of here and be a hero."

"I've *been* a hero," said Bear, "and it didn't do anything for me, except get me some medals that I keep in a cigar box and a piece of metal I carry around in my leg."

"So you're not gonna help me?"

"You heard my deal."

"*Your* deal? Hey, you're the one under arrest."

Bear shrugged and said nothing.

Ragg exploded. "You got sand, boy, I'll say that for you! Telling me what I gotta do in my own jail. Well, let me spell it out for you. I'm gonna lock you back up, and as far as I'm concerned, you can stay in there till Santa Claus comes, and the way I'm feeling right now, I just might lock *him* up, too."

He motioned for Bear to head back toward the cell. Bear gave no indication he was ready to move, and Ragg pulled out the sap from his rear pocket, pounding it into his palm. "Hey, Tonto. We can do this the easy way or the hard way."

Bear shrugged again, gave a half smile and walked back into the cell, keeping one eye on Ragg all the while. Ragg slammed the door shut behind him with a resounding clang, turned around, spit on the floor at the edge of the bars, then walked back up front and slumped down in his chair. The phone rang.

"This is Ragg ... Oliver, where you been, boy? ... Yeah, well, I need you to get your dogs down here real quick like. We got an escaped killer on our hands, and I want you to track him.... Huh? ... Sometime late last night.... Who? ... Yeah, I know Bear knows the Gut better than anybody else, but he happens to be in jail right now, so that's why I'm calling you while the scent's still fresh. ... Who? ... It's BB, that's who."

The instant the words left Ragg's mouth, he knew it was no good. The only other man who had ever tracked BB with dogs was Lump Bodine, for that time it had been the sheriff's show, and Lump had made the mistake of letting his dogs off the leash to run. They had found them a day later floating in Dark Creek, both with broken necks, the jaws completely separated at the hinge. Two days after that, BB showed up at his mother's house, just like the psychiatrist said he would, and they managed to get a net over him, and then one of the medical guys from Dix rushed in and gave him a shot that put him out like a light.

Oliver: "Ain't no way I'm gonna risk my dogs for a crazy like BB."

Ragg: "Don't you care about the people he killed?"

Oliver: "Sure I care, but finding him ain't gonna bring them back to life. Hey, Ragg, that Jesus at the tomb stuff is for preachers."

Ragg: "It's your duty as a law abiding citizen."

Oliver: "Ragg, you're forgetting I know you from high school, so you know what you can do with your duty."

Ragg begged, bargained and pleaded, but Oliver was not buying any of it. Finally, the policeman slammed down the phone with a string of curses. There wasn't anybody else he knew locally who would show up sober and with dogs that could track, and if he went to get outside help, the word would get out, then the state boys would take over, it'd be in the newspapers, and he'd be up the creek. Sweetwater didn't need or want any bad publicity. The mayor had made that very clear to him.

Ragg closed his eyes and cradled his forehead in his right hand. He had one dead man, not counting Maggie's cook and the yellow gal who would be better off if she *did* die. A messed up office. An escaped killer on his hands. He was out of cigars. No coffee. Had a cell block that still smelled like a slaughterhouse. Plus a hardheaded Indian who didn't want to play ball.

The phone rang. He snatched it up, growling a yeah into the receiver, listened for a few seconds, then put it down. It was the hospital. Maggie's dishwasher had gone into a coma during surgery earlier this morning and never came out. Her heart stopped ten minutes ago. The hospital thought he would like to know. Ragg had to laugh. *We thought you'd like to know.* What he *really* needed to know is what would it take for Bear to go into the Gut.

And the truth was, the chief of the Sweetwater Police Department didn't have a clue.

10

9:47 AM, Saturday, the fourth . . .

Charity was thrilled. With Joshua by her side, she was teaching once again, just as the Lord had called her to do. As a young girl graduating high school in 1881, she'd wanted to go to college, but her parents didn't have the money in those days. Few people did. Finally, when Decatur Female Seminary opened in '89 on the edge of Atlanta, she was 26 and had a savings account built up from clerking at Mears Dry Goods and Notions. Her mother had told her that 26 was too old to go to college, but that did not deter Charity Abigail Whitley. She had already written the school, and though they had told her there was no room and not to come, she packed her suitcase, kissed her mother good-bye and took the train to Atlanta. Once there, she sat on a wooden bench outside the dean's office for the better part of a day until he agreed to see her. He said he could only spare her 15 minutes, but they wound up talking for two hours. Charity was not only admitted but received a scholarship as well.

In her third year, a young, handsome evangelist named Caleb Trace came to preach. She fell in love with him halfway through his sermon, and they were married 24 hours after graduation. In 1906, the college changed its name to Agnes Scott, but Charity would always tell people she went to seminary, knowing that would set off skyrockets in their heads. A woman going to seminary? Now see here, young ladies don't do that. Of course, she hadn't gone to become a preacher, but a Christian teacher, because if there was one thing churches needed more than preaching, it was teaching. However, she had learned that far too many pastors were either ignorant of this fact, too lazy to do anything about it, or fearful of putting new ideas in the heads of the congregation who more often than not were "sot in their ways," as Caleb used to say. Her husband had also said to her, "Charity, you know more about the Bible and what it means than most preachers, but darling, don't be telling this in public or they'll have my hide for breakfast and yours for dinner."

After Charity cleaned up the kitchen, she took Joshua onto the sun porch and sat him down in a chair. Then she asked him to close his eyes, and when he did, she said, "Now before I start to talk to God, first I'm going to listen, and I want you to listen with me. And then I'll let you try it."

Joshua sat there with his eyes closed, feeling very relaxed in the warm sun that streamed through the windows. After a moment or two, he heard her begin to speak, and he was amazed. It was as though she were talking to somebody in her family. When she finished, he told her so.

"Well, son, now that's exactly who God is. He is our Father, you know. That's the first two words in The Lord's Prayer, and they're not there by accident." She moved over closer to him. "Now Joshua, I know you lost your earth father, but now you have a chance to have *another* Father, and this one can never be taken from you. Never. He will hear everything you tell Him, and He'll understand."

She paused. Joshua nodded, his eyes fixed on hers.

"And didn't you tell me that you always wanted a brother?"

"Yes ma'am."

"Well, now you have one. Jesus is always going to be there for you, for you both have the same heavenly Father."

Joshua furrowed his brow. Charity saw this and continued.

"Something else, too. You have the same name."

"We do. Jesus and me?"

"Yes. His Hebrew name was Yeshua. It was the Greeks who named Him Jesus. And you see, Yeshua is the same as Joshua."

Joshua squinted. "It doesn't sound like it."

"Oh well, you have to put the accent on the first syllable. Say 'yeah.' "

"Yeah."

"Good. Now say, 'shoo-ah.'" He said it.

"Now put them together. Yeah shoo-ah. You see how close it sounds to Joshua?"

The boy pronounced it as she had, then looked at Charity, his eyes wide in amazement. "Wow, Charity! Jesus and I have the same first name." He grew quiet for a moment, his eyes slowly widening in amazement.

"Uh, Charity . . . what does my name mean?"

"God delivered," she said, capturing him with her gaze, "and that's exactly what He did. And one day, God will deliver *you*, Joshua. Just wait and see. My Caleb always used to say that God was slow as molasses, but always on time." She laughed, then dabbed at the corner of her eye with her apron.

The boy was filled with wonderment, but remained silent.

Then he said, "Charity . . . why are you called Charity?"

"Oh, so now we're on *my* name, is that it?" she laughed. "Because my mother named me that."

"But I thought 'charity' meant . . . well, like giving money to the poor."

"Oh young'un, it does, but it means so much more than that. It means 'love,' and that's the best thing you can give to *anyone*. And you know something else?"

Joshua shook his head.

"Love is the one thing that the more you give away, the more you have left." Charity recalled how when she was a little girl, her mother told her that at the moment of her birth, she had prayed that God would bring Sam Whitley home from the war to see his baby daughter. Then one day not long after Lee surrendered, she had looked up from where she stood near her mother in the garden and seen a solitary figure in the distance, walking slowly toward her and had tugged at her mother's apron and pointed down the road. Soon the three of them were holding one another in a fierce embrace, weeping tears of joy in the bright sunlight.

Charity blinked hard and collected her thoughts. "Now, Joshua, when you feel the urge to talk to Him, don't put on airs. Just talk to Him the same way you would talk to me or your mother—or to yourself. You talk to yourself, don't you, young'un?"

"Well, sure, Charity. Mom says everybody does that."

"This is a little bit like that, only better. Because when you talk to yourself, you're the only one who's listening. But when you talk to God, *He* is listening to you, and you're not alone anymore. You have Father and Son to hear you, and the two of them send the Holy Ghost to give you what you need."

"Like what?"

"Oh . . ." she pursed her lips. "I guess courage and strength come at the top of my list. But there are other things, too, and you'll find these out the older you get. But all you need to know is, the next time you feel the need to talk to Him, when you have something you need to get off your chest, you just up and tell Him, then when you've finished, say, 'Lord, make me strong. Keep my faith solid like a rock. And give me courage so I can do Your will and not be afraid.' Can you remember that?"

Joshua nodded.

"Well, I have to hear you. Say it back to me."

Joshua had to try twice until he got it right. Charity got up from her chair, came over and hugged him, then clapped her hands and said, "Let me see, now. Wasn't this the morning you were going to cut my grass, and I was going to pay you a dollar and a half?"

"Yes'sum. Except you said a dollar."

Charity smiled. "Did I say that, really?"

"Yes ma'am."

"Well, so be it. But a worker is worth his hire, so when you get through, which I calculate will take you till about . . . hmm, just before noon, you come on in and I'll have lunch waiting on you."

"Yes ma'am. You got a deal!" Joshua flew out the screen door, and Charity smiled to herself, thinking all the while if she and Caleb had been blessed with a son, she would have wanted him to be just like Joshua.

An hour and a half later, the boy came in all flushed from the heat, and she gave him a towel soaked in ice water to cool him down. Then after he washed up, she put his favorite lunch before him: A BLT with a big glass of milk and peach cobbler with whipped cream. Charity had already eaten an apple, and all she wanted was a glass of water with a little lemon juice in it. Her mother had always said it was good for her skin. With a third of the sandwich in his mouth, Joshua managed to get out the question that had been plaguing him.

"Charity, how can God be, well, you know, three people?"

"Not people, Son. Beings!"

"Okay, beings, then."

"Well, now you take water — like this glass I have here in front of me. Without it, there would be no life on earth, right?"

The boy nodded, chewing, then wiping his mouth.

"If I boil a pot of water on my stove, what comes out of the top?"

"Steam."

"That's right. And when wintertime comes, what happens to the water in the birdbath I have by the garden?"

"It freezes . . . into ice."

"Uh huh. Now you're getting it, Joshua. Water can be liquid or solid or vapor, but it's still water, isn't it?"

The boy nodded, already into his cobbler, pausing in midmouthful, a thoughtful expression on his face.

"Son, it's the same way with God. He can reveal Himself to us in whatever form is necessary at the time. And the Messiah came so that God could find out what people were really like and feel what we felt. I mean, mortals like us—we get toothaches, skinned knees, broken toes, we get sick, we're frightened of this, tempted by that. People beat us up, call us names, imprison us . . . well, Jesus knows all about these things because He's human just like you and me. That's why we can tell Him everything, and He will understand and forgive us. He knows what it is to laugh and to love and to lose and to cry and. . . . "

"God can cry?" asked Joshua. He was utterly amazed.

"Of course, God can cry," said Charity. "I've heard Him. And one day, you'll hear Him, too. You have my word on it. And you have something even better than that, too."

"What's that?" asked the boy.

"*His* Word," responded Charity, her face beaming. "His Word. Oh, hallelujah!" She took a deep breath then let out a long sigh. "Joshua, all this will become so clear to you one day,

I just know it will, and then you'll come to know Him as I do, and you will come to love Him. Do you believe me, Son?"

"Yes," he replied, nodding solemnly, for he knew Charity would never lie to him. Then he watched as Charity picked up the glass of water and drained the contents, then sat it down with a smile.

"Water," she said. "It's what life is all about. People need to drink more of it, just like they need to have God fill their hearts to overflowing with His spirit. Don't you ever forget that, Joshua."

He swallowed hard. "No ma'am, I won't."

"Good. Now carry your dishes over to the sink and rinse them out, then go play or whatever boys do on a beautiful afternoon like this. I have a whole basket of sewing to take care of. Whoa, now, boy! Don't I get a hug before you go?"

"Aw, Charity. I'm going to see you later this afternoon when Mom comes back, won't I?"

"Sure you will. But I need a hug anyway."

He hugged her, and was out the door in a flash, Buddy jumping up from where he had been lying on the porch. Joshua spent the rest of the afternoon at Jimmy Woolard's with Billy Manning, the three of them deciding it was too hot to play outside, and going upstairs in Jimmy's bedroom to pore over his comic book collection, the largest in town.

When he returned to the cottage, he looked at the clock on the mantle and realized his mom wouldn't be home for another thirty minutes or so, and that meant he and Buddy could play some more. He flew out of the house, the dog following, and ran up the trail that led between the field of tobacco and the woods, the naked, ragged stalks having long since been stripped of their rich harvest. It was a good day to play war. He had put on his high tops and was wearing a knapsack he had gotten at the army surplus, and he had on the canteen that he had gotten from Jimmy Booker in a swap. As he walked, he kicked at dirt clods, and every now and then he'd swoop down, pick one up and hurl it at a stalk and say, "Gotcha!"

Buddy would bark and run over to inspect the dead enemy soldier. This was the best time for him, when he and Buddy were out here alone, just the two of them. After running after some soldiers that were trying to get away, he collapsed on the ground almost out of breath, Buddy coming to his aid with a series of licks and barks. Joshua remembered what Charity had said about just speaking right out and not being afraid. Like he was talking to his father. . . . "Lord. . . ." He tried again. He had to tell somebody. "Lord . . ." again, the words caught in his throat. Then he made up his mind he was going to tell God what happened even if it killed him. . . .

Lord . . . I was down at the library one night getting some books, it was back in June, and I had to use the bathroom, but the only one is in the police station. . . . Well, I went in there and while I was, you know, unzipping my fly, a man came in and stood next to me and he reached over and patted my behind, and then he tried to touch my . . . you know, God . . . and when I pulled away, he laughed and said that if I let him touch mine, he would let me touch his, but I didn't want to, and I was scared and I ran out of there, but he grabbed me by the arm and said if I ever told anybody, he'd come one night and cut my thing off, and Lord, I didn't go back into the library to check out my books, but rode home as fast as I could. And . . . and . . . I felt bad about it for a long time . . . I felt like I had done something dirty, and I could still see him looking at me, his hand reaching out to touch me, and I was ashamed . . . and I just wanted You to know, God.

There, Joshua thought. He had told God his worst, deepest, darkest secret, and Charity said that once he did that, it would make him feel better. She was right. It *did* feel good. He lay there waiting for God to answer him. Waiting to hear something, sitting there on the warm soil cross-legged with his eyes still squeezed shut.

The rabbit bolted out of a clump of broom straw where it had been hiding, waiting for them to leave. Buddy gave chase instantly and Joshua opened his eyes in time to see both dog and rabbit disappear into the woods. Joshua called out, "Buddy, come back here. You hear me? Come on back, Buddy! I mean it."

But Buddy did *not* come back, and Joshua could hear the sound of his barking. It seemed he was getting farther away. The boy had been in the woods only once and not very far, for he knew his mom would have been furious if she had known, since she had forbidden him to go there, but Joshua didn't figure he had to tell her. Shucks, a boy didn't have to tell his mother everything. It would only worry her to death, and anyway, he thought, she had enough on her mind.

Buddy began barking again, this time sounding more excited, and without hesitating further, Joshua found an opening in the thick growth and plunged into the woods. The land began to slope downward, and he ran pell-mell through briars and fallen branches, calling out again and again. Buddy had gone after rabbits before, but had always come back when Joshua called, and a sense of growing fear began to overtake him. What if Buddy went too far into the woods and couldn't find his way back? What if some kind of animal got hold of him and hurt him? What if it had him right now?

Joshua could feel his heart pounding, as he half walked, half ran through the woods, sweeping the low-lying branches and vines away from him, freeing himself when the briars caught on his trousers and all the while calling, "Buddy, c'mon back, Buddy. C'mon, boy," until finally, he felt the ground grow spongy underfoot, and then he came to the edge of the swamp. He stood motionless. He heard the dog bark once far off, the sound echoing over the black water.

Joshua hesitated a second, turned to look over his shoulder as though someone might be watching him. He couldn't go back without his dog. He just couldn't. His mother wouldn't have to know. He took one last look around, then plunged into the water, calling out *Buddy* with every step he took. Here in the outer reaches of the swamp, the water seemed to soak up what little light managed to find its way down through the thick green canopy overhead.

"Budde-e-e!"

He heard the barking again, but fainter. He changed his course, thinking the barking came more from the right now. Buddy barked again, but the sound seemed to come from everywhere because of the water and the dense growth of trees.

He would pause. Call out. Wait. Then plunge into the undergrowth again, thinking his dog couldn't be far away. He tripped and fell, then got up and leaned over for a moment, his hands on his knees, breathing heavily. A cloud of gnats swirled around him. He moved up onto a hummock of land and knelt down, his back leaning against the trunk of the cypress. He listened to the sound of his breathing. A mosquito whined in his ear. He slapped it away.

It was a lot darker in here than up in the piney woods. It was . . . different. Joshua didn't like it. But he had to find Buddy. He could not go back without his dog. He knew that.

"Buddy. Here, Buddy . . . c'mon, boy. Buddy, where are you?"

The sound of the word *you* came back at him in a lingering echo, and Joshua turned around, then again, realizing that the trees and the moss and the vines all seemed to run together. He had no idea of where he was or the way he had come. And at that moment, a feeling of dread began to well up within him, making his stomach flutter. If he could find Buddy, maybe *he* would know the way home.

"Buddy," he called.

"Buddy. . . ."

His voice came back, the word floating in the thick wet air. *Buddeeee!*

Joshua stood there, his lips still parted, and he realized he had never before been in a place that was so quiet. He couldn't hear a thing but his heart beating wildly in his chest, and though he told himself he was not lost and was not going to be afraid, he knew that he was.

"God," said Joshua, "I'm lost. Help me, please." And he waited to hear God speak to him as Charity said He would, but all he heard were the raucous cries of the birds overhead and the sound of his heart as though it would leap out of his chest, and then he would be dead for sure, and he didn't care what Charity said because then, God, it would be all Your fault.

Not knowing what else to do, Joshua fell on his knees and wept.

11

1:28 PM, Saturday, the fourth . . .

Four miles east of Sweetwater lies the small community of Dark Creek. It takes its name from the meandering stream that flows by the old landing, then empties into the Roanoke a mile or so farther on. There is a scramble of houses, their clapboards worn by wind and weather, the tin roofs on some having long since turned to rust. Another building sits along the road, this one stooped on wobbly stacks of bricks with a slight tilt to the right. A small sign reads Dark Creek Independent Bible Church. Next to it lies a garage of sorts that still doubles as a blacksmith's shop. Finally, across the road stands *Hardison's Store, Raymond and Kate Hardison, Proprietors,* the faded letters barely visible on the sign Raymond had painted and put up the morning after they got married 20 years ago this September the 25th.

Kate remembered . . . there hadn't been any honeymoon. Right after they said *I do,* they moved their things into a tiny clapboard dwelling that had been a storage shed. She fried a chicken for their wedding supper, and afterwards she snuffed out the candle and with a full moon shining through the window and playing on their bare bodies, the two of them giggling and blushing, Raymond pulled her down onto the bed that was too short for his long legs. Afterwards they talked all night long about the wonder of what they had shared, their eyes wide, hearts bursting with the secret joys of a man and a woman, the gifts of a loving God.

From the start, the two of them had agreed they would share equally in the work, whatever had to be done to make a go of it out here in the middle of nowhere. She and Raymond had kept that promise through good times and bad until that day came. The day that had been permanently etched in her mind. . . . It was a Monday afternoon. He was plowing their corn, 50 yards distant from the little house that he had built with his own hands before the twins had come. She had just put Jeremiah and James down for their nap, when she heard the thunder, looked out the kitchen window and saw the black cloud that was almost directly over Raymond. She ran outside and yelled to him, pointing up at the cloud. He stopped, looked up, gave her a wave and bent down to unhitch the plow. In a minute or so, he'd join her in the store, but as she had stood there watching him, she saw the long crooked streak of lightning fork down out of that dark cloud and find its way right to her husband.

One second he was there smiling and waving at her, and as she broke into a run, suddenly she saw him lit up in an orange-blue light that lasted only a second. She thought she heard him cry once, but when she arrived at his side, there was nothing to be done. His body lay on the freshly plowed ground, the work shoes she had bought him for his birthday having been ripped off his feet now charred black and still smoking where the lightning had left him to go into the ground. His warm body still twitched intermittently, and she knelt down, cradling him in her arms and crying, *Oh, baby, baby, don't leave me. . . . Dear God, don't take him, please don't take my man.*

The funeral was the next afternoon, and the following morning, she was back in the store because it was just her and the twins now, and they had to make it. By grannies, they were *gonna* make it. And they did for the next 17 years. Pearl Harbor came, then in the spring of '43, the twins reached 17 and graduated from high school. Over the years, a dime at a time, Kate had saved enough money for them to go up to Chapel Hill, and she had seen to it that they always got up their lessons, made good grades and behaved like proper gentlemen. But a week after graduation, they came home from town, their faces flushed with excitement, the words tumbling out of their mouths.

Momma, Momma, we're going to be paratroopers in the 82nd Airborne... see, we already got our bus tickets for Fort Bragg, and the recruiting sergeant told us we'd be the first set of twins ever to go to jump school at Fort Benning. . . .

She knew they would have been drafted soon enough anyway, and her initial anger subsided, turned into tears, and finally she knew she had no choice but to accept their decision. They had one good dinner together, and the next morning they were gone. After that, they had come home only once, looking so handsome in their new uniforms and shined jump boots with their paratrooper wings, and she had taken them to church, being proud of them, but hiding her fear. The following week, they were shipped overseas; she got letters from them every week or so for a year. She would listen to the radio daily to keep up with the war, and as Christmas drew near, she knew the 82nd had been fighting in Belgium, near a town whose name she couldn't pronounce — it started with a "B."

The day after Christmas, the telegram arrived just as she was closing up earlier than usual since it was so cold and wet and there was no business anyway. Russell Corey brought it out from town, with his long face looking down, not wanting to meet her eyes, but she knew what it was before he even put the yellow windowed envelope into her trembling hands. She hung two gold stars in the window, and a week later, they shipped her boys home; two soldiers, a sergeant and a captain came for the funeral and gave her two folded American flags, the two Bronze Stars and Purple Hearts that she kept in the trunk with the rest of their things from high school. Kate buried Jeremiah and James beside their father, then went on with her life. First Raymond, then the twins. She would have gladly gone in the place of either of them, and she would often ask God why He didn't take her instead, but she never got an answer; however, she knew that getting no answer *was* His answer. And she knew she would have to be content with that.

Kate walked out to the gas pump and began to work the handle back and forth, until the red liquid slowly gurgled up to the top of the clear glass cylinder. More and more people were getting electric pumps, but she didn't have the money to put into one. If she did, she'd only have to raise the price of her gas, and if it went up just one penny, there would be some people that would never let her hear the end of it, and the one who always came to mind first was Blackbird. It was generally said around Dark Creek that Blackbird would squeeze a nickel till the Indian rode the buffalo.

He had been baptized as Blake Bird after his grandfather, but everybody called him "Blackbird," because when he was a little boy going to school, he'd had the dirtiest feet of anyone. It wasn't because he went barefoot, though, because *everybody* went barefoot till cold weather came. Maybe he didn't like to wash, or maybe some folks were just naturally dirtier than others. Anyway, the nickname had stuck, and even though he had indoor plumbing now and could buy all the shoes he wanted to, somehow she thought the name still suited him because everytime he came into the store, he always had a scowl on his face, like he was getting ready to cloud up and rain. Immediately, she closed her eyes, looked up, feeling the sun on her face and said aloud, "Lord, please forgive me. I don't mean that man no harm."

"Miz Kate, you must be talking directly to God sure nuf."

She opened her eyes to see Goodboy standing there wearing that huge dazzling smile of his, with the two gleaming gold teeth.

"Oh! You scared me, Goodboy. I didn't even hear you."

"Yas'sum, that's what people say about me all the time. They say, 'Goodboy, you be so quiet, you could sneak up on a rabbit fo' he knowed you was there.' "

Kate shielded her eyes and looked at the black man in his worn overalls. Raymond had been six feet, but Goodboy stood an inch or two taller. His huge arms hung down by his side, the long, ropy muscles the evidence of years of working Doctor Reardon's farm. He was one of the few men she had known, other than Raymond, who could lift a 100-pound sack of fertilizer under each arm and walk off with it. The story was that one Sunday morning when Dr. Reardon went out to get his paper, he found the baby on the doorstep lying in a bean hamper. The doctor's wife had been alive then, and she took the baby in without a moment's hesitation and let their maid rear it. The baby seldom cried and never gave them any trouble, and since they didn't know who his parents were, they named him Goodboy Lincoln Found.

As the child grew, they realized he was different from other children. It wasn't that he was addled or retarded or anything like that. Kate had learned that Goodboy was innocent of the way the world really was and how evil men could be. Yet he knew right from wrong, he could read his Bible, and he could look at a truckload of fertilizer and tell you how many sacks were on it. In fact, sometimes, she would fill a scoop of beans from the sack and ask Goodboy to guess how many were in it. Every time she did this he had guessed correctly.

One other thing he was good at: *throwing*. If he had gone to school, she reckoned he might have been a big league baseball pitcher. She could remember that when the twins were growing up, Goodboy would come home from the field and walk up to the store, and they would ask him to show them how good he could throw. She could hear them hollering now, "C'mon, Goodboy, show us what you got!" He would pitch to them, the ball coming so hard and fast that whoever was brave enough to catch would be knocked right off his feet. It was said that Goodboy Found could chuck a rock and knock a squirrel right out of a tree good as a man could with a rifle.

Kate wasn't sure she understood why God gave him those gifts other than they made up for what he *didn't* get. Plus, sometimes Goodboy knew just what you were thinking.

"Goodboy, let me ask you a question. How old are you?"

"I'm, lem'me see now . . . twenty-seven."

"And when? . . ."

"Ain't rightly sure of my birthday, Miz Kate. But Doctuh Jesse say it be some time in June."

She smiled at him, then laughed aloud. "Goodboy Found, you are a child of God, you know that?"

"Yas'sum . . . deed I do."

"Now, what can I do for you?"

Goodboy began to recite a short list of groceries without hesitation as the two of them entered the store, trading the August heat for the welcome coolness of the interior, the big fan circling lazily overhead. While Kate was getting up his order, the small bell on the screen door tinkled, and she looked up to see who it was, then felt her teeth pressing on each other.

Blackbird.

She spoke first, just as she did with everyone, but though she generally called everyone by name, she didn't do it with him.

"Yes sir, how are you today?"

"Okay, I reckon. I need to pay you for my gas."

"Yes sir. I'll be with you as soon as I finish getting up Goodboy's list."

A scowl formed on the white man's face.

"Kate Hardison, I'm in a hurry, and I ain't got time to wait on no nigger." The ensuing silence filled the store instantly, its presence something Kate could feel pressing on her chest and squeezing her heart, then moving lower to tie her stomach in a knot.

Goodboy spoke first. "Miz Kate, if Mistuh Blackbird be in a hurry, it's. . . . "

"No, that's all right, Goodboy. You were first, and I always wait on my customers the way they come in."

Now Blackbird had never liked this woman from the day he first came in the store, and with the passing of the years, he had grown to like her even less, and maybe it was the heat or the nigger or what all, but he decided he'd had about a bellyful of Kate Hardison. He moved toward her as she stood at the end of the counter near the scales.

"Now you listen here, Kate. I don't cotton to no uppity women, specially when they're nigger lovers to boot, and I'm gonna give you what somebody should of done a long time ago to shut up that smart mouth of yours." So saying, he drew back his arm intending to slap her, surprised that Kate did not flinch, but met his gaze squarely, then even more surprised when he felt his wrist caught in a vise. He stared with shock to see the hand so large it totally encircled his wrist, the fingers meeting each other. He could not believe it. A black hand on his white wrist.

"Mistuh Blackbird, suh, you know you don't need to go round hitting on no women folks, specially not Miz Kate. She ain't never done nobody no harm."

Blackbird couldn't find his voice. Before he could, Kate found hers with no problem. "Blackbird, I'm gonna tell you something. You ain't nothing but a bully. You always have been and you always will be, and everybody in Dark Creek knows it, but is too scared to tell you. You're a mean man, that's what you are. You're mean to your wife, you were mean to your momma and daddy while they were living, and if you had had children, you would have been mean to them, too. You been coming into my store for 20 years now, and I reckon that's enough. You might be a big shot in the Klan, but that don't mean doodley squat to me, and you can walk in here again, many times as you want to—the law says I can't keep you out—but I'm going to tell you this, *Mister* Blackbird. From now on, your money ain't worth nothing in here. It won't buy you spit."

Kate stood there, her face no more than 12 inches from his. She could see the tiny red veins in his skin, his upper lip curling in the trace of a sneer showing the small crooked teeth, a muscle twitching along his cheekbone, his eyes blazing in a mixture of shock and anger.

"Nigger, get your black hand off me, you hear me, boy!" His face was contorted with rage, but the vise did not loosen.

A long moment passed. They could hear the sound of a car going by. A fly buzzed overhead. The fan hummed.

"Goodboy, let him be now," said Kate, quietly. "It's all right. Mister Bird is not gonna be any more trouble, are you?"

Blackbird stared back at her, his lower lip trembling.

"*Mister* Bird, I asked you a question."

Blackbird shook his head as an answer.

"All right, Goodboy, let him go."

"Yas'sum." Goodboy relaxed his grip.

Blackbird felt his wrist to make sure it was not broken, the imprints of Goodboy's fingers still showing red. He turned on his heel and stormed out the door, letting it slam behind him, took a step or two toward his car, then turned and raised his fist, the words coming out mixed with spittle. "You . . . you ain't heard the last of this. Both of you. You just remember that."

The two of them stood there watching as Blackbird climbed into his truck and drove off, the wheels spinning, enveloping the storefront in a cloud of dust. Kate sat down behind the counter, letting her breath out in a sigh, glad the ordeal was over.

"Whooee!" said Goodboy. "I ain't never seen *nobody* that mad before, has you, Miz Kate?"

"Well, maybe a couple of times, but one thing's for sure. I reckon he could have chewed a tire iron in half and spit nails."

Goodboy laughed uproariously, took off his cap and pounded his thigh. "Miz Kate, you are a caution sure nuf—now that's the truth."

"Well," she said, "I need to finish getting up your order, but I plumb forgot where I was."

"Uh ruh, I believe you'd bout gotten to the sack of corn-meal."

She nodded and turned to the shelf of staples behind the counter, then wheeled around to look at him. "Goodboy," she paused, not knowing how to say it, then decided she would say whatever popped into her mouth. "You are my friend, and I thank you for being here . . . for helping me," the words coming out in that warm, rich voice that any choir would give up its robes to have in their alto section.

"Yas'sum, well, one thing's for sure. We *all* brothers and sisters in the Lord, and thass a fact, ain't it?" He looked at her, and as she met his glance squarely, she knew she was not look-ing into a man's face, but into his very soul.

"Yes, Goodboy," she said, "that *is* a fact." She totalled up the groceries, and the black man pulled out two crumpled one dollar bills and paid her. As though to break the mood of the previous moment, Kate grabbed the worn wooden scoop, plunged it into the sack of pinto beans, then held it up. "You want to guess for a free Coke Cola?"

"Well, yas'sum, if you wants me to." Goodboy stared at the scoop for a moment, knit his brow and said, "87."

"Here's your Coke," said Kate with a sigh and waved good-bye to her friend as he went out the door. "Be sure to bring the bottle back." As the door closed behind Goodboy, the bag of groceries in one hand, the Coke in the other, she looked at the scoop of beans lying on the counter. She knew there was no need to count them, for when she finished, there would be not 86 or 88 but exactly 87 beans. She did not know how he did it, but she also knew it was a gift from the Holy Spirit, like his rock throwing, and that God had anointed Goodboy in a very special way.

Kate kept staring at the beans and staring . . . and staring. Finally, as with all the other times, she could no longer resist and began picking them out of the large scoop one by one, lay-ing them on the counter in neat rows until she counted out the last three beans . . . "85, 86, 87." She nodded her head slowly and said, almost in a whisper, "Lord . . . I know the Holy Spirit gave Goodboy something special, and I know he is my brother, and I love him just the way You told us to. And even if nobody else understands what I'm talking about, I know *You* do, and that's all that matters. Now if You'll excuse me, Lord, I got work to do. You got Your job, and I got mine."

12

6:47 PM, Saturday, the fourth . . .

The heat, the trip, the interview and everything else had just about worn Deborah down to a frazzle. When she had arrived in Rocky Mount, Mr. Clippard had met her bus and taken her to the store where they spent an hour together talking in his office. Then he showed her around the store, introducing her to his entire staff.   After that came lunch, and more talk and more questions. Finally, he told her she would fit in good at Clippard's and that the job was hers.   The whole thing had taken longer than she thought and when he dropped her off at the station, she realized she had missed her bus.   The next bus wouldn't get to Sweetwater until six-thirty. She tried to get hold of Charity, but there was no answer, but Deborah didn't worry.   Joshua could take care of himself until she got there, and if he got lonely, he could always go up and visit with Charity.   When she finally arrived home, she splurged for a quarter for a taxi and after paying the driver, went into the cottage, eager to see her son.

"Joshua, where are you? I have the most wonderful news!" When no answer came, she realized he was probably out in the field playing with Buddy. She stepped onto the small back porch and yelled. "Joshua, I'm home."

Of course, he could be playing at one of his friend's houses, but then, he always left a note by the phone if he went anywhere. She went back into the cottage and looked, but there was no note. She looked up the numbers in the book and called both friends. He was not there. Well, maybe he was out riding his bike, but she'd check with Charity to make sure. She walked out the screen door, letting it slam behind her, started to walk toward the house, then without realizing it, broke into a dead run, even though it was barely 50 feet away.

"Charity! Charity?"

She snatched open the screen door and went into the kitchen. No one.

"Charity?"

She went into the huge parlor, her eyes having to adjust to the darkness. Charity always pulled down the shades to keep out the blazing afternoon sun. Deborah found her sitting in her favorite chair, smiling at her, the Bible in her lap.

"Charity, didn't you hear me calling? Where's Joshua?"

"Oh yes, I know. Caleb will be home for dinner soon, and I have to get things ready, child," said the older woman, a distant quality to her voice.

"Caleb . . . Charity, what on earth? . . . " Deborah broke off and going over to the older woman, knelt by the chair, taking hold of her hands. She noticed Charity's glasses had fallen to the floor.

"Charity, what is it? Tell me, what's wrong? Where's Joshua? What's happened?"

Charity looked at her and smiled sweetly. "My Caleb, now, he always wants meat loaf on Sunday evenings."

Deborah shook her head. It wasn't Sunday, it was Saturday. And Caleb had died a long time ago. She said, "Charity, I don't understand." She gripped the older woman's wrists and shook her. "Charity. Where's Joshua? Where's my son? I want my son!"

Charity just looked at her and smiled. It was as though she was looking *through* her.

Deborah ran out of the house, down the back steps, past the cottage and into the adjoining field of tobacco stalks, half stumbling as she ran through the soft dirt, her high heels digging into the ground at every step, screaming her son's name over and over, until she tripped and sprawled headlong into the dirt, her fists starting to pound the earth.

"God, what did You do with my son? I want my son . . . do You hear me, God! I want Joshua. You took my husband, but You're not going to take my son from me. You're not . . . You can't. Do You hear me, God? *Do You hear me?*"

13

7:12 PM, Saturday, the fourth . . .

Carlyle Woolard was Charity's closest neighbor, though he lived 50 yards away on the other side of a small patch of woods. He was just putting up his lawnmower, and hearing what sounded like a woman screaming, came over at a dead run. He first went into the house and found Charity in her chair. Not being able to make sense out of anything she said, he called Doctor Reardon and told him something was bad wrong with Charity and to come over right away.

Then he heard someone moaning softly and turned just as Deborah walked into the room, her hair disheveled, one shoe off, the heel on the other broken, her stockings torn, dirt stains on her face and hands, and her eyes wild looking as though she'd seen a ghost. Carlyle recognized her as the Grayson woman who rented the cottage. She was babbling something about her son, but Carlyle could make no more sense out of her than he had Charity, and he picked up the phone and called the police.

Ragg had been sitting there behind his desk, just having finished a hamburger, and knowing he was going to have to do something about BB and fast. The mayor had already been in, and they'd had a long talk, if you could call it a talk, thought Ragg. Johnson had told him that by God there was a killer out there on the loose, and it was his job to find him and bring him in. Ragg had told him that Oliver Hagy was not going to go into the Gut with his dogs to hunt BB, and furthermore, by now BB was so far back in that swamp he wasn't going to hurt anybody else because there wasn't anybody back in there to hurt. The phone rang, and five minutes later, he was sitting in the large parlor, waiting for Dr. Reardon to finish examining Charity. It took Jesse only a moment to determine that she had suffered a stroke. As to its severity, he wasn't sure, but at her age, any incident like that was serious. Now the Grayson woman was another story. She was hysterical, and Jesse made her sit down, asked Ragg to bring her a glass of water, then held her hands and made her take slow, deep breaths. Finally, she was able to tell them. She had been gone most of the day on a job interview in Rocky Mount and had come home to find Charity like this, and Joshua gone. She added that her son knew better than to go off without leaving a note or . . . her voice trailed off.

"Mrs. Grayson, do you know who I am?"

Deborah focused on the face and thought it seemed familiar.

"I'm Police Chief Ragg. Now, where do you think your son might be?"

"I don't know," she said softly, shaking her head slowly back and forth.

"Well, could he have gone over to somebody's house, a friend that maybe you don't know?"

"No . . . he wouldn't do that. He knows better."

"Uh huh. Well, let's see now, Ma'am. Could he be out playing in the woods behind the tobacco field?" Ragg gestured with his hand.

"He . . . he knows he's not to go in the woods."

"Well, you know, Miz Grayson, sometimes boys that age know one thing and do another. He might have lost all track of time." Her look told Ragg she was not even listening to him.

"He had a dog," said Carlyle, who had stayed on after the two men arrived.

"What kind of dog?" asked Ragg.

"Just a dog. I don't know. Looked to me like it was maybe six months old or so. Still a puppy, I guess you'd say."

"It's part collie, part chow," said Deborah. "His name is Buddy."

Ragg went out of the house, ran through the field, up to the woods and walked along the edge of the woods looking for something. Anything. He whistled loudly and called out the boy's name several times, shouting with all his might in the direction of the swamp. He walked into the woods 50 feet or so, calling and still whistling, knowing that if the boy were within hearing distance, he would give some kind of response. As he stood there in the deepening twilight, an idea began to take shape in his head. He turned and went back to the house. The mayor had arrived and seeing Ragg, beckoned him to join him in the kitchen. There was an ambulance out front, and two men were carrying out Charity on a stretcher while the doctor accompanied them.

"I figured I'd better come on over," said the mayor. "Is the boy lost?"

Ragg nodded grimly. "More'n likely."

"In the Gut?"

"Yes sir, Mister Mayor. His dog probably spooked a rabbit, took off after it, the kid followed, then probably got turned around one way and then another and panicked. It's awful tricky in there, and remember, we've had two grown men who never came back, so for a boy who doesn't know his way around—well, it don't look good. Thing is, by now, there's no telling how far into the Gut he's gone."

"Well, we have to get up a search party or something. We need to find him."

Yeah, *we* sure do, don't we? thought Ragg. He came back into the living room. "Miz Grayson, do you happen to have a picture of your son?"

She nodded, left the room for a moment then came back and put the wallet sized photo in Ragg's hands. "It's a school picture. They had them made last March."

The inside of Ragg's mouth went dry as a stone. His hands got hot. He felt his face flush. It was the same kid he had approached in the bathroom at the station. He fought for control, managed to keep his voice calm as he thanked her, then left the group for a moment to walk out onto the back porch. He had to sort all this out. He stared at the woods. The idea kept coming together like pieces of a jigsaw puzzle slowly putting themselves into place. Bear might not go in the Gut after BB, but

Ragg's hunch told him the Indian would definitely go after the boy. He reached for a cigar then remembered he was fresh out.

BB was out there roaming around in the Gut like a wild animal that needed to be shot. Plus, there was the kid who one day might decide to blab about what had happened and make it into something it wasn't. Ragg didn't know whose word people would take if push came to shove, and he didn't want to find out either. He knew Standing Bear could track down BB. And now, the boy, too. But that wouldn't solve anything. Unless. . . .

Ragg drove his fist into his palm and came back into the parlor. He looked at Johnson. "Mister Mayor, I wonder if I could have one of your cigarettes." Johnson, who knew his police chief to be an inveterate cigar smoker, puzzled over this briefly, then shook one out of the pack. Ragg stuck it in his mouth and lit it. He drew deeply, blew out a cloud of smoke then watched it swirl up toward the chandelier. The plan kept forming in his mind, and suddenly, the pieces came together.

"Mayor, are you gonna tell her about BB?"

"No," said Johnson. "Somehow, I don't think this is the right time or place. It would be more than she could handle."

"Well, I'll let you decide that. In the meantime, I think I've got an answer that'll work. Yes sir, I surely do."

Ragg turned and looked at Deborah who sat on the sofa, her shoulders slumped. "Miz Grayson, we're gonna find your son for you, so don't you worry about a thing. You hear? I'm gonna take charge of this thing personally, Ma'am. I give you my solemn word."

14

8:12 PM, Saturday, the fourth . . .

When Ragg left Charity's house and walked out to his car, he was surprised to find the mayor waiting for him, leaning up against the Ford and having a smoke.

Johnson explained that if Ragg found BB and the boy, it would be a feather in his cap and would cinch his raise with city council. Plus with his own campaign for the legislature next year . . . well, he was sure the chief could understand how something like this could have a great effect on both their careers, and wasn't that the way Ragg saw it, too. Ragg chewed on all this on his way back to the station. Johnson had it part right and part wrong. If Bear went in and brought the boy back alive, *he'd* be the hero, not Ragg, and he didn't want that. Then, too, there was the chance the kid would blab to somebody about what happened, and Ragg would never work as a policeman again.

But if Bear tracked the boy, and Ragg went along with him, it just might be that the Indian would not make it back alive. For that matter, something might happen to the kid, too. After all, BB had already killed three people, so the story would come back sounding something like this: Bear spied BB and went after him, telling Ragg to stay behind. He waited, but Bear never came back. The next morning, Ragg found what was left of the boy.

Miz Grayson, please accept my deepest sympathy. God knows I did all I could, and I only wish I could have done more.

And if Bear *did* luck up and snag BB, Ragg would take care of him so that his body would never be found, though he hadn't figured out just how yet. Dead or alive, BB couldn't testify to anything, and it was easier just to leave him there dead. No one would want to go back in for the body, and no one would expect Ragg to carry a man that size out of the swamp. The other thing was, nobody cared whether BB was alive or dead except that nuthouse doctor. So that was the plan: no BB. No Bear. No kid. No problems.

By the time he had made his swing through town and returned to the jail, Bear had just finished his supper. Ragg walked back to the cell block, dragging a chair with him. He turned it around, slid it up to the bars and sat down with his arms folded over the top. He looked at the man whom he wanted to see dead so bad he could taste it. He smiled at him.

"The grub okay?"

"I've had better, and I've had worse." There was something in Ragg's voice that set off an alarm in Bear. The white man wanted to pow wow. Talk trade. Set a snare. They always did.

Ragg started to offer the Indian a cigar then remembered he didn't smoke. He lit one up and tried to read the stolid face three feet away from his. Hard to see into those dark eyes. Like looking down a well at midnight.

"I just got back from Charity's house. Charity Trace. You know her?"

"I know her name."

"Well, anyway, she had a little stroke and is in the hospital. The Grayson boy, him and his momma live out back in that little cottage, and while she was out of town today, the boy went and got himself lost in the Gut. It's too dark to go looking for him now, so I figured we'd wait until morning and go in after him."

Bear sat there, unblinking, not smiling. No response.

"You know the kid, Bear?"

"I met him once. A friend of his brought him to a Scout meeting right after school let out."

Ragg started to respond, then checked himself just in time.

"Well, now, we both know the Gut ain't no place for a little kid, specially with somebody like BB running around loose."

"You got that right, Chief." Bear looked right at Ragg, then shifted his eyes upward so he was looking right over the man's head so that Ragg could not catch his glance. His daddy had taught him how to do that—said it drove the white eyes crazy.

"Bear, I know that BB's none of your business, like you said. Anyway, by now, he's probably so far back in there ain't nobody gonna ever find him. We got two dead niggers, but that ain't no big deal. We lose one every Saturday night anyway. Eldon's gone, too, but that comes with the job. But now the boy ... that's another story. You know, Bear, let's just say that, uh, I was to let you out of here and wipe the slate clean. No record of your arrest. And if you was to go into the Gut and find that kid, the town would owe you a big thank you. At least, that's the way I see it. How do you see it?"

"What I see is you want to tag along with me and take part of the credit, right?"

"Yeah, the thought did cross my mind," said Ragg.

Bear managed a little smile. He stood up and walked over to grip the bars with his hands, looking down at the policeman. "You wouldn't be dead weight on me in the Gut, would you? I move pretty fast."

"Oh, I can keep up."

"And once we're in there, I'm the boss. You have to do what I say. And if you can't keep up, I'll leave you behind."

Ragg made a face. "That ain't the way it. . . . "

"I deal one hand in this game," interrupted Bear. "Play 'em or fold 'em."

Once again, his face became that impenetrable mask. Ragg felt himself start to blow, tried to puff on the cigar and realized it had gone out. The Indian had him—for now. He set his mouth in a hard line and got up from the chair.

"Well, let me run this by our mayor, and see what he says."

"The mayor's gonna do whatever you tell him to do," said Bear.

"Yeah, I guess he will at that. You got it all figured out, don't you? You're pretty smart for an Indian."

"And you're not so dumb for a white man."

Ragg felt his skin prickle, a rush of heat running through him, but he knew this kind of talk wouldn't get them anywhere. The plan was the important thing. He had to keep that in mind for now because later on when it was all over, none of this would matter. Lose the battle, but win the war.

"You don't think anything bad might happen to him before we find him, do you?"

Bear took a breath, clasped his large hands together and cracked his knuckles. "Well, there's four things out there that could give him a problem. Water moccasins, quicksand, BB and the gator. They're all bad, but the gator's the worst."

"You really think there's an alligator in the Gut?"

"I *know* there is. A big one, too."

A moment of silence hung in the air that still reeked with Lysol.

"All right, you got yourself a deal," said Ragg. He stuck his hand through the bars. Bear looked at it, then took it.

"You gonna unlock this door or what?" said Bear. "I have to get cleaned up and pack my gear."

Ragg took the key ring from his belt, unlocked the cell door, and Bear swung it open, walked by Ragg and said, "Five o'clock, sharp. Pick me up at my place. You'll need boots. Wear long sleeves. Don't carry anything that makes a noise like keys, metal, stuff like that. Pack yourself enough food and water to last two days. We may not need it, but then again, we might. Got it?"

Ragg nodded, turned to lay the keys on the desk, and when he turned around again, Bear had vanished. The policeman took off his cap and wiped the sweatband, laying it on the desk. Even with the fans going, it was hot in here, but he knew where they were going, it would be a lot hotter. He also knew he had a plan that would work. He sat down in the chair, propped his feet up on the desk and in spite of the odor which stabbed at his nostrils and his office which was still a mess, Ragg began to laugh out loud, nodding all the while. Everything was gonna be sweet. Real sweet.

15

9:09 PM, Saturday, the fourth . . .

Kate had counted up the day's receipts from the Tampa Nuggets cigar box that she kept the bills in, added up the change, and made a careful notation in the ancient ledger she kept under the counter. She turned off all the lights but a small bulb, locked the door, then walked the hundred or so feet to her little house that sat behind the store in a grove of oaks and willows. She had not been home more than ten minutes when she realized she had left her Bible at the store, the first time she had ever done that. She always kept it with her during the day so that when she had a break she could turn to the Word and find solace and strength. Kate sighed deeply, then raised herself from the rocker that had been Raymond's favorite, walked out into the darkness and along the path that led to the store. Just before she reached the corner of the building, however, she heard a murmur of voices and flattened herself against the outside wall.

She craned her neck around the corner and saw a pickup parked on the other side of the pumps. The outside of the station was dark since the bulb in her sign had long since been burned out—just one more of those things she needed to take care of. A cloud was passing over the moon, and all she could make out were the shapes of three men. They were wearing sheets with the hoods hanging down over their necks. As she listened intently she could make out the voices. One was Blackbird's, the other belonging to Mash Gannon, a longtime bootlegger and Klan member. She thought the third was J.D. Elrod, a shade tree mechanic who stayed drunk more than he did sober. At that instant, the moon freed itself from the cloud, and she could see Elrod clearly.

Blackbird: "Here, you want some of this?"

Mash: "Yeah." He took the half-pint that Blackbird handed him.

Blackbird: "You shoulda heard what that nigger did to me today. I'm talking about right here in this store."

Mash: "Yeah, you already told me."

Elrod: "Well, tell me. *I* didn't hear about it."

Blackbird: "He put his hand on me, that's what. A nigger laying hands on a white man! If I'd had a gun, I'd a shot him dead on the spot, and no jury in this county would convict me."

Mash: "You mighty right about that."

Blackbird let out a whoop.

Mash: "Blackbird, keep it quiet. Kate might hear you. Besides, you better not drink anymore if we're gonna go ahead with this thing."

Blackbird: "Hey, don't worry about me none. I ain't never too drunk to go whup up on niggers. Nosirreebob."

Mash: "All right, all right, that ain't gonna get us anywhere. Now if we're gonna do this thing, let's do it."

The three of them got into the pickup truck, two in the cab and one in back, and she watched as they headed out onto the tar and gravel, then turn off on the dirt road toward Goodboy's cabin. Kate broke into a run back to the house. There wasn't a whole lot of time left.

Goodboy was out back bathing by the well thinking about how he had left Doctor Reardon's house at the age of 12 and come to live here with Sim Bell who had farmed for the doctor since he was 14. Sim was a widower, a hard worker and a good teacher, and he had taught Goodboy all that he knew. Just before Goodboy reached his sixteenth birthday, Sim's heart quit on him right in the middle of plowing a row, and the 80 acres of tobacco and peanuts had become Goodboy's sole responsibility. He finished rinsing off the soap with a bucket of cold water and dried himself with two flour sacks sewn into a towel. He stepped into his clean overalls that he would wear to church in the morning, and as he did, he heard the sound of the pickup, then the voices.

"Hey, nigger, come on out of that house."

"You heard him, boy, and that means now!"

He went in the house, walked through the hall and onto the porch. There were three of them standing there about 20 feet away, wearing sheets and hoods and carrying torches. One of them had a rifle, the other a shotgun. The third had a bull whip. The pickup sat back another 30 feet toward the road.

"Nigger, 'bout *time* you got out here. You due for a whipping, you know that? As a matter of fact, boy, according to my watch, you're past due!" said Blackbird. They all laughed.

Goodboy stood there, his body shivering in spite of the warm August night. He hadn't gotten his gun, because he knew if he did, he might shoot someone, and if that happened, then he'd be found hanging from a tree by morning.

"White folks, y'all need to go on home now. Everybody knows Goodboy is a good nigger."

"You're good for nothin', that's what you're good for," said Blackbird. "You think you can go around acting uppity, but I'm here to tell you we ain't gonna allow that in Dark Creek."

Goodboy recognized the voice instantly.

"All right, boy, that's enough talking. Step on down here in the dirt and draw your time." The tallest of the three men stepped forward brandishing the torch and cracked the whip, sending a chill down Goodboy's spine. If he ran back into the house, they'd come in after him. If he ran away, he'd come home to find a pile of ashes where his house had been. If he went for his shotgun, he'd be dead. He dropped to his knees on the worn boards of the front porch, clasped his hands and began praying, saying the words softly to himself.

"O, Lord Jesus, save me from the white folks' evil, Lord. I forgive them for not knowing what they be about, but Lord, You know my heart is pure and that I love You, and. . . . "

"Hey, this ain't no prayer meetin'," said Mash. He cracked the whip again, the end of it biting into the black man's bare shoulder. A line of blood appeared and began to trickle slowly down his arm. Goodboy realized how frightened he was, but he was determined not to let them see it.

"BOOM!"

It was the loudest sound Goodboy had ever heard, and he knew it weren't no shotgun. Dirt clods rained down all about the three white men for what seemed an eternity, staining their robes with splotches of dark brown.

"Jesus!" cried Blackbird.

"Next time, call on somebody you know," shouted Kate. She was standing out near the road at an angle from the pickup about 30 feet away from the men. She had run all the way from the house cutting across the field and down the road, hoping she would get there in time. Kate had not run that far or that fast since she was in the fourth grade, and she stood there now, her chest heaving as she gulped down great draughts of air.

"Hey, you crazy woman, what are you gonna do with that dynamite. You trying to kill us or something?" Blackbird brandished his torch.

"No," said Kate. "If I'd a *wanted* to kill you, you'd already be on the devil's doorstep."

"Now looka here, Kate," said Mash, "this ain't none of your business. We're just over here to teach this nigger a lesson."

"A lesson, huh? Well, y'all are the first teachers I've seen who come to school dressed in sheets. And anyway, you can take off those silly hoods 'cause I already know who you are."

Blackbird ripped off his hood and threw it down with a curse.

"Kate Hardison, if you was a man, you'd be dead by now."

"Praise God," said Kate. "If I *was* a man like my Raymond, I'd whip the lot of you and shout hallelujah the whole time I was doing it."

"I don't like your tongue, woman," said Blackbird.

"Well now . . . I don't like your truck," snapped Kate.

"What's that supposed to mean?"

Kate's breathing had finally returned to normal as she raised the stick of dynamite. "It means that all I got to do is light this and toss it in the back of that truck, and y'all gonna be walking home instead of riding, and it's gonna be raining spare parts all over Dark Creek. And if I know anything about insurance companies, you would have a powerful hard time trying to explain what happened to your truck."

"You're just bluffing, woman," said Blackbird.

"You try me," said Kate. "Cuz I'm about to start singing 'Amazin' Grace,' and by the time I'm finished with the first chorus, if y'all ain't in the truck and going down that road, there ain't gonna be no truck to get into."

Goodboy was still standing on the porch, taking all this in. He did not doubt for a minute that she would do it.

"Well, you can just. . . . "

"Amazing Grace, how sweet the sound. . . ."

"Now, Kate," hollered Blackbird. "You stop this foolishness right now, you hear me!"

" *. . . that saved a wretch like me."*

"Woman, you 'bout as crazy as. . . ."

"I once was lost . . ." Kate held the lighter near the fuse . . . *"but now am found. . . ."* She raised her arm.

"All right, all right," yelled Blackbird. "C'mon, boys." The three men ran to the truck nearly knocking each other over in the process, two scrambled into the cab and the third, Kate thought it was Elrod, jumped into the back, the engine caught, and with Mash shaking his fist at her and flinging curses, the truck spun its tires in a circle, throwing Elrod out onto the dirt. He yelled as though he were hurt, let out some curses, jumped back in, and the trio went jouncing down the dirt road that led to the tar and gravel, and then finally, the night was silent again. Goodboy sat down on the top step and let out his breath slowly. Kate came forward and stood at the bottom of the steps. The black man looked up at her, and the smile appeared, the teeth flashing even in the darkness.

"Miz Kate, the good Lord ain't *never* made no woman like you before, white or colored."

"Well, if He has," came the reply, "I hope I never meet her, I'll tell you that." She broke into laughter, and then he joined in. When it was over, he said, "I ain't got nuthin' to offer you but a drink of well water, but you're welcome to it."

"Well water would be just fine," said Kate.

"You just come up on the porch then and sit in this chair, and I'll be right back."

Kate was more than glad to sit down, and when he returned with the jelly glass of water, he sat in the other chair and rocked silently for a moment, then asked the question he'd been struggling with the whole time.

"Miz Kate, how in the world did you know they was gonna do this?"

She cradled the large glass in her hand, smiled at him and said, "Goodboy . . . one thing I've learned in my life. If you stay close to your Bible, it'll tell you all you need to know."

Her black friend looked puzzled for a moment, then gulped down the contents of his glass and nodding his head slowly said, "Yes ma'am, Miz Kate. That is a natural-born fact." He set the glass down on the worn boards of the porch.

"But where in the world did you learn how to use dynamite?"

"Raymond taught me not long after we were married. He was using it to blast out some stumps, and he said if I was gonna be a storekeeper and a farmer's wife, I had to learn all about things like that. Then, just after Easter, a man came by and wanted to trade me a half box of dynamite for a stock of groceries since he didn't have any money, and we made a deal."

Goodboy shook his head slowly again, sighed and let his huge shoulders droop.

"Miz Kate, you must like 'Amazing Grace' a lot."

"I sure do. That's my favorite hymn."

"Well, I like it a powerful lot, too. How 'bout we give thanks to God and sing it together?" said Goodboy.

"All right," replied Kate. "Do you know the last verse?"

He nodded and the black man and the white woman sat on the porch of an ancient tenant shack and sang the last chorus to a song written by a former slave trader who finally found God, their voices blending beautifully, her alto and his baritone, the sound riding on the night air, soaring up into the starry reaches.

When we've been there, ten thousand years
Bright shining as the sun.
We've no less days to sing God's praise
than when we'd first begun.

16

4:04 AM, Sunday, the fifth . . .

In room 106 of Barnwell Community Hospital, Charity suddenly opened her eyes, feeling the rush of wind on her face, knowing it was the Holy Spirit. She could feel the strength of the Lord pouring into her by the second. Then she saw Caleb standing in the doorway.

"Honey, I've been waiting for you so long."

"I know, Dear," Charity said, "but the Lord isn't ready to call me home yet. I have work to do and until I'm finished, I can't leave here."

"Well, I miss you awful bad."

"And I miss you, my wonderful man, but I'll be all right now. The Lord sent the Holy Spirit to heal me. I felt His power go right through me, and it was wonderful. Oh, Caleb, darling, my mind is so clear and fresh, it's like I'm a young woman again, when we first met. God is so good to me."

"All right, Charity, I'm going back now. I'll be waiting for you."

"Yes, Dear. You go along now."

Bernice Tappen, the night nurse, would not be relieved until six. She had just finished reviewing the chart for Charity, that stated when the patient was admitted she could neither walk nor speak, the results of having suffered a moderately severe stroke.

That had been less than eight hours ago. She had a catheter in, and there was a wheelchair beside her bed. All of a sudden

Bernice thought she heard voices, got up to investigate and saw a person walking down the far end of the hall.

"Now just where do you think you're going?" said Bernice. At that point, the patient turned around.

"Honey," said Charity, her voice strong and clear. "I crave a Coke Cola in the worst way, and that's the gospel truth."

With that, Bernice, a nurse of uncommon strength and single-minded purpose, of whom Dr. Barnwell had said, if she'd been born a man she might have been General Patton, did something she had never done before, even after 27 years of nursing, four children, two husbands, a house burning down on Christmas eve, and a black snake showing up in her bathtub.

She fainted.

17

4:48 AM, Sunday, the fifth . . .

Bear awoke and looked at the luminous dial of his watch, with its black face and ragged canvas strap, the one he had worn all through the Pacific campaigns. Three-thirty on the dot.

It took him less than 30 minutes to select everything he needed and lay it out on the kitchen table: his K-bar knife, a coil of rope, a poncho and light blanket, matches, some C rations, two apples, two chocolate bars, a bag of peanuts, toilet paper, a small bottle of iodine, gauze bandages, a sterno stove, a large canteen of water, water purifying tablets, a flashlight with a spare set of batteries, a compass, his M-1 carbine from combat that the commanding officer had made him a gift of, four clips of ammo, and as a last thought, he decided to take his father's Colt .44 which was the only possession he had left to give Bear when he died.

He packed everything in the knapsack, then turned off the kitchen light, unpacked it and familiarized himself with the location of every item in the pack and on his cartridge belt. Then he turned on the light and repacked everything. He dressed in his battle fatigues with jungle boots, a canteen on his cartridge belt as well as his assault knife and machete. He stowed the .44 in the outside pocket of the pack, making it easy to get to in case of an emergency.

When he heard the horn blow, he turned off the lights, locked the door and walked out to the car. Bear told Ragg where he wanted him to drive, and after arriving, they left the car and entered the swamp at the point where Bear figured BB must have gone in the night before. From what he'd seen and knew of BB, he would have made a beeline for the quickest and closest means of cover.

A week ago, the remnant of a hurricane had come inland and dumped two inches of rain on the area, and the water was still up in the swamp. Tracking would be a bit harder, but Bear was confident he would pick up something. It was all a matter of being patient and watching for the signs, just as his father had taught him.

"I want to pick up BB's trail first," he explained to Ragg. "If I don't find out where *he* is, then with the boy wandering around out there lost and we start calling for him, he might get so excited, he'll start yelling. And, if BB's anywhere around when that happens, he'll jump on Joshua like a hawk on a sparrow. So we'll take our time. I know the boy'll be that much hungrier when we get to him and half-eaten up by yellow flies or mosquitoes, but that's a lot better than finding him in little pieces."

Ragg listened with a nod. Bear set off into the swamp in a loping gait that alternated between a walk and a trot. The swamp was an endless procession of cypress and gum, the trees festooned with Spanish moss. A thick growth of vines and creepers seemed to block their path at every turn, and briars tugged at their clothing. Bear led the way through the black water that from time to time would give rise to a hummock of ground, a small island of spongy earth beneath their feet. He knew that someone as large as BB ought to be easy to track, but an hour later, after crossing back and forth, he realized he was up against someone who knew how to cover his tracks. He paused and wiped his brow with the sleeve of his shirt, then took a small swallow of water.

"What's the matter?" asked Ragg, who was breathing heavily, the sweat rolling off his face in droplets.

"He's good, that one. He keeps doubling back on himself. That's okay. I can still smell him."

"Smell him? In this swamp?" Ragg let out a sour laugh.

"That's what you white eyes always say when Indians do something you *can't,*" said Bear. He rubbed the back of his hand across his eyes, sighted his compass then headed off in a northeasterly direction. His eyes scanned every branch, every leaf, every inch of every hanging vine, and every tree trunk. Ragg followed behind, each step harder to take than the last one. They hadn't been in here that long, and he was already worn out, the thick, stifling heat sapping the strength from him. He didn't know how much more of this he could take, but he wasn't about to be outdone by an Indian. The yellow flies and mosquitoes kept after them. Ragg swatted at them a couple of times, and Bear turned around at the sound, a frown on his face.

"Something bothering you?"

"What do you think? Aren't they biting you?"

Bear shook his head and smiled. "The boy is having to put up with them same as us, and he's been out here a lot longer. Something to think about."

Ragg started to reply, then shook his head in tight lipped silence, wiping his sweating face with a large bandana.

Bear led them into dense thicket that had him cutting a path through the thick brush with his machete. An hour became two. Two turned into three. Just when the policeman thought he was going to collapse, Bear stopped.

"What is it?" said the policeman.

"It's him," said Bear in a quiet voice. "Look." He reached down and picked up a small branch that had been broken in two.

"So what does that mean?" asked Ragg.

"See where it was lying?" Bear glanced up and pointed. "It couldn't have fallen from overhead since the only tree it could have come from is three feet shy of that. BB didn't mean to, but he stepped on it, breaking it, so he threw it to one side. No animal would do that. There haven't been any strong winds, and nothing else could account for it."

"Could of been the kid."

"Nope. Best of my recollection, the boy is too small to break a stick that size. It would have taken a full grown man. Anyway, Joshua would have had no reason to throw it out of his path."

Ragg had to admit he was impressed. "So what now?"

"Now that I know he's been through this way and heading deeper, I can double back and zigzag till I pick up the kid."

Ragg grunted and took out a cigar, but the minute Bear heard the click of the Zippo, he spun around, snatched the cigar from his lips, field stripped it, then scattered the remains.

"Hey, what's that all about?" said Ragg, his anger flaring.

"In a place like this, BB can smell this smoke before he even sees us."

"Okay," said Ragg. "I'll just chew one, unless you got any more objections."

"Chew away," said Bear with a shrug, shifted his pack and pushed on. Ragg gave a silent curse and fell in behind the Indian as he moved off through the water. Bear's motions seemed effortless, and his steps barely made a sound. From behind, the policeman realized that the Gut was like a second home for his enemy. Well, hi-yo silver, thought Ragg. I reckon I'll just have to watch my step. Yes sir, Mr. Tonto. I'll do just that . . . until my time comes. He shifted the pack on his back, pleased with himself for having brought along his little surprise.

18

5:39 AM, Sunday, the fifth . . .

Joshua awoke with a start and for a moment did not realize where he was. He had tucked his small frame into the recesses of a cypress on a small hummock of ground, first gathering some ferns and underbrush and layering them over his face to help protect him against the mosquitoes. Now, as he threw them off and unwound his cramped body, his mind replayed everything that had happened to him. All he knew was that he wanted to find Buddy and go home.

He had slept fitfully during the night, his skin itching furiously from the insect bites all over the exposed parts of his body. The hunger gnawed at his stomach, and he thought about how good one of Charity's biscuits would taste. Getting lost was all his fault and he knew it. Running and stumbling, he had penetrated well into the heart of the Gut, then wandered aimlessly for another hour before nightfall.

Joshua took a healthy swallow from the canteen and wanted more, but first sloshed it around and figured he had enough to last him another day. He had no idea what time it was since he had never worn a watch, but morning announced itself with splinters of light darting into the swamp. He walked a few steps to the edge of the creek, knelt and washed his face and arms as best he could. That made him feel better, though it did nothing for his fear. If only Buddy were with him, it wouldn't be so bad.

Joshua thought about everything Charity had told him, and he decided to pray again. Clasping his hands together and closing his eyes, the words began to come out slowly. . . .

God, please don't let my mother worry too much and take care of my dog, Buddy. Did God have anything to do with animals? Joshua didn't know.

Charity says that You're my brother and You know everything about me, so I guess You know how scared I am. I'm not a sissy, Lord, but I'm more scared than I've ever been before.

Joshua wondered if he should say anything else. Then he remembered that Charity told him he should always pray for those people he loved. Yes, he would pray for Charity.

Lord, please look after Charity because she has been so good to me and my mother, and I know she believes in You and trusts You because she told me she did.

He broke off here, not knowing how to continue. He paused a second, then said aloud . . . *Amen.*

It grew lighter by the moment, and he could make out the shapes of the trees that stretched away into the distance, standing like so many grey sentinels on watch. The mist that formed during the night drifted through the cypress in ghostly wisps, as the warmth of the early sun began to find its way into the Gut. As he sat there, he thought he heard a sound to his right, then out of the corner of his eye, he saw movement. A hundred feet away, a man suddenly emerged from the mist. He seemed to be moving through the water as though he were part of the swamp itself, the vines and creepers parting before him as he moved through them. Joshua had never seen a man this large before. He reminded him of the giants he had read about in storybooks. The man's hair was long and matted together, his mouth hanging open. His clothes were in tatters, his face smeared all over with something dark. Joshua squeezed his body tightly into the recesses of the cypress. The man stopped suddenly and began to sniff the air, turning his large head first one way and then the other.

uhhh
ooof

Joshua watched and listened intently. Who was he and what was he doing here? Could he be somebody who had been sent to look for him? Joshua didn't think so. He felt his throat tighten and his breathing start to come in short gasps, his mouth growing dry. The man looked right in his direction, but Joshua didn't think he could see him. He squeezed his eyes shut, his heart pounding furiously.

uhhhh
yuh yuh
bb look momma
find momma

Joshua forced himself to open his eyes and watch as the man took a few more steps in his direction. The sudden urge to urinate came over him, and he felt the first few drops start to flow, but squeezed his eyes shut and forced it back.

God, don't let him find me, please God . . . help me hold it in. . . .

The man sniffed the air, turned abruptly toward Joshua and began to walk in his direction. Then he paused, sniffed again, then plunged off toward his right, until he seemed to be swallowed up by a green wall. Joshua opened his eyes but could hold it back no longer and felt the urine streaming down his legs. He was ashamed of himself. Only little kids did that. He wondered if Jesus had done this when He was little and scared. Charity had said that Jesus had suffered all the things that we did. Joshua wished He were here now. He went down to the water's edge again and tried to wash his legs, made a mess, then collapsed in frustration on the marshy ground.

Lord, why don't You come and help me? Charity said You would, and she never lies.

Joshua felt hopelessly and miserably and completely alone.

God, I want to go home. I miss my mother. I need You . . . where are You?

The only answer he heard were the sounds of the birds overhead, as the sun informed them it was time to begin looking for food as others of their species had done every day in the swamp for thousands of years. Joshua heard them singing, but their songs did not help. It made him even sadder, and sitting there, with the animals of the Gut coming to life, he began to sob softly to himself, tasting the tears as they slowly coursed down his cheeks.

Where was God?

Charity promised.

Where *was* He?

19

11:01 AM, Sunday, the fifth . . .

Dark Creek Church had its usual worship group of 27 faithful members who filed in on schedule and sat where they always did, knowing they would stand up on cue, sing, deposit a few rumpled bills and coins in the collection plate, listen to the sermon with great solemnity, then file out by Reverend Yelton at the door, shake his hand and tell him it was another good message, then go home to Sunday dinner. This was their once-a-week ritual, interrupted only by an occasional funeral, Christmas and Easter.

Kate was there along with them, though she was not a member in the strict sense, meaning her name was not on the roll. She knew many people actually believed if their name was not on a church roll, they were not going to heaven. It was so silly it was all she could do to keep from laughing when people brought it up, which, sooner or later, they always did.

She knew every person in the church by first, middle and last name, as well as their closest kin, and could recite a litany of what they ate, smoked, drove, wore to church and gossiped about the minute church was over. As was the case in most churches that she had ever known, a handful of people from two families controlled everything, from what hymns would be sung to how much they should pay the preacher. Blackbird and his wife, and his cousin, Ben and his wife, were one of these two groups. The other was Ida Beth Ware and her husband who tagged along behind her considerable bulk, looking like a sick mule tied behind a wagon. Kate, being as outspoken as she was, would talk openly with those customers who would listen about how people wanted to "own the church and God along with it," and by doing so, she had not exactly ingratiated herself with these two families.

She had asked herself time and time again why she continued to go here, and the answer was always the same. She had a few good friends among the congregation she could count on, but if she went to a church in town, she wouldn't know a soul. Besides, you went to church not to please people, but to please God. The sermons by Preacher Yelton meant little to her, and she seldom listened. His preaching was what Raymond would have called sawing sawdust. He had a bald head, horse teeth in front, one of them gold, and eyes that looked as though they were about to pop out of his head. He had a habit of joking about his high blood pressure by telling people that when he preached and got red in the face, it meant the devil was hearing every word and was mad as a hornet.

The tiny choir of four people sang the call to worship, Rev. Yelton made his usual announcements, then came another hymn, the collection was taken and once the choir had come down into the congregation, he launched into the sermon. As the words fell upon her ears, Kate felt her body start to tighten up, muscle by muscle, limb by limb. She glanced down and realized she was squeezing her Bible so hard her knuckles were chalk white.

" . . . The Almighty knew what He was doing when He created the races, and He meant for the black race to be in servitude and bondage to the white race. That's why He made them inferior and us *superior*. And when those among us begin to treat the black man as an equal, then you are going directly against Scripture, and this is happening right now in our little Christian community.

"God Almighty has put these words in my mouth, and I have no choice but to share them with you. Yesterday, a nigger had the audacity . . . the nerve . . . the downright, unspeakable gall to put his hand upon a member of this church. Not only a member, mind you, but a deacon, our beloved brother Blake Bird. A white man, whose grandparents settled this land, having his good name besmirched by an uppity, low-down, no-count nigger!"

Kate stared straight ahead, clenching her teeth, fixing her gaze on the flower arrangements. She closed her Bible and clasped her hands in her lap. She didn't know how long she could take this, but she prayed silently, asking the Lord for direction.

"Oh, but there is more to this story," continued Yelton, his voice continuing to grow in volume. "All this happened while someone . . . *someone* in this very church stood up for the black man and ignored the white man, and as sure as God is my witness, this kind of behavior cannot be tolerated in America. These people are next to animals, beasts of the field, and that is where they should remain. And if they try to break their traces and slip the bonds God ordained for them, then by heaven, they will know the vengeance of the Lord and of His faithful servants!"

"Amen, brother!" Blackbird put in his two cents.

It was the sign Kate had been seeking. She had heard enough. She stood up, her jaw clenched tightly, yet managing her sweet smile as she stepped into the aisle and turned to walk toward the door. She took a quiet delight in the looks of astonishment on people who kept their heads facing forward but whose eyes were stuck on her like fuzz on a peach.

"Sister Hardison? Where do you think you are going?" Yelton bellowed. Every head in the church turned as though at a prearranged signal.

"Not where *you're* going, that's for sure."

This was met by a few gasps, a barely muffled giggle and one outright guffaw from Junior Holden.

"By the Almighty, woman, *nobody* walks out when I'm preaching. In the name of all that is holy, I command you to take your seat and be reverent!"

"My *Lord* commands me," said Kate. "No men, and dang few preachers." She turned on her heel and walked to the doors, and as she did, she could hear his voice bellowing after her.

"Sister Hardison, I order you back in this church, or you will be damned to hellfire and perdition. God will not be mocked!"

She turned and hesitated, and Yelton paused in his attack, thinking perhaps she'd had a change of heart.

"Preacher, first of all, I reckon everybody in this church knows that our Lord said, 'Love thy neighbor as thyself.' The only thing is, I don't recollect His saying that only applied to white folks, and if you find out that Jesus said otherwise, I'd be much obliged if you let me know."

"Now, you just. . . . "

"No, *you* just hush, preacher, because I've been listening to you long enough, and now it's *your* turn to listen. I am going home to fix Sunday dinner for Goodboy Found, and yes, he is a colored man, and yes, I stuck up for him last night because he is also my neighbor and good Christian brother in our Lord, and if any of you would like to join us at our table, there's more than enough food to go around. And preacher, I will pray for you mightily so that, praise God, whatever happens to you ain't on my conscience 'cuz I sure don't want to be responsible for your soul."

As she turned to leave, the last thing she saw was Yelton's face all puffed up and glowing like a stoplight, his mouth puckered as though he had just sucked on a lemon. As she went out the door into the fierce heat, she could hear his voice rising again, shouting, screaming, but she could not make out the words and thanked the Lord for that.

She had told Goodboy before she left his house last night that he was invited to have Sunday dinner with her, and if he would come on up about 12:30, the two of them would sit out back under the big pecan tree and eat the chicken she had fried before leaving for church. Kate knew she had spoken the truth in church, about his being her neighbor. And she knew that when Raymond was alive, he had always shown kindness to colored people.

Since Goodboy didn't have any family to care for, and for that matter, neither did she, the fellowship was good for both of them. She often wondered why he had never gotten married, but she knew the reasons were none of her business. Kate reckoned maybe it was because the Lord made him a little different and just didn't intend for him to have a wife. She knew God worked that way sometimes. While musing over all this, she set out the chicken, potato salad, biscuits and pitcher of iced tea and not long after she finished, Goodboy showed up.

"Miz Kate, now you know you shouldn't of gone to all this trouble for Goodboy."

"No trouble at all. It's just as easy to fix for two as one, and anyway, I hate to eat by myself, and of all meals, Sunday dinner. It . . . well, it just reminds me of, you know . . . family."

"Yas'sum."

They sat down, Kate asked Goodboy to pray, and he gave a simple blessing. As they began to eat, she was glad to see that the events of the previous evening had not lessened her friend's appetite.

"Miz Kate, you know . . . ain't many colored folks that have a white friend like you. God sho is good to me." He demolished a leg and buttered a biscuit that suddenly disappeared into his cavernous mouth.

Kate nodded. "Goodboy, what do you reckon might have happened if the Lord hadn't sent down an angel to tell me to get over there last night?"

He washed down the last of the biscuit with a swig of tea. "Well, now, I can't rightly say for sure, but I reckon they would of given me right smart of a whuppin'. Maybe somethin' worse. It would have been about the baddest thing that ever happened to Goodboy. You know, they's some mean white mens out here in Dark Creek, and I don't know why they hate this poor nigger so much."

"Oh, I don't think it's just you." Kate sipped at her tea, thinking it was maybe a mite too strong. "See, my daddy taught me to respect all kinda folks, and my Raymond was the same way. And I taught that to my boys, too."

"Yas'sum, them boys was crackerjacks sure enough."

Goodboy chewed the last of the meat off a drumstick, then put it down and licked his fingers. "Well, I tell you this, Miz Kate. Peers to me that Mistuh Blackbird has got something inside him, way down deep that's about as nasty as anything I ever seen in a man, white or black. And he sure don't like Goodboy, not one bit. No ma'am."

"No, he doesn't. Course, he doesn't like Kate Hardison either."

"No'm, I don't suppose he does. But one thing you can count on. God's gonna work it all out, if we just wait on Him."

"Oh, I believe that all right," said Kate. She filled both their glasses and took a sip while her friend downed half the glass in one swallow.

"Goodboy, who do you think God is?"

"Ma'am?"

"I mean, when you talk to God, do you see somebody?"

Goodboy wiped his mouth with the paper napkin, then folded it neatly before putting it back on the table. "No'm, it ain't like I see someone, you know. It's more like . . . I *feel* Him. Yas'sum. That's it. I feels Jesus getting so close to me, He could be holding my hand."

"I reckon last night He was, wasn't He?"

"Oh, yas'sum, deed He was. And you know, I was thinking about that after you left. You told me if I stay close to my Bible, it'll tell me everything I need to know. Was you reading something in Scripture that told you to go outside and hear what them mens was fixin' to do?"

Kate explained how she had left her Bible in the store and gone back to get it. Goodboy listened intently, then reared back on the bench and laughed, showing a mouthful of teeth.

"Yas'sum, now that's the Holy Ghost working sure nuf. That's how He does, you know? Our preacher, Brother Elijah, he be telling us that just when you think God has forgotten all about you, He will up and do something just to remind you that He is still God, and He ain't gonna run off and leave you."

Kate was listening to him, knowing that if they had tied Goodboy to a tree last night and whipped him, the blood that came out of his wounds would have been as red as her own. She sat there, shaking her head slowly. Goodboy saw the thoughtful look on her face transform itself into a smile.

"What you thinking, Miz Kate? God saying something to you?"

"Yes, Goodboy, indeed He was." She stood up abruptly and clapped her hands. "Now, Brother Found, what would you say to some fresh peach cobbler?" But before he could respond, a small boy burst in upon them, his chest heaving like a robin's. It was Billy Purvis, grandson of Elsie Muncie, one of Lois' best friends and good customers.

"Miz Kate, Miz Kate!"

"Lord, child, what is it?"

"He . . . he. . . ."

"Now, young'un, sit down here and catch your breath, then maybe you can get the words out."

"No'm, I can't stay, but Granny told me to come on over here as fast as I could and tell you the news."

"Well, Billy Purvis, I *never*! Anyway, now that you're here, go ahead and tell me."

"He. . . ."

"Who?"

"The preacher. He kept on hollering and shouting after you left, and then he kinda leaned one way and then the other, and fell smack down on top of the altar rail. Daddy said he looked like he'd been kicked by a mule. They called for an ambulance, and everybody's saying he musta had a heart attack or somethin'."

"Is he alive, child?"

"Yas'sum, I reckon."

"Praise the Lord." Kate reflected upon all this for a moment, feeling a sudden heaviness well up in her own heart. "Well, I am sure sorry to hear that," she said, knowing it was the truth and that she had not wished the man any harm. "But the best thing we can do now for Brother Yelton is pray. Goodboy . . . Billy, let's join hands with each other and bow our heads in prayer.

"Dear Lord. . . . " As she started praying, and as Billy Purvis bowed his head, he found himself looking at his small hand that appeared even smaller cradled in the gigantic hand of Goodboy Found. He realized this was the first time in his whole life he had ever held a colored person's hand, and he was nine years old, going on ten. Billy realized something else, too. Something he had never noticed before. The palm of Goodboy's hand wasn't black at all. It was kinda pinkish looking like the bottom of the foot of his six-month-old baby brother, Calvin.

"Amen," said Kate.

"Amen," said Goodboy.

"Amen," mumbled Billy, freed his hand from Goodboy's, then ran like the wind.

20

1:20 PM, Sunday, the fifth . . .

Deborah had taken one of the pills that Dr. Reardon had given her, and it provided her with a few hours sleep, but she awoke feeling emptied out. She spent most of the morning house-cleaning, scrubbing with a vengeance, and dusting, anything to keep her mind occupied. The fact that Chief Ragg and Standing Bear had gone into the Gut to find her son gave her some hope. When she heard the car drive up in the yard, she glanced out the window and saw that it was Dr. Reardon and someone else whose face she couldn't make out because of the sun reflecting off the window. Reardon went around to open the door. His passenger got out, and Deborah could barely contain her astonishment. It was Charity! Deborah ran out to greet her friend.

"Charity, I thought you were . . . I mean, well, what on earth are you doing home from the hospital?"

"Child, you'll just have to ask the Holy Spirit about that. I figure the Lord just needed me to be here with you, to give you comfort when you needed it most. Don't you reckon?"

Deborah cast an inquiring glance at Reardon. The physician raised his eyebrows then threw his hands up in the air. "Deborah, I've been practicing medicine almost 25 years, and every now and then somebody throws me a curve ball, and this is one of those times. I guess Charity's explanation is as good as any." He laughed and put his arms around the younger woman. "Did that pill I gave you help much last night?"

"Yes," she lied. "Well, some. Actually, I just can't. . . ." She fumbled for a word, then shook her head in exasperation.

"Yes, I know what you mean." He was going to add, I know what it means to lose a son, but he thought better of it, for the truth was, the chances of Joshua's being alive after this short a time were pretty good, barring having been snakebit or . . . the image of BB flashed into his mind, and Jesse let his thoughts trail off, as they walked into the house and sat down in the kitchen. Immediately, Charity busied herself with making a pitcher of lemonade.

Reardon looked at Deborah who was watching Charity and smiling, glad her friend was well and back home in spite of what had happened to her. Jesse sat there, his hands clasping and unclasping in uncharacteristic fashion. He debated whether to tell Deborah about BB. If she *did* know, she couldn't do anything, and something like that might push her over the edge. He decided against it. Charity put the full pitcher and three glasses along the table, then set down a dish of parched peanuts.

Deborah took a few, munched for a moment, then turned to the doctor. "Do you think Standing Bear will . . . I mean, is he capable of finding Joshua?"

"Oh, I think he's very capable," said Jesse. "Standing Bear is very good at that sort of thing, and with the two of them in there, it's just a matter of time," unless, he thought, BB gets to Joshua first.

"Why, land, Deborah," added Charity. "Everybody knows that nothing can get away from an Indian in the swamp, and I'll just bet you we'll be hearing something before dark. Don't you think so, Doctor Reardon?"

"Well, you might be right, Charity. You just might be right."

The phone rang from the parlor. Charity went in to answer it.

"Hello?"

"Yes, he's here. Whom may I say is calling?"

"Doctor who? Dr. Maynard? Certainly, one moment, please."

She looked at Jesse. "It's for you. A Doctor Maynard from Dorothea Dix in Raleigh."

Jesse thanked her and went to the phone. He talked for a few minutes, keeping his voice low, his back to the two women in the kitchen. Maynard explained that somehow the newspaper boys had gotten wind of the story, about BB having come back to Sweetwater, the murders, and now his being on the loose in the Gut, and they were going to break it as a page one story in tomorrow's *News and Observer*. Maynard assured Reardon he had tried to squelch it, but to no avail. Jesse thanked his fellow physician, hung up and came back into the kitchen with a grim look on his face. If he didn't tell her now, tomorrow would be too late, and he could never live with himself if she read about it in the papers before hearing it from him.

"Deborah," he said, setting his mouth in a firm line.

"Yes?" She looked at him, a mother missing her only son. He didn't know how to do this, but Jesse knew he had to. He took a deep breath and placed both his hands on top of hers. "There's something I think you ought to know."

21

6:20 PM, Sunday, the fifth . . .

"I've picked up the boy."

"What?" said Ragg thickly. He was in a half stupor from the heat and the exertion of the day, every square inch of clothing drenched with sweat. Even with three rest breaks plus an hour for a light lunch at noon, he was so exhausted he could barely put one foot before another and was grateful for this interruption. At this point, he didn't care about finding the boy or BB or anything. All he wanted right now was to get out of Devil's Gut. They named it right, he thought.

"See this?" Bear pointed down at a patch of soft mud where the imprint of the sole of a sneaker was faintly visible. "Now if I can follow this trail without losing it, we'll run right into him. He can't be more than a quarter of a mile from us."

"How can you tell?"

"Track's fairly fresh. He must have been by here, oh, maybe five, six o'clock or so, and he's probably getting tired and not moving too fast. She said his canteen is missing, so he's probably still got some water. I don't guess he has any food, but kids that age are tough."

"Why don't we just call out for him and let him know we're here?" asked Ragg.

"I told you. If he heard us, he'd get excited and yell back, but unless you know the Gut, you can't tell where a sound is coming from. He could start running in the wrong way, and if BB's anywhere around, no telling what he'll do. Like sometimes, when little kids get scared and run from a dog, the dog figures they're rabbits and goes after them. Anyway, I'll feel better once we have Joshua with us, then we'll let BB take care of himself. Long as he doesn't bother us, we won't bother him. At least, not this go around."

"Wait a minute," said Ragg with a scowl. "You mean, we're gonna bring back the boy and not BB?"

"Hey, the deal was to find the *boy*. I'll complete the mission, and then we'll go back. You have to remember something," said Bear. "BB could be watching us right now, but he won't do anything. He knows we have guns. He'll wait like the great hunting animals do and come for us in the dark. He thinks we're here to capture him and take him back. For my money, he could stay out here for the rest of his natural life, which probably isn't too long anyway. He's already crazy, so they're not gonna give him the electric chair or anything like that. They'll just put him back inside."

"Yeah, well if I see him, he's gonna be a *dead* crazy."

"You mean, you'd shoot him on sight?" asked Bear, his eyes narrowing.

"You better believe I would. He killed a police officer, in case you've done forgot, and there ain't no way I'm gonna let him go back up to Dix and take life easy."

"Ragg, you're talking about a man who doesn't know right from wrong."

"He doesn't *have* to. That's my job. Besides, shooting him is no different from shooting a mad dog."

Bear was going to argue the point and decided not to. "Well, before long we'll make camp for the night."

Ragg's eyes widened at the prospect of this. "I thought you said that's when BB will come for us."

"I did, and he probably will, but we can handle it if we're smart. Anyway, we're out here now and I'm not going back until I find the boy. We couldn't go back tonight even if we had Joshua with us. Walking through the Gut in the dark is a sure ticket to get snake bit. Man, I thought cops were supposed to be smart. Ragg, you disappoint me."

"You watch your mouth, boy."

"No, you watch yours, white eyes. I could go off and leave you here, find the boy, take him home, and you might not find your way out of here before BB catches up with you. And I expect he'll remember you."

"You trying to scare me?"

"I don't know, Ragg. *Are* you scared?" Bear locked the man's eyes in an unrelenting stare.

Ragg had never hated another human being as much as he did this Indian. Just a day ago, Bear had been his prisoner under his control and now *he* was the one giving the orders. Things weren't working out the way he had planned. If Bear came back with the boy, then *he* would be the hero, and on top of that, the kid might decide to blab about what happened. And once the story got out, people would side with the kid. If that happened, his reputation and his job would go right down the drain. Ragg needed time to sort through all this. He also needed to do something else. All the walking and the heat had gotten his bowels in gear.

"Listen, I got to take a crap, okay?"

"You asking my permission?" said Bear, hiding his smile.

"No, I'm not asking your permission. I'm just saying don't go running off or anything until I'm through."

"I'm not going anywhere. You just watch where you walk. This isn't Main Street."

"Don't worry about me. I can find my way around," lied Ragg. The truth was, hc had been uneasy since the moment they had entered the Gut.

Bear sat down, his back against a cypress, picked up a twig and began to chew it. He heard the policeman walk off the trail about 30 feet away, then turn and disappear behind a large gum tree. He could hear him stomping about, then silence. Bear looked around and one by one, he silently recited the names of the flowers and herbs. There was the pale blue hepatica, good for a sick liver. Over there near the juniper was some lungwort, that his mother would make into a poultice when he had croup. He could smell the honeysuckle, too, his father's favorite, and with the scent of it in his nostrils now, he recalled the first time his father had taken him here trapping, and how he had taught him the Indian names of each flower and animal. Tom Running Elk had known the Gut like a farmer knew his land. He had even. . . . "

"Godamighty! What the—hey, I can't get out! *Hey!*"

Bear sprang to his feet and ran toward the sound. Ragg was now screaming, "Help me. I'm sinking!"

Bear knew what had happened before he even got there. When he found him, Ragg was already up to his mid-thigh in the quicksand, a look of sheer horror on his face.

"Quit struggling," said Bear.

Ragg squirmed all the harder, the fear showing in his eyes.

"I said, quit struggling, Ragg. It'll only suck you down faster!" Bear was shouting at him now. "I'll be right back." In ten seconds, he had extracted the rope from the pack and was back, having already made a loop on the run. He threw this around the policeman, yelling, "Get it under your shoulders and hang on." Ragg would not stop squirming and now the quicksand had reached his waist.

"I told you once . . . *keep still!*" Bear's command shouted at the top of his voice worked. The policeman went limp, though he had his arms free enough to work the loop under his shoulders. Bear looped one end of the rope around a small cypress, then dug in his feet and began to pull.

"Pull harder!" cried Ragg.

Bear would have yelled back at him but needed every ounce of his strength to overcome the deadly suction of the quicksand. Finally, he saw the man's body heave itself up on the hummock of earth. The Indian undid the rope from under his shoulders. Ragg lay there, his lungs heaving. He was hyperventilating. Bear had seen it on the battlefield, and he did the only thing a man *could* do. He slapped Ragg as hard as he could.

"Come on, Ragg. You're safe now. You didn't die. You're okay. Just take long slow breaths, and you'll be fine." The policeman's face was covered in a sheen of sweat, the eyes glazed, his lips trembling. Bear fetched his canteen and gave Ragg a few sips of water. Gradually, the man began to gain control of himself, and in a few minutes, he was sitting quietly against the trunk of the tree.

"You'd best change clothes and wash yourself off as best you can," said Bear. "Otherwise, the smell of that mud will draw the yellow flies, and they'll be all over you like white on rice. And next time, if you're not sure where you're walking, stick one foot in up to your ankle. If it's bad, it'll start sucking at it, and when it does, just pull it out nice and easy, but always look behind you when you're backing out."

Ragg had forgotten all about the quicksand. It was no longer of any consequence. He was burning from the sting of the man's hand on his face, and the shame created a heat within his own to rival that of the swamp. No grown man had ever slapped him before, least of all an Indian. Bear might have saved his life, but that didn't change anything. When the time was right, he would have the satisfaction of knowing he had killed him. And he was looking forward. . . .

"I'm over here. Help, somebody. I'm over heeeeere!"

22

7:05 PM, Sunday, the fifth . . .

Joshua had been on his knees praying, just like Charity told him to. He had been wanting to call out for help, but once he had seen that man, whoever he was, he had been afraid to. Now, after splashing water on his face to cool him down, he took a brief sip from the canteen. He felt a growing emptiness within him, but it had nothing to do with food. He knelt by a sweet gum, looking up momentarily at the Spanish moss hanging down in long fluffy streamers, like an old woman's fine grey hair that had grown curly and long. Like Charity's. . . .

. . . Lord . . . Charity says You love me and that You sent Your Son to show us how much You loved us. . . . God, I wish I could have known Him. It's just that . . . well, I want to find Buddy and go home to my mother and Charity and all my friends. Lord, I'm not angry with You about my father. Not anymore. I know Mom is, but I'm not because Charity told me You didn't come and take little boys' fathers away from them, and I believe her. But Lord, I'm awful scared. Charity said if I put out my hand, You'd take it. . . .

Joshua closed his eyes and stretched out his hand, and at that instant, he heard what sounded like a man screaming, though he really wasn't sure since it seemed to come from far away. He didn't think it was the big man he had seen earlier. He craned his head in the direction of the sound. Maybe it was someone looking for him. If he didn't shout back, he might not have another chance. They might go off in another direction, and then it'd be too late.

He hesitated. Should he answer? *Lord, should I?*

Suddenly, he knew what to do. "Help, somebody. I'm over here . . . help!" The sound of his own voice startled him.

Bear heard it, and before the echo had even faded, he had set his course and was off splashing into the shallow water, high stepping, the carbine held out in front of him. Ragg had his clothes half on, tried to pull up his pants, stumbled, tried again, then fell to the ground, letting out a string of curses.

From a sumac thicket on a small knoll about 50 yards away, BB crouched there hidden, watching. He had been observing them, trying to understand what was going on. He had known the night before that someone else was out here. His thoughts were clumsy, large shapes moving slowly about in his head. He remembered both men. One had been there when he killed the bad man in the jail place.

Now, ever so slowly, pieces of the picture began to come together. . . .

badmen come to get bb
bb kill them
night soon
bb wait

Bear stopped suddenly, hearing the cry of birds roosting for the night.

"Joshua! Call out again so I can find you. This is Standing Bear. Can you hear me?" The Gut played it back, his voice . . . *me . . . me . . . me?*

He listened intently. Then he heard the boy's high voice.

"I'm over here."

Bear changed his course slightly and set off again. Another minute of running, splashing through the water, tearing through the vines and creepers, feeling the briars catch at him, low-lying branches swatting him in the face, but paying no attention . . . like that time on Guadalcanal when he went after his Choctaw friend Jimmy Two Rivers who had been hit and had called out for him. . . .

"Joshua. I'm coming . . . where are you?"

"This way. Over here." *Here . . . here.* The echoes were shorter, he was getting closer. Night was coming on fast.

Three minutes later, he broke into a small clearing of gum on a hummock and saw the boy sitting there against a tree, knees drawn up to his chest, hugging himself. The boy leapt to his feet when he saw Bear, and literally flung himself at him, his eyes wet with tears.

"Standing Bear! It's me, Joshua . . . do you remember me? I was so scared . . . I didn't think anybody would ever find me . . . I saw a snake once . . . and I thought my dog, Buddy, would find me, but he didn't . . . and . . . and then I saw this other man, he was huge like a giant, but he scared me the way he looked, so I didn't move or anything . . . and he didn't see me and he went away, but I don't know where. . . . " Joshua stopped long enough to draw in a breath, and when he did, Bear drew the boy to him in a big hug. He could see at a glance the mosquitoes had drunk their fill of him.

"Do you want me to carry you?" asked Bear, indicating Joshua could get on his back.

"I . . . no, I can walk. I'm okay, Standing Bear. How did you find me?"

"Aw, us Injuns can smell you white eyes from a mile off." Bear laughed and tousled the boy's hair. "And just call me Bear. Everybody else does."

He gave the boy a smile. Brave kid, thought the Indian. To be out here all alone, especially having seen BB. It must have scared the daylights out of him, and Bear was amazed Joshua hadn't broken from cover and run. As they made their way back, Joshua wanted to keep on talking, but Bear touched his shoulder, pointed out into the swamp, then put his finger to his lips. The boy nodded, his eyes widening. By the time they rejoined Ragg, the light was almost gone, the last pale streamers of it lancing through the trees and reflecting off the water, creating an eerie effect. Ragg was lying there with his cap over his face, using his pack for a pillow, unaware that while Bear had been gone, BB had been debating whether to rush the bad man and kill him while the other man was gone. But he knew about guns, and it would be better when it was dark. He had sat there in his place of concealment watching Ragg.

Smelling him. Tasting his flesh. Hating him.

Ragg ground his teeth. He knew the kid would recognize him. So what. He'd just throw him a hard look, and that would be the end of it.

"Joshua," said Bear, "this is Chief Ragg."

"Hello, boy. Say, your momma sure has been worried about you." He didn't meet Joshua's glance, but nonetheless, Joshua recognized the voice before he even made out the man's features in the twilight. It was the man from the bathroom at the police station. He didn't understand. Why was he here? It didn't make sense to him, but he was so exhausted he couldn't think about it right now. Besides, Bear was here to protect him now.

"She . . yeah, I know. I didn't mean to get lost or anything. I hope she's not angry with me."

"Your mother's okay," said Bear, but instantly, he had caught the abrupt change in the boy. Fear? Anger? He wasn't sure, but he knew there was bad medicine between him and Ragg. He'd find out when the time was right. He retrieved the bottle of lotion from his pack and as he applied it to the insect bites, he kept up a running narrative . . . "Ahh, don't worry about your mom," said Bear. "My grandfather was a Cherokee chief, but when he was about your age, maybe a little older, he had to go through the initiation to become a brave. He had to spend a month out in the mountains by himself with only a bow and arrow and his knife. If he could do that, then the tribe would let him back home and accept him as a brave. And he made it." He finished the last of the lotion. "There, does that feel a little better?"

Joshua nodded. Bear set himself busy gathering some green wood and building a small fire. If they sat close enough to it, the smoke would keep the mosquitoes at bay. Then he broke out some food from his pack: dried beef, crackers, apples, chocolate bars and water. Ragg sat a few yards away from them, having laid out his own food, eating it in silence. Every now and then he would cast a furtive glance in their direction, and Bear could see the change in him as well. Sooner or later, whatever it was that lay between Joshua and Ragg would have to surface. He watched with pleasure as the boy wolfed down the food until it was all gone, then started munching on the apple.

"Good, huh?"

"Wow, yeah, Bear. I didn't know how hungry I was." Joshua paused, belched suddenly and laughed. He took another bite of the apple, then looked up with a frown on his face. "Bear, who was the other man I saw?"

Bear explained as best he could about BB, trying to leave out some of the bad parts. He didn't want to frighten the boy any worse than he already was. Then he turned to Ragg. "Why don't you tell him?"

"Boy, I'll give it to you straight. BB is like an animal that growed up wrong. Doc Reardon said that the wires in his head are kinda scrambled, and he ain't ever gonna get better. In fact, the doc says he'll just keep getting worse and worse. But in my book, he's a killer and a criminal, and he needs to pay for it."

"Pay for it?"

"Well, you know. Like the Bible says—an eye for an eye and a tooth for a tooth. BB killed one of my officers and two niggers, and some years back, he hurt a man pretty bad, but the state, well, they decided BB was some kind of special case or something, so they didn't give him the chair like they should of. Say, Bear, since we got this fire going, is it all right if I smoke, *boss?*" Bear could see the smirk in the firelight. He nodded.

It was dark now. Joshua moved closer to the fire. "Is BB out there now?"

"Yep," said Bear.

"Could he be watching us, I mean, right now?"

"Probably."

"But if he's afraid of being shot or taken prisoner, why doesn't he just run far away and hide where nobody could ever find him?" asked the boy.

"Joshua, it's like he wants to get away from us and yet he doesn't. Something in him wants to get close to us because we're people, but something else scares him off and makes him not like us. The other thing is, I don't think he even knows who or what he is. My father told me that sometimes in the tribe, a baby would be born and the medicine man knew that an evil spirit possessed it. Maybe it was that way with BB."

"Will he try to get us tonight, while we sleep?"

"Nah." Bear figured there was no need in telling the boy the truth. After what he'd been through, he couldn't handle it, and since he'd seen BB, it'd probably give him nightmares. If BB thought they had come to get him, to take him back, he would definitely come for them tonight to kill them. All of them.

Ragg sat there watching the two of them out of the corner of his eye. If BB took care of the boy, then he would take care of the Indian. It would be nice if things worked out that way. Or if BB got Bear, Ragg could take care of the kid. He wasn't crazy about that, but he knew he could make it look like an accident. In any case, Ragg was going to look out for Ragg.

Bear put some more wood on the fire. "The way I figure it, we're about two miles from where we came in, and if we get up at first light, I'll have you home in time for a real breakfast."

"Yeah, like Charity's ham biscuits," said Joshua. "Boy, they're the best things you ever tasted."

Bear nodded, smiling. He remembered his grandmother who cooked and his mother and the smell of the food, and the scent of his mother's hair and how she sang to him when he was little. He remembered how strong and brave his father was, and then his life was gone. He knew there was a Great Spirit who was the father of all men, and that his life, like that of his parents and their parents, was in the hands of this Spirit.

"Bear . . . do Indians believe in God?" said Joshua.

Ragg gave a little laugh from where he lay on his side. "Boy, you're asking the wrong man."

Bear bristled at this and then told himself that the white eyes had no knowledge of the Great Spirit. He told Joshua that yes, he believed in God and that when he was a small child on the reservation, a Methodist circuit rider had baptized him. His mother had been for it, and his father against it, but his mother finally won out. The Cherokees knew there was a Great Spirit, and for those who had become Christians, like Bear, they regarded him the same as God the Father. Bear told Joshua how much the Great Spirit loved all the creatures He created, and after a few minutes of this, he saw the boy yawn and figured he'd told him enough to satisfy him. Bear looked at his watch and said, "I'm gonna put some more wood on the fire, then you two get some sleep. I'll take the first watch. Ragg, I'll wake you at midnight."

"Suits me fine," said Ragg. "After running around in this swamp all day, I'm plumb tuckered." He moved his roll closer to the fire, curled up in a light cotton blanket, pulling it over his head as partial protection against the mosquitoes. Bear pulled a blanket out of his pack, and fixed it for Joshua, then told him good night. The boy stared into the fire and thought he saw a face, then the face went away and he was asleep.

Bear checked the fire one last time, then sat cross-legged next to the fire and Joshua. He chambered a round in the carbine. He would keep the fire burning through his watch and tell himself the stories that his grandfather, Red Hawk, used to tell him, and he would not fall asleep. Cherokee warriors, like U.S. Marines, did not fall asleep on watch.

From where he hunkered down in the water behind a large cypress, BB watched and waited.

badman
want hurt
soon
bb wait

23

9:04 PM, Sunday, the fifth . . .

Jesse had just finished listening to H.V. Kaltenborn give the nine o'clock news. He preferred him to Walter Winchell who was a bit too showy for his taste. Lucy had fixed him a wonderful dinner of spare ribs, limas, baked acorn squash, biscuits, iced tea and cherry pie. That woman could cook like no one he'd ever known, and he hated to think what his life would be like without her. Practicing medicine was a full-time calling, like being a minister, and if a man did it properly, there was neither time nor energy left to keep up a house and all the other stuff that went with it. Lucy took his car down to be repaired when something was wrong with it, bought his Christmas cards and even knew when his shoes needed repairing and his underwear needed replacing. Jesse realized what a blessing she was to him.

His thoughts returned to the war. According to Kaltenborn, the Allies already had the plans for a full-scale invasion of the Japanese mainland and had estimated the cost in lives on both sides to approach a half million. Jesse heard the figures and shook his head slowly. It just wasn't worth it. But then he realized as though to balance bad news like the war and BB, you got treated to the miracle of a Charity. He got up from the table and pulled down some reference books, but after a cursory search, realized there was very little in the literature to support what had happened to her since her stroke. So how to explain it then? He couldn't. His grandmother had been a woman of incredibly strong faith, who spoke in tongues and had believed in healing services. Jesse had never thought much about that, but on the other hand, he had read enough and seen enough firsthand accounts of people near death that he, himself, had given up on, only to have someone who really loved them come in and pray over them, and they would recover. We call it spontaneous remission, he thought, but he knew it was God's hand working through the healing power of the Holy Spirit. There simply was no other explanation, and it surely wasn't luck. Luck was one thing Jesse Reardon had never believed in.

When he had told Deborah about BB being in the Gut, she had gone to pieces. He had to give her a shot to calm her down, and he had suggested to Charity that the woman stay with her so she could keep an eye on her. In light of what had happened, that's a real switch, he thought. Charity at 82, having suffered a stroke, is keeping an eye on Deborah. He hoped that tomorrow would bring good news. If the boy were still alive, surely Standing Bear would find him with or without Ragg's help, whatever that might amount to. If he *was* alive, and if nothing had gone wrong and if BB . . . too many if's, he thought. Jesse fetched his glass and poured his nightcap.

He knew that Elliot Maynard was determined to get BB back up to Dix in one piece, but Jesse had been careful not to give him any reassurance on that score. He had told him he thought if anyone could do it, Standing Bear was the man. But again, he told Maynard, it's in God's hands, to which the only answer had been a snort and then a very long silence on the line. Some people simply did not believe in God. A lot of people *said* they did, but saying was one thing and believing another. Yet, one thing he had observed in all his years of practicing. He would come to find himself with patients who said all this God stuff was a lot of hokum. Then he would tell them there was nothing else that he could do for them as a doctor, and did they need to see a minister, and every last one of them would say, "Yes, how soon can you get one?"

He mused upon that while sipping at the Jack. Lord, those boys up in Lynchburg, Tennessee, made about the best whiskey there was. He was glad he had never developed a taste for it beyond his nightly drink, and praise the Lord for that. What was it Timothy or somebody had said about a little wine now and then being good for the stomach? Well, wine for them and Jack Daniels for him. Of course, if he had ever let it get control of him, it could have easily ruined his life and destroyed his practice along with it, and oh Lord, he did love being a doctor. He couldn't imagine having done anything else with his life. It was just the thrill of experiencing a case like Charity's that enhanced the mystery and wonder of it all. He realized, as one of his professors at Johns Hopkins had told him, that during their careers they would discover that God picked up where science left off, and Jesse knew this was one of those cases.

BB was another interesting study. Maybe a chromosome was missing or something else—a chemical imbalance, although he didn't know very much about that. But something had gone haywire in what, given different circumstances, might have been the mind of an ingenious inventor, a great writer, a superb artist. Jesse had scrubbed on enough brain procedures to know that even the best surgeons were playing a guessing game once they sawed off the top of the skull and went in. It was still all one big mystery.

He hoped that Standing Bear would be successful. He had to be. It was apparent that the Grayson woman loved her son more than life itself, and he did not want to think what she might do if they came back with bad news. Clearing his thoughts, he dialed to WPTF to get the weather for tomorrow. The announcer was saying, "And now the forecast for Monday, August 6th. *Folks, summer is still very much with us, and tomorrow won't be any better. Look for temperatures to be in the low nineties with a few scattered showers in the far eastern portion. Other than that, we hope you're all ready for Monday and the start of a brand-new week. Before long, school will be starting, and we want to remind you that. . . ."*

Jesse switched it off. He sat there in the dark, then went out onto the veranda and got in his favorite rocking chair. A man deserved a few moments of peace and serenity at the end of a day, since he never knew what tomorrow would bring. He had learned that each day brought the incredible gift of life and the good news of grace evidenced by the fact that when we least expected it, God would surprise us with joy. As He had with Charity. As Jesse hoped, He would also do that with Deborah.

Hope was all we had . . . all there ever was. Hope was stronger than memory. It was stronger than intelligence and more lasting than talent. It was God's gift to us.

He sat there rocking, sipping and listening to the cicadas. Their sound was changing now, just as the hues of the butterflies, once brilliant in July, were beginning to lose their radiance. Nature was telling us something in that wonderful way she had of sharing her secrets. Jesse sought comfort in the fact that he was glad there *was* a God so that poor dumb Jesse Reardon didn't have to figure all this out. So Lord, then how come I didn't stay at Johns Hopkins? I'd be chief of surgery now. How come a good man like Caleb Trace had to be beaten to death by a bunch of hate-filled klansmen? How come I lost my wife? How come I never remarried? How come I'm a doctor, and Ragg's a cop and BB's a monster? Or is it Ragg who is the monster? Jesse knew that being God was one job he never wanted. He drained the glass.

Praise the Lord.

Charity had invited Deborah over for supper and was in the midst of preparing the meal when it happened. The Holy Spirit came to her and gave her a vision . . . there was Joshua sitting by a fire and he was smiling. He was all right. Praise God! Standing Bear had found him, and the boy was going to be fine. She knew that.

Neither spoke very much during the meal, but after the table had been cleared, Charity told her young friend she wanted to pray with her, and holding hands, the two sat there while the words poured from Charity's mouth. When she finished, she told Deborah that prayer was how we talked to God and how God talked to us. It was conversation, she said, and if you don't converse with someone, then the two of you become strangers.

"I want you to believe in a living God, Deborah. A God who can work miracles."

"You mean miracles like in the Old Testament? With Moses and the Red Sea? The burning bush and stuff like that?"

"Yes, only they're still happening today. All around us. Child, look at me. Here I am up and around talking to you, and I know those people at the hospital still don't believe it. There's pills and shots and such, and then there's God's medicine, and it's so much stronger."

"I don't know, Charity. I know what you're saying, and I want to believe, but it's awful hard when you've lost your husband, and six months later, your only child is lost in the swamp with a mad man running around loose. God may have done great things in your life, but I can't say much for what He's done in mine. It's no wonder I feel the way I do."

"Maybe that's because you never took the time to know Him," said Charity. She was going to say more, then decided this was not the time. "Let me ask you this," said the older woman, a smile forming on her lips. "Were you happy with Martin?"

"Yes, of course."

"Did you love him?"

"Certainly I loved him. You know that."

"Well, I loved my Caleb, and now I'm going to tell you a story."

Charity settled herself into the chair, clamped her hands down on the arms and began. "All his life, Caleb had preached the very heart and soul of the Gospel and when it came to Negroes, he was color-blind. Well, I remember it all, now. It was a Saturday afternoon, and the rumor started that a colored man from Dark Creek actually smiled at a white woman and said, 'Good afternoon, Ma'am,' though later on, no one could verify this, including the woman herself. Well, in those days, for a colored man to even *speak* to a white woman on the street was forbidden. And as a lesson to the rest of the coloreds, the Klan hung him from a large oak that grew beside the church. You see, a good many of the church members belonged to the Klan as well.

"Well, when Caleb heard about it, he sent word to the colored preacher that he would be coming out there Sunday evening to preach a sermon about this, and he did. But oh, my Caleb. It wouldn't do for him to preach it anywhere than right under that tree where that Negro was hanging. What happened later, I found out from the Negro minister who had come to hear Caleb. My man told the people that the Klan was the very spawn of Satan right here in Dark Creek.

"After it was over, the people left, and he was there all by himself, and I don't know for sure, but I guess it happened just before he got into his car . . . a group of men attacked him with axe handles and clubs and left him lying there bleeding on the ground, with a sign saying 'nigger lover' around his neck. When he didn't come home, I called the sheriff, he went out there and found him and took him to Dr. Reardon's. He had severe internal injuries and was hemorrhaging, and Dr. Reardon managed to get him on the operating table, but a clot broke loose, traveled to his lungs and he died. Not one church in this town, not one preacher had the gumption enough to go up against the Klan. And after he died, they still didn't speak out, and I haven't set foot in a church since. The Lord and I have our special time together in my room and in the garden and . . . well, wherever I happen to be, that's church. I've had 19 long, empty years to think about this, child, and if it hadn't been for the Lord healing me, I would have been broken up into little pieces a long time ago." She dabbed at the corner of her eyes with the small handkerchief she had been holding in her hand.

Deborah wanted to weep with her, to share her tears, but somehow she couldn't.

"I always knew something terrible must have happened," said Deborah, "but I never knew what. Charity, I'm glad you told me."

Charity nodded, blew her nose delicately, then straightened up in the chair, her face firm with resolve and gave a brief nod of her head.

"Deborah, I know Joshua is all right."

"I don't understand . . . how do you know?"

"I just know, that's all."

"Charity, I *want* to believe you, but please don't get my hopes up. It's more than I can take."

The older woman held up her hand and opened the worn Bible that lay upon her lap. "Here," she said, "read this, starting right here . . . Hebrews 11:1."

Deborah found her finger and read. " 'Faith is the assurance of things hoped for; the conviction of things not seen.'

"You mean that if I have faith that Joshua will be all right, he *will* be. Is that what you're telling me?" The doubt was a cloud over her face. Charity saw it.

"If you trust God enough to put it all into His hands, then yes."

"That's all I have to do? Believe?"

"Yes. That and a couple of other things."

"Such as?"

"You have to obey Him and love Him," said Charity, closing the Bible.

"But how can I obey if I can't hear Him talking to me?"

"Ahh, child, that's what praying is all about, and that's what we're going to do now. Come on, come close to me and let me put my hands on you. We're going to pray for Joshua. For deliverance."

Twenty minutes later, Deborah walked down to the cottage, her head reeling. If she could only believe like Charity. What was it that made her so different, so trusting of God? Could she really hear Him talking to her. And Caleb's death—for what? Deborah thought about the woman's terrible loneliness all these years. The old, empty house with all its memories. She turned to look at it, then glanced up at the night sky.

"God," she said, feeling clumsy and awkward. She had never spoken to God before in her entire life.

"Lord, I'm so lonely and frightened. I need You for my friend. I don't have anyone else to lean on . . . to talk to. I want to know You, Lord. I want You to talk to me. Please. Now."

"I believe, I believe," she said fiercely, kneeling there in the dark, but she did *not* believe, and she knew it. And the worst part, she thought, was that God knew it, too. She took a deep breath, the night air hot and thick in her lungs, pressing her down like a great weight, squeezing whatever hope was left right out of her body. She wanted to cry, but there were no tears left in her. There was nothing left but an overwhelming, nameless dread.

24

4:12 AM, Monday, the sixth . . .

BB was hunkered down beside a cypress where he had remained most of the night. He heard the voice.

do it now

He could see the embers of the fire that had all but died down. Under slivers of moonlight, he moved forward silently in a half crouch being careful of every twig and branch lying in his path. As his feet came out of the water, they made no sound. No telltale drips or splashes. He was as silent and invisible as the night. He was not walking through the Gut.

He had *become* the Gut.

Joshua lay in a deep sleep. Ragg had been awakened by Bear at midnight and taking his blanket with him, propped himself up against the tree with his gun in his hand. He had stared into the fire, put more wood on it twice, then began to nod until his body finally surrendered to sleep.

Beyond, in the darkness, BB grunted softly to himself, feeling the heat rise in his loins as it always did when he was ready to hurt the bad men. He inched closer and closer.

badmen in food place
found bb
bb killed one
bb kill again

He waited until the embers from the fire cast no light, and in a move as a great jungle cat would make, BB leapt from his hiding place and pounced on the man propped against the tree, letting out a yell. As he did, Ragg awoke half in shock, his limbs paralyzed with fear. In his panic, he reached for his gun, but by now, BB was on top of him reaching for his throat. Ragg, panic-stricken, was screaming into the face that snarled at him, "I'll kill you, I'll kill you!"

At the same instant Joshua awoke, but before he could even move, a hand went over his mouth, and he was whisked away into the darkness to a place behind a large gum. Bear put his finger over his mouth, told him not to move and then vanished. The whole thing took no more than five seconds.

Ragg was still trying to get to his gun. He felt the hands closing around his throat and knew he did not have long left before his breath would run out.

"Bear, help! Get him off of me!"

The heavy stick hit BB in back of the head once, then again, just above the neck in a blow that would have rendered the average man unconscious. Stunned momentarily, he relinquished his grip on Ragg, let out a yell and wheeled around to find only the empty darkness. He shook his head, then received another blow from someone he could not see. He growled and snarled like a wild animal. Ragg managed to find his gun that had been knocked away in the dark, before he could get a grip on it, it was knocked out of his hand, but not by BB. He saw Bear to his right.

"You crazy Indian, what are you doing?"

Bear pushed him away with a straight arm, and turned to face BB and as he did, he turned on his flashlight and shone it directly into BB's eyes, then let out a bloodcurdling war cry. BB jerked back, blinded momentarily by the light and startled by the sound. It was the interval of time that Bear needed. He jabbed the pole into BB's stomach and heard the air go out of him in a loud *whoof*. The huge figure dropped on all fours, gasping for breath, but immediately began to get back on his feet.

"C'mon, Ragg!" shouted Bear. "I'm gonna hit him again and try to knock him out. Then you give me a hand so I can get him tied up. I need you to hold the light." Bear felt something hit the back of his head, and the last thing he remembered as he pitched forward was the sound of a gun going off in his ears.

Ragg had realized it was now or never. He would not get another chance. He struck Bear behind his ear with the gun with all his force, then turned to shoot BB who was now barely visible in the dark, but as he pulled the trigger, the sound deafening in the stillness of the night, BB spun and dove, the bullet entering his right side, instead of his heart where Ragg had aimed.

Yarrrrgh!

The yell brought terror to Ragg, and he kept turning around pointing the gun, kicking with his feet to find the flashlight. Finally, his foot made contact, and he picked it up and shone it around.

BB was gone.

Bear was lying on the ground motionless.

The boy was gone.

"Joshua, where are you? You can come back now. It's okay."

Joshua froze. He did not trust this man. The flashlight's beam had frozen the image in his mind. He had seen Ragg hit his friend behind the head. He remembered what Bear had told him. He would not answer the policeman.

"Boy, quit playing games with me. I know you're out there, and by God, when I find you, I'm gonna fix you good, you hear me!" Ragg was yelling at the top of his voice, half from anger, half from fear. As dark as it was, if BB came back to finish what he started, Ragg knew he wouldn't have a prayer. He heard Bear moan and move slightly, and he bent over and tapped him again behind the ear. After fumbling around, he found the rope in the pack and tied the Indian's feet, already knowing what he was going to do, having worked it out in his head hours ago. Satisfied his prisoner couldn't get away, he took the flashlight and started to look for Joshua.

"Boy, you better come back here," hollered Ragg. It would be light before long, and once he found the boy, he'd have to decide how he wanted to play this thing. He didn't think he could kill a kid. No, he needed to come back a hero with the boy. Anyway, weren't him and his mother moving away to Rocky

Mount soon? Out of sight, out of mind, and the whole thing would blow over and be forgotten. But right now, he'd put a good scare into the kid.

"Hey, boy. I know you can hear me, so you listen up good. It's gonna be daylight soon, and I'm gonna find you, and you know it. If you're getting any funny ideas about what you're gonna tell people when we get back, let me tell you something. You blab one word of this, and I'll come after you and your momma in Rocky Mount or wherever y'all go. You can't hide from me. I'll find you and when I do, I'm gonna slice up your momma's face real good so she won't be so pretty anymore. And you'll be to blame, you hear me, boy? You want that on your conscience? Huh?"

Joshua thought that if he ran fast enough and far enough, once daylight came maybe he could find his way out. He had to tell somebody what had happened. He felt something brush by his bare leg, and knowing it was a snake, he screamed and broke loose from his cover, running blindly through the swamp. In his panic, he tripped over a rotting log and plunged headlong, the cypress knee rushing up to meet him, striking his forehead in a glancing blow.

After searching for a few minutes, Ragg found him and bringing him back to the small clearing, he laid him down. He could not get him to respond, but at least he had a pulse and it was steady. More than likely, he got a concussion, thought Ragg. And when that happened, he knew it generally wiped out somebody's memory for a while. And whatever they *thought* they knew, came out kind of scrambled. People wouldn't take the word of a kid with a concussion over that of a police chief. Standing Bear would be leftovers for the swamp varmints, and Ragg would be a hero after all. Everything was playing out just right. It might take him a while, but he knew he could find his way out of here after daylight by using Bear's compass. But before he and the kid left here, there was work to be done. Yes! He would bring the boy back. That would be a feather in his cap. The kid couldn't have seen anything, and his brain would be so scrambled, he'd be lucky if he remembered any of this.

Ragg rummaged around in his pack and brought out the small entrenching tool he had bought the day before. He had to fix up Tonto good and proper. It was something Ragg had been looking forward to for a long time, and now the time was here. He was no longer worried about BB. He figured the man had hit the trail for good, but Ragg knew he had wounded him, and he'd be somebody else's problem.

The good news, thought Ragg, was that *his* problem was about to be solved.

25

4:47 AM, Monday, the sixth . . .

Charity awoke suddenly and lay there motionless.

Directly overhead lay a huge cobweb connecting the four posts of her bed, the thick strands suspended like a shimmering canopy.

In the center lay the spider.

Its swollen body was the size of a softball, the hairy legs a foot long and when it moved, the strands of the web shook. She could see its venomous fangs glistening in the light from the hallway. Now, the spider began to let itself down slowly by a thread of silk . . . lower . . . lower . . . until it was barely 12 inches from her face. She closed her eyes and told God how much she loved Him and that she was not afraid because He was there. When she opened her eyes, the web and spider had vanished.

Thank You, Lord.

She prayed for Joshua and the men in the Gut and for Deborah, then dressed hurriedly and went downstairs to fix coffee and read her devotional. Ten minutes later, after she'd had her coffee and biscuit, she was standing in her garden, smelling the freshness of the new day, when it reappeared.

The bird.

It stood at the end of the row, then squawked loudly. Its beak was dripping with blood that was splashing onto the ground in big droplets. She could smell the blood. It was foul, the stench filling her nostrils. She fell to her knees on the earth, still cool from the night and damp from the dew. Charity's voice rang out clear as a church bell.

"Satan, you have no business here with me. I deny you, and you have no choice but to depart. Go back to hell where you belong. You are utter filth, an abomination of the world, and by the power of God Almighty, I order you—be gone!"

Charity saw the bird flap its wings and take to the air, then as though struck by an unseen object, fall to earth. When it hit the ground, it broke into little bits and pieces that scurried about like black beetles, the ground then seeming to swallow them up. Charity Whitley Trace burst into song, and Edgar Davis drove up in time to hear her and whistled in unison as he left the pint of buttermilk on her doorstep.

5:20 AM . . .

Within the small cabin at Dark Creek, on the Reardon farm, Goodboy roused himself from his bed and after pulling on his overalls, he knelt by his bed.

"Lord, thank You for this day. Thank You for all Your blessings, Lord, and most of all for Miz Kate. I know she is an angel, and that You sent her . . . and oh, Jesus, I am so blessed and sanctified by Your love. Yes, indeed, Lord. Amen."

He put on a pot of coffee, and fried some fatback, eating two of the biscuits Miz Kate had given him to take home. Today there were peanuts to be plowed. Oh gracious Lord, yes. Your faithful servant, Goodboy, is ready to go to work.

5:43 AM . . .

Blackbird stirred in his sleep from his vantage point in the woods. He awoke, glancing at his watch. He had left the house on Sunday evening, telling his wife, Lucinda, he wanted to be at the cattle auction in Raleigh early in the morning, and that he would spend the night at the motor court near the auction barn. He knew it made no difference to her one way or the other.

While he was preparing to leave, he made certain she didn't see him take his deer rifle and slide it into the truck behind the seat. That night, after pulling out of the driveway, he had driven out onto the hard surface, then doubled back to the old logging road that after years of neglect was barely a pair of ruts, all but concealed by the undergrowth that had overtaken it. He drove into the woods so that his truck couldn't be seen from the road. Then he got out, taking the rifle case and a flashlight. He walked deeper into the woods then circled the lower edge of the field of peanuts and took up position behind some thick bushes. Sitting here, he knew he could not be seen by anyone, even someone up close plowing in the morning . . . someone like Goodboy Found.

Blackbird was wide awake even before the sun came up.

He didn't need any breakfast.

He didn't need any coffee.

He didn't need nothing, by God, but to see that nigger lying on the ground dead. He'd take care of him like they took care of that big mouth nigger lover, Caleb Trace, 19 years ago this month. He remembered it like it was yesterday. Of all men, a preacher coming out to Dark Creek and stirrin' up folks, giving niggers ideas they had no business having. In four generations of his family, no nigger had ever laid his hands on a Bird, until Goodboy. Well sir, thought Blackbird, he would be the first and the last. That boy's plowing days were over. Then tonight or tomorrow night, he and Mash would take care of Miz Kate Hardison. They'd torch her store, and by sunup, there wouldn't be nothing left but ashes.

Nigger lovers just didn't belong in Dark Creek, and this would send out a strong message. Might be a good time to start reorganizing the Klan, too. Get people interested again now that the war was winding down. America had fought for something, by God, and it was to keep our nation clean of kikes, coons and whoever else Hitler didn't get to fry in them ovens. Hitler might have been on the other side, thought Blackbird, but he sure had the right idea. Only problem was—that ol' boy didn't live long enough to finish the job. Anyway, after he took care of this little unfinished business, he would head on up to Raleigh, knowing he had done a good day's work.

5:54 AM . . .

BB lay flat on his back on the damp ground, his breathing labored. He had run as far as he could from the bad man with the gun, then when he sensed he was safe, he had tended to the wound, stuffing it with a mixture of moss and mud. With each pulse of the pain that throbbed within him, his anger grew, transforming itself into blind rage.

badmen hurt bb
bb want hurt badmen

Now with the light coming up fast, he knew he had to stay away from open places. As the sky turned a bright pink, he found a spring and drank his fill, then splashed the water over his face and felt better. The picture of a bad man with a gun came into his mind, and his body shook with rage. He wanted to hurt back. He needed to hurt back. Just as he decided to move on, he picked up the unmistakable scent.

badman
gun
close

6:05 AM . . .

Goodboy took the mule out of the stall and leading it by a short rope, walked down the path by the edge of the field to the last row that skirted the edge of the swamp. The plow was where he had left it Friday evening. On the way, he talked to the mule as he always did.

"Now ain't we a sight, jes the two of us walking out here all by our lonely selfs? You know, mule, if you was the one what had the sense, you'd be leading, and I'd be followin'. But the good Lord knew what He was doin' and that's why I'm Goodboy and you're ol' mule. Sometimes, though, seems like you know more'n I do, and that's something can't nobody figure out. How come a mule is smarter about some things than a man is. But praise God, I ain't got to worry 'bout that 'cuz the Lord done figured it all out a long, long time ago." Goodboy gave out that deep, rolling musical laugh, and the mule flapped its ears at the sound and swished its tail at a fly trying to light on its hind leg.

6:14 AM . . .

Blackbird saw them coming. The mule and the man.

He knew there would be no one else out here at this time of morning, and by the time Goodboy showed up missing, he would have gotten to Raleigh, established his alibi and returned home again. The pair were about 30 yards away now and coming closer. Blackbird cocked the rifle and drew a bead on the familiar head under the straw hat. Just a few more seconds now.

Almost. . . .

As his finger tightened on the trigger, the rifle was seized from his grasp and thrown to one side. In the same instant, he was snatched up from the ground in a crushing hug, and he heard a distinct crack as three of his ribs snapped under the pressure. The pain drove into his chest like a ice pick. He could not get his breath.

Goodboy heard the commotion and stopped dead in his tracks as he watched in disbelief. What he saw was a man unlike any he had ever seen before, leaping out of the woods onto the edge of the plowed rows. He was holding another man by his wrists and swinging him around as a parent would do playing with a child. Except this was a grown man, but he was being slung so fast, Goodboy couldn't even make out who it was. The larger man spun faster and faster, letting out a yell, but as loud as it was, it could not cover up the man's screams.

Suddenly, BB let loose of the body, and it hurtled upward through the air slamming into a tree with a loud *thunk* some 15 feet off the ground, impaled on the broken end of a short branch. The arms and legs were splayed from where the body was lodged in the tree, the short branch sticking out through his chest, blood pouring out around the stick, the eyes staring wide open in horror.

Goodboy stood rooted to the ground. He had long since dropped the rope, and the mule had brayed and taken off across the field in a dead gallop. BB and Goodboy eyed each other from a distance of 50 paces. BB did not like what he saw. Neither did Goodboy. Then, BB raised his arms and started toward Goodboy in that loping run of his, the eyes glazed over and spittle coming from his mouth.

"Holy Ghost, help me," said Goodboy, and continuing to say it, looked down, and in that instant, his eyes fell upon a rock slightly smaller than a baseball. He picked it up and in one unbroken motion, let it fly out of his hand with all the force he could muster, hearing the words come out of his mouth, "Lord, send this rock where it belongs."

It hit dead center in BB's forehead, the sound like a watermelon being dropped on a cement floor. BB stopped in his tracks, a look of bewilderment on his face, stared at Goodboy for a split second, then fell forward flat on his face and was still. Goodboy was still trembling from the excitement, but he was not afraid. He went up to the body, bent down and rolled him over, looking at the man's face, blood trickling out of his nostrils, the crude features now even more misshapen because of the caved-in skull. Goodboy knelt in the earth beside the man, taking off his hat.

Oh, Lawd, if this man be dead, then I sholly did not mean to kill him and I ax You to forgive me, Lawd. I ain't never done nothing like this before, and Lawd, You know that. But Jesus knows I had to do something. I'm powerful sorry. Lawd, and please bless this poor soul, whoever he is, and find a place for him. Amen.

9:27 AM, Monday, the sixth . . .

"Lucy," hollered Jesse. Then again. "Luuuucy."

There was no response, and he looked puzzled and shook his head. "Be back in a minute," he said to his patient, a man named J.D. Elrod who had sprained his ankle falling out of a hayloft. Jesse muttered to himself, for having smelled the liquor on his patient's breath, he figured the man had probably been drunk when it happened. Too, he didn't believe he fell out of a hayloft at all. He grimaced. Doctor, he told himself. You're not a judge here to try people, you're here to heal them. He walked through one door, then down a short hallway, then into the kitchen to find his nurse hunched over the small radio that sat by the sink.

"Lucy, didn't you hear me calling you? We have patients to treat." There was a mild tone of annoyance in his voice. She turned around, her eyes open wide and staring right at his, and she pointed at the radio.

"Lordy, doctor, I'm sorry, but it's President Truman! He said we just dropped some kind of big bomb on Japan!"

26

9:34 AM, Monday, the sixth . . .

Goodboy had been sitting in the field for a long time, talking to God.

After a while, he walked over to look at the body of Blackbird hanging in the tree, then at the other man who lay there in the earth, and that's when he noticed the blood ebbing out in a thick, red flow from the wound in the man's side. He knew what a gunshot wound looked like, and he figured somebody had shot him before he hit him with the rock, but it couldn't have been Blackbird or he would have heard the shot. In the growing heat, the blow flies were already swarming around the wound, some lighting on it to lay their eggs that would later hatch into maggots. Without even knowing what he was doing or saying, he began praying. . . .

. . . *Lawd, You know I didn't mean Mr. Blackbird no harm, it just that he have these wicked thoughts in his heart when he come visiting me Saturday night and Lawd, I doan know what makes people want to hate us so, but I sholly didn't want nothing like this to happen to him. And then, this here other man, he come out of the woods like the devil hisself, and Lawd, I jus know he was gonna kill me, you could see it in his eyes, so I didn't know what else to do but chuck a rock at him, but I sho didn't mean to kill him. Sweet Jesus, You know that. And now I got these two dead mens here, and white folks is gonna think I kilt both of them, and then they gonna wanna hang this nigger for sure. Lawd, have mercy. . . .*

Goodboy sat there in silence for a moment, his head bowed, his hands clutching his straw hat, then after a few minutes, he realized he had to go tell Miz Kate. She would know what to do.

Kate did not have her radio on during the day except to hear the weather and farm market report at six. She thought it distracted people and was not good for business, thus she had not heard the news of the bomb being dropped until someone burst into the store hollering about he'd just heard it on his car radio, and then two other people stopped, and before long, the store was filled with people shouting, laughing, cracking jokes, buying each other Coke Colas and telling their versions of the stories.

Some said the war was over.

Others said it wasn't.

Some said it was all made up.

Others said no, they'd heard Truman say it his own self, and by grannies, whatever else he was, Harry Truman wasn't a liar.

Children were running around in the store, people asking how much was this and that, the expensive stuff that she never sold much of, men pounding each other on the back, talking about what this would do to the price of tobacco and cotton and peanuts, and in the midst of this furor, Goodboy entered the store holding his hat, his face a dark mask. He ignored everyone else, went up to the counter and said, "Miz Kate, there's somethin' I needs to show you, and I'd be much obliged if you could come with me right now."

Kate's first impulse was to tell him about the bomb being dropped, for she knew he had no radio in the cabin. But after noticing the look of concern and fear on his sweating face, she shooed everybody out of the store after considerable effort, and then the two of them started to talk. Goodboy told her what happened as she sat there her eyes wide in fascination, shock and finally horror. When he had finished, she called the sheriff's office, told them where they would be, turned the sign around from OPEN to CLOSED, took Goodboy by the elbow, and after locking the door, the two of them got into her car and drove down the road that skirted the edge of the field dead-ending at the woods.

Within 20 minutes, Sheriff Wade Handy pulled up in his car, and the three of them walked down to the body of BB, the sheriff taking note of what appeared to be a gunshot wound in the man's side and the blood spotted rock lying two feet away. Then Goodboy led them over to the tree from which Blackbird hung suspended. Handy stared up at the dead man in the tree for a long moment, then came back to where Kate and Goodboy stood there in the blazing heat.

"Goodboy," said Handy, fishing for a cigarette in his shirt pocket, "I want you to tell me exactly what all happened here."

Goodboy told him, pausing only to take a deep breath, then continue. He did not stutter or fumble with the words.

"Uh huh," said the sheriff. He pointed with his hand. "Well, I know that there fella is BB." He escaped from Dix Hospital about five days ago. Killed two colored people at Maggie Ware's cafe and a policeman, and more'n likely, he killed Blackbird as well. Leastways, based on what I see, that's what I think happened, but now, just so I get all this straight, tell me the whole story again." Handy had learned that people who had nothing to hide and therefore didn't have to make up anything would tell the story almost the same way they had the first time.

Goodboy did what the sheriff asked, speaking slowly, sometimes pausing to find the right word. When he finished, Wade asked him to point where he had seen BB emerge from the swamp with Blackbird in his grip. When he did, the sheriff told them to wait, and he walked over, disappearing from sight within the thick undergrowth. A moment later, he came out, holding the rifle in his hands, shaking his head slowly. He worked open the bolt, saw that it was fully loaded, then draped it over his shoulder.

When he rejoined them, Kate said, "Sheriff, I know this man, and I'll vouch for him. He's a good colored man and a Christian. Goodboy's been living out here for 14 years, farming this land for Doctor Reardon, and he ain't never told a lie to nobody. It just ain't *in* him to lie, and God knows it. Why, he would no more. . . ."

"All right, all right, Kate. I believe you." Wade waved her quiet with his hand but he did it nice and easy-like with a big smile. Kate Hardison's reputation was countywide, and nobody—it didn't matter whether you were a law enforcement officer or a Hoover FBI man—nobody wanted to lock horns with her.

"Thing is, I still gotta bring Goodboy in for questioning and get all this down in the record. If I don't, somebody down the line is gonna raise a ruckus. The way it stands, I got two dead men on my hands, and I want to be mighty sure my records are clean. You know, next year I'm coming up for re-election, and if somebody running against me decides to bring it up and make an issue out of it, I need to make sure all my cows are in the barn. You know how that is, don't you?" he said to Kate.

"I surely do. But now, you ain't gonna charge him, are you?" asked Kate, her eyebrows raised.

"No, I'm not." Handy bent down and retrieved the rock. "I mean, this here is the rock he threw at BB. And I don't think any man in his right mind would climb a tree to put a dead man up in it. That just don't make sense. First of all, *how* would he do it, and second of all, *why* would he do it? Like I say, it don't make no sense at all other than that it happened just the way he said. And I will tell you this: I have witnessed a lot of crazy, bad things since I put on this badge back in '37, but this beats all I ever *did* see." He pulled out a large handkerchief, removed his hat and wiped his brow.

"All right, y'all, I've seen and heard enough. We need to be getting on back to town. I'll send an ambulance out to bring in the bodies. Goodboy I'll be taking you in to get your statement down, but you ain't got nothing to worry about. You ain't gonna be charged, and nobody is gonna mess with you. So why don't you just get in my car? I ain't gonna cuff you or anything like that, and I'll be over there in a minute after I finish talking with Miz Kate."

Goodboy shuffled over to the car, opened the back door and got in.

Handy glanced at him for a second, then turned to Kate and spoke, lowering his voice. "Now, Kate, it ain't so much that I'm a protector of colored people, though people have said that about me, but I *am* a protector of the law. Thing is, if I don't do this proper-like, then by the time election comes around, somebody will start picking on me like I'm a banjo. I got two dead white men on my hands here, and one live nigger. Now, you ain't got to be no college graduate to know that a lot of people are gonna jump to conclusions in a heartbeat. If Goodboy was guilty, that would be one thing. But my gut says he ain't, so I just want you to know that if the Birds or anybody else try to take on the law, they better pack themselves a lunch 'cause it's gonna be the longest day in their life."

Hearing this, Kate nodded her head, then told Handy about the incident that had happened at the store. He listened gravely, nodding his head from time to time and giving an occasional grunt. "Well, I reckon that explains why he had it in for Goodboy. I guess a lot of white men might have felt the same way, but it don't call for killing a man. Not in my county, it don't."

Kate eyed Handy up and down as though she were measuring him for a suit. "Sheriff, you got sand. When election comes around, you can put your posters up at my store."

"Well now, Kate, that's mighty kind of you. Now, let me get on back to town and take care of all the paperwork. The sooner I do, the sooner it'll be over."

Before he left Dark Creek, Handy stopped by the house of Blackbird, telling Goodboy to wait in the car. He walked up the path to the door, knocked, and when Lucinda answered it, he went inside. Goodboy watched the door, wondering. In five minutes, he came back out, holding his hat and shook hands with her. When he told her, the news shocked her at first, but then it seemed as though she looked relieved. Like a weight had been lifted off her shoulders. Of course, Handy wasn't about to tell this to anyone. A law man had to learn to keep secrets, and that was one lesson he had learned well since he got elected.

Now, back in town, Handy sat down with Goodboy in his office and called Doctor Reardon, explaining what happened and reassuring him that the black man would not be charged. Then he let Goodboy talk to the doctor while he left the room. When he came back in, he had Doris Morgan come in and get it all down on her steno pad, just for the record. Finally Handy said, "All right, Doris. Thank you. Goodboy . . . I'm letting you go. As far as I'm concerned, and as far as Martin County and the state of North Carolina is concerned, there ain't no need for a hearing or nothing else. You're a free man, and I'm gonna take you on back to the farm."

As he rode back from town Handy glanced over his shoulder and said, "Goodboy, what do you think about the bomb?"

Lost in thought, Goodboy raised his eyebrows, looked at the white man's face in the rearview mirror and said, "Bomb? Lawd, Sheriff, I don't know nothin' 'bout no bomb, but whatever it be, suh, I didn't have nothin' to do with it."

Handy laughed so hard, he almost choked on his tobacco, and he thought he would make sure that story got around all over the county. He'd heard Doc's nigger was a little funny in the head, but he was okay. Yes'sir. Goodboy Found was okay.

I didn't have nothin' to do with it. He laughed again, and Goodboy felt good, hearing him laugh, knowing that was a good sign. The car pulled up in front of the cabin, the dust swirling around them.

"Thank you, suh." Goodboy stuck his hand out, and the sheriff took it, thinking he had not shaken the hands of too many colored folks in his lifetime, but there was a new day coming, no two ways about it, and it might just be a good time to start.

Someone came by the store and told Kate that Blackbird's funeral would be at three on Wednesday. She knew she didn't have any business there. None whatsoever. Kate always believed that if you didn't get along with a person when he was alive, his being dead didn't change anything. She knew she was supposed to love Blackbird just like God loved her, because that was what He expected from her, from all of us, and that God's love was like the sunshine. It fell on crabgrass just like it did on cotton. But nowhere in Scripture did it say she had to *like* the man. Still, she knew there must have been some good in him somewhere, and if there was, God would already have found it on the day of judgment.

If it had been *her* job to find it, she knew she would have had a powerful hard time coming up with anything good. Then a hot wave of shame swept through her. "Lord, forgive me," said Kate, "because I know if You graded us on the basis of what we've done, there'd be a great old big passel of us standing on the edge of hell, and Lord, You know that's one place I don't ever want to see."

27

11:40 AM, Monday, the sixth . . .

Sweetwater was not the same town it had been at sunrise.

The fire sirens started wailing just after the news broke, and *The Enterprise* went to work putting out a special edition. Up and down Main street, store owners set out flags, and clerks and customers alike ran out into the street yelling, hugging and clapping each other on the back.

Pete Hines, the fire chief and also the town's best known barber, had a customer sitting in the chair all lathered up when the siren went off. He tossed his razor in the sink and moved his considerable bulk at an amazing rate of speed to the firehouse where he and his volunteers got out the big American LaFrance and drove up and down Main, blowing the siren, ringing the bells and honking the horn while people of all ages tried to clamber on board. Those who were able and sober made it. Those who were already well on their way toward getting drunk tried to catch hold of something or someone, failed, fell off in the process, but nobody seemed to notice or care, including themselves. The war wasn't over, everybody knew that, but they also knew something big had happened, and the end wasn't far off. *Couldn't* be. The experts on the radio were saying this new kind of atomic bomb would put an end to wars forever.

On top of all this had come the news from the sheriff's office about what had happened out at Dark Creek, news that ordinarily would have had everyone in town buzzing and the entire switchboard lit up, but now that was relegated to second place. That crazy man, BB, who had killed Eldon Carver, and the two colored people that worked for Maggie, had all of a sudden come running out of the swamp, killed the man they called Blackbird out at Dark Creek, and then had started after Doc Reardon's nigger, Goodboy Found, when that ol' boy threw a rock at him, hit him slam in the middle of his head and killed him stone dead.

Jesse had tried to sort all this out during the morning. He wanted to call the sheriff back and ask him some more questions, but the switchboard was jammed. Lucy had already tried to call two prescriptions into the drugstore only to have Grace tell her, "Sweetie, I reckon you're just gonna have to get in line like everybody else."

As a result, they had seen only a handful of patients during the morning, but it was just as well. It gave Lucy a chance to tidy up what they called "the little hospital," that consisted of four beds in the space that had once been a large formal dining room. Sometimes, patients were better off here where the doctor could keep an eye on them than they would be at home.

Lucy had kept the radio on the whole time. In fact, she had brought it into the examining room, after asking his approval, since both of them wanted to hear the news the minute it broke from Washington. There had been endless speeches by this politician and that general, the governor, senators and just about everybody else, and Jesse shared their great relief that soon the struggle would be over. The monstrous evil that had taken his son and millions of other young men and women was about to end, and he grieved for their death and the other kind of pain that now had to be borne by the living: parents, husbands, wives and children who had to go on knowing that nothing would ever fill that emptiness in their hearts. He sipped from the fresh cup of coffee Lucy had brought him, then bent to the task of examining a friend of Lucy's, a young woman who was in her fifth month. After checking to make sure his ears were not deceiving him, he told her that it might be twins. She grinned at her husband whose eyes appeared as though they would bulge out of his head.

Jesse said, "Now, I can't be sure, you understand, but I have seen lots of twins in my time, and this sure does look like it."

"Well, is dey gonna be boys or girls?" asked the woman.

"Oh, I don't know that."

"Doctuh, Miss Lucy here, says you know everything."

Jesse blushed and cast a reproving glance at his nurse. "Well, I sure appreciate that, but even so, I guess we'll just have to wait until. . . . " He was interrupted by the sound of a horn blowing outside.

"Good Lord, I wonder how long this is going to keep up," he said, turning to Lucy with a laugh. As he turned to take off his gloves, a man in overalls burst through the doorway, his face flushed with excitement: "Hey, Doc! I found 'em. I found 'em!"

"Found who?" said Jesse, wondering what all this was about.

"You know. Chief Ragg and the boy. The one who was lost. Ragg must have been carrying the boy on his back and passed out in the heat, and I almost ran over them. They were on Deer Lick Road where. . . . "

Jesse didn't stay to hear the rest. He dashed out to the ancient mud splattered pickup, and sure enough, there were Ragg and Joshua lying in the back. Dear God, let him be all right, thought Jesse. He motioned to the man, and they carried the boy inside first, laying him on the examining table, then Ragg who was already starting to moan. Heat exhaustion, thought Jesse automatically, and after he and the farmer laid Ragg in one of the beds, he gave Lucy instructions to put ice cold compresses on his face and let him know when he came around.

The ugly bruise on Joshua's forehead indicated the boy had taken quite a blow. Pulse weak, but steady. Breathing regular. He pulled back the eyelids and could see the tiny blood vessels that had ruptured in the eyes. It was clear the boy had suffered a concussion. He would be unconscious for some time, and chances are he would come out of it, but possibly with some short-term memory loss. It all depended on the severity of the blow he had received, and there was no way to tell that. Still, children seemed to fare better than grown-ups. He was comforted by Lucy's quiet presence by his side.

"Call his mother," he said, his fingers still roaming over Joshua's face, neck and skull, looking for further damage. Then he glanced at her. "No, the lines are probably tied up anyway. Besides, it's better you go fetch her in person. Take the car."

"What if she asks me about his condition?" said Lucy. Jesse had expected that.

"Tell her . . . I said I thought he was going to be okay, but that I couldn't be sure, and we'd know more about it by morning. You might have her bring some things so she can stay the night with him. I'm sure she'll want to do that."

"Yes, doctor." Lucy vanished in a white-stockinged blur with only a starched rustle.

By now, Ragg had come around. His conversation was a bit muddled, but he was able to sit up in bed. Jesse gave him a salt pill and made him drink a large glass of Lucy's fresh lemonade.

"Feeling a little better?" he asked Ragg.

"Yeah, doctor. I . . . guess I must have passed out from the load and the heat and everything. How'd I get here?"

"A man brought you. Said he found y'all on Deer Lick Road."

Ragg shook his head slowly from side to side.

"Godamighty, Doc . . . I didn't think we were gonna make it."

"Can you remember what happened?"

And with that, Ragg told his story that he had rehearsed over and over every step of the way while carrying the boy on his back. It was a good story. In fact, it was a great story. About how they looked and looked and finally found Joshua and had been camped out for the night asleep when BB attacked. . . .

"It must have been about an hour and a half before sunup. I reckon. I had taken the first watch, and then Bear, he was on. The next thing I knew I woke up, hearing Joshua yelling and screaming as he ran by me in the dark, like the devil was chasing him. I could see that BB had hold of Bear something fierce . . . holding him in his arms and shaking him like he was a rag doll. I reached for my gun and got off one shot, but that's all, 'cuz I was afraid I would hit Bear. But it must have done the trick 'cuz

BB turned and ran off into the swamp, and dang if Bear didn't get up and go after him. I tried to call him back, but he wouldn't stop. In a minute or two, I heard him yell out, but in the swamp, you can't really tell much about a sound."

The policeman paused and licked his lips. Jesse watched him intently, berating himself for ever having thought ill of the man.

"Well, naturally, my first concern was the boy, but it didn't take me long to find him. He was about 40 feet away. I guess he had panicked, being so scared and all, and running in the dark, he'd fallen and hit his head on a cypress knee. Well, I knew I had to get him out of there and back here, and I couldn't wait around for Bear any longer. So I did what I thought was right. We left out a little bit after daylight, and I guess . . . we wandered around a good bit . . . plus carrying him, it was slow going, and I had to stop and rest every bit . . . and. . . . "

"It's all right," said Jesse. "Lucy, bring the Chief . . . oh, I plumb forgot. She's gone to fetch Deborah. Well, here, I'll get you some more lemonade. After all, you've had quite a day." When he returned with the pitcher, he filled Ragg in on the events of Blackbird, BB and Goodboy, then told him about the bomb. The policeman seemed stunned by the news, then recovered himself.

"Well, I reckon the war's about over, and maybe all this is, too, except for Bear missing. There's no telling what happened to him. I have a pretty good idea of how to get back to where we were, and as soon as I feel up to it, I'm going back in there and look for him." Before anyone else finds him first, thought Ragg.

Reardon looked at him, knowing that if Ragg hadn't been there, Joshua might never have come back at all. Deborah and son owed the chief their thanks. Ragg lay there motionless, then blinked hard and looked up at Reardon, with a look of genuine concern on his face. "Is the boy gonna be all right?"

"I don't know," said the physician. "He appears to have a concussion and is in a coma. That's just another way of saying he's in a deep state of unconsciousness and not able to respond. We have him on glucose to keep his body fluids up, and other than that and monitoring his signs, there isn't a great deal we can do. In cases of this sort, the first 18 to 24 hours are the most critical. His vital signs are good, but that doesn't necessarily mean much."

"A concussion, huh? What does that do to him?" Ragg seemed genuinely concerned, and again, Jesse was impressed by this apparent shift in the man's character. It was a side he had not seen before.

"Oh, he could have temporary amnesia—short-term memory loss. Or worse." It depends upon the severity of the blow.

"But he *is* gonna be okay, right?"

"Well, Chief, I don't know how to answer that. The blow he took must have been a powerful one. With someone else, it could easily have killed him. It might be a good while, though, before he can get things all straightened out in his head. On the other hand, I've seen some miraculous recoveries from this kind of thing. At this point, it's all very hard to tell, but you needn't worry yourself about this, Chief. I'd say you've performed a great service for Miz Grayson and her son . . . and for the whole town."

Ragg smiled. "Thanks, doctor. It's what I'm paid to do. I just keep thinking about Bear. He and I weren't exactly buddies, but I feel responsible for him."

"Mmm." Jesse nodded slowly. "Yes . . . well, from the little I know of Standing Bear, if he's able to at all, that is physically, he will certainly find his way back, and when our young patient in there recovers, and if and when the Japanese decide to surrender, we'll all have something to celebrate, won't we?" He smiled broadly and clapped the chief of police on the back.

"You're right, doctor. We sure will," said Ragg, summoning all his willpower to return the smile. He was so pleased with the way things had worked out, it was all he could do to keep from laughing out loud.

The news traveled fast. The farmer who had picked up the pair went downtown to enter into the celebration, and within 30 minutes, the word had spread all over town. A stringer from the

News and Observer happened to be at the sheriff's office following up on the story that broke this morning about BB, but when he heard about the latest events, he smelled an even better story and showed up on the doctor's doorstep wanting to interview Ragg. Jesse gave him a definite no, saying he wouldn't countenance that kind of thing in his office. Moreover, he said, that even though Chief Ragg would be released this afternoon, he would still be a little weak and it might be better if the reporter talked to him in the morning. The reporter persisted. By this time, Lucy had returned with Deborah. While he began explaining things to Deborah, the reporter, having struck out with the doctor, tried his luck with Lucy.

"Mister newspaper man, sir," she said, her arms folded as she fixed him with that stony stare of hers. "We got two sick people here, one of them a boy who's bad off plus his momma who needs peace and quiet, and we surely don't need any more commotion than we already have. So my advice to you is to march straight back downtown and get a room at the George Reynold's hotel. Then you come by here about nine in the morning, not before, and we may let you talk with the boy's mother, that is, *if* she's willing. What you do with Chief Ragg, well, that's between you and him."

The reporter listened, swallowed and said, "Uh, yes ma'am," suddenly realizing he hadn't ever said that to a colored woman before.

By the time the reporter left, Jesse and Deborah were sitting by Joshua's bed. The shades on the two large windows were pulled down to keep out the harsh sunlight, and this only added another dimension to the gloom that lay in Deborah's heart. She keep looking at her son and stroking his hand, while Lucy kept bringing new cold compresses. Jesse patiently went over all the issues he had discussed with Ragg. He paused.

"And . . .?" she prompted.

He stroked his chin. "Well, I didn't tell this to Ragg or to anyone, but I can tell you. Deborah, a blow of this severity could easily cause long-term brain damage. I've seen it happen before."

The silence rose like a wall around her.

"How long is long?" she said, almost in a whisper.

He didn't flinch. "Six months, a year . . . maybe permanent."

"When will we know?"

"Probably by sometime late tonight or early morning."

"I want to stay in here with him. Is that all right?"

"Certainly. Use the bed right next to his or you can sleep in the easy chair. Of course, I'll be close by if—" he corrected himself, "*when* he says something or makes any kind of sound. It could be a sign that he's regaining consciousness. The one thing I fear most in conditions like this is convulsions. A head injury can often bring these on, and coupled with the heat and the frightening experience he's had, it's a miracle he's doing as well as he is. I've brought his fever down, but it's still higher than I'd like it to be."

He stood there for a moment, observing her, then touched her on the shoulder and left. Deborah remained motionless in the chair, trying to sift through everything he had said. Finally, the events of the past two days took their toll, and she fell into a deep sleep.

"Ma'am? Miz Grayson . . . Doctor says you need to eat, and I fixed you a little tray."

Deborah shook the sleep from her. "Oh! What time is it?"

"It's after seven, ma'am. All the patients have gone home. You had a good long nap, and Doctor says, that's just what you needed."

Deborah tried to wave off the food, but Lucy would not be deterred.

"Now, Miz Grayson, when Doctor Reardon tells me to do something, I have to do it, and he told me to fix this and make sure you eat it, so please don't be giving me a hard time. We all got enough to worry about without that. Besides, you need to be strong for your boy, and having some food inside you is going to help. Course, you need to be doing some powerful praying, too."

Deborah did not know how to respond. "Yes . . . Charity said she would be praying too, and that gives me courage."

"That's true, but you know, sometimes, we just got to get on the line and talk to God directly. I appreciate when folks pray for me, but like I said, there are times I have to do my own praying. I think that's what God wants. Don't you?"

Deborah gave a polite smile and nodded. This kind of talk still made her very uncomfortable. Her mind shifted gears suddenly.

"Is Chief Ragg still here?"

"No'm. He got to feeling so good the doctor let him go on home."

"I can't believe I could be so unthinking," said Deborah, a tone of dismay in her voice.

"Ma'am?" Lucy said, wearing a puzzled look.

"I never got to thank Chief Ragg for bringing my son back to me. How could I be so inconsiderate!"

"Well, I'm sure you'll have time for that tomorrow. I understand there's going to be some kind of press conference at city hall around ten o'clock—for the newspaper folks, but you'll probably be wanting to stay close to Joshua."

Deborah nodded.

Lucy said, "Now, it sure would do this nurse's heart good if you'd try some of that chicken. It's baked, just the way he likes it, and there's candied yams and fresh garden peas and some peach cobbler."

Deborah nodded, trying her best to smile. "I'll eat . . . I promise."

Lucy smiled, patted her shoulder, then left the room to the two of them, mother and son. Deborah looked down at the tray. It did look good, and she picked up her fork and started to work on a yam, when the thought suddenly hit her, causing her to let the fork slip from her hand.

Standing Bear.

No one mentioned him. Where was he? What had happened to him? At that instant, her son's body began to move in the bed, as though a giant hand were moving the bed back and forth, and then his head started to jerk, his body rocking, and from his mouth came a series of "uh-uh-uh" in time with the jerks. Deborah sprung out of the chair, the tray falling off her lap, and blind with panic, dashed from the room, the words stuck in her throat, the scream coming out at full volume.

28

5:47 PM, Monday, the sixth . . .

The pain slammed Bear into consciousness.

He felt as though someone had taken a rubber mallet and pounded on every square inch of his body. But along with that, there was another sensation, his mind struggling to identify it. All he knew was that he couldn't move his limbs. He wanted to, but they would not respond. When he managed to get his eyes fully open, the first objects that came into focus were leaves, twigs and rotting vegetation. Then he realized why his body refused to move.

He was buried in the wet, thick swamp earth up to his neck.

He might have been a post driven into the ground for all the movement he could generate. From where he was, the bank sloped downward to the edge of Dark Creek barely five feet away from his mouth. His eyes being at ground level gave him an entirely new perspective, and he watched as a small salamander scurried over the mud hunting for insects. It was not more than 12 inches from his face, and paused to look at this strange creature, then vanished from sight.

Ragg. The word lay in his mouth, its bitter taste almost making him gag. Bear had underestimated the policeman. His father would have been very disappointed in him and would have reminded him of the old saying: a rattlesnake is small, but its bite is worse than a bear's. He had been snake bit. Bear gave a small grunt of displeasure with himself.

Ragg must have had this plan in his mind all along. He had done to Bear what Apaches used to do to their enemies, except the Apaches refined the torture by pouring honey on the man's eyes and lips and tongue. Soon, the desert ants would come and feed voraciously on these parts until there was nothing left but shreds of cartilage and bloody, bony sockets.

Bear licked his lips and tasted dried blood, and he knew Ragg must have pistol whipped him. All this must have happened while he was unconscious. He had not realized until now just how treacherous and evil the white eyes really was, and he tried to think back to the moment when BB had attacked them. All he could remember was hustling Joshua away to safety then rushing back to confront BB, and then . . . nothing.

What had happened to them? What if Joshua had been killed? On the other hand, if they had managed to survive the attack, had Ragg taken the boy back with him? If he did, surely the boy would tell everyone what happened. But what if he had *not* taken him back. What if Joshua were out here, too, and BB still wandering around on the loose. Too many what ifs.

His face and neck itched furiously from the hordes of mosquitoes that had fed on him, but he had encountered far worse in the jungles of the South Pacific. But worst of all was his raging thirst. He wanted a drink of water more than he had ever wanted anything else in his life. Then, as he adjusted to seeing the world at ground level, he swiveled his head to the left as far as he could and saw his pack sitting there about six feet away. At first, he did not understand why Ragg had done that, and then he realized it was a kind of torture, a little game. *Hey, Indian: there's everything you need—water, knife, gun, food, flashlight, right over there. You can look at it and think about it and imagine what a drink of water from the canteen would taste like, but you can't have it.* Clever, he thought. Maybe Ragg *did* have Apache blood in him from way back. The Cherokees had not been cruel. Tough, brave fighters, but never cruel.

Bear listened to the songs of the birds, each note familiar to him from the times he and his father had roamed the swamps years ago, but now their changing cries signaled that darkness would come over the Gut in another two hours. And then? A few small swamp animals would find him, and the more brave ones would probably approach within a few feet or so to check him out. A raccoon might decide to come even closer to sniff him, but Bear knew that by yelling and growling, he could drive him off. But only for a while. However, it was not raccoons or the small animals that worried him.

It was the night hunting animals, starting with the wildcats who would track down the scent of blood from his bruised face. A black bear might come to investigate, but if he did not look the bear in the face, he knew it would not bother him. They were after live, running game. No, there was something far worse to deal with—the animal that his brothers, the Seminoles, had learned to fear in the Everglades. The perfect killing machine.

The gator.

He knew it was here, and he had felt its presence from the minute he entered the Gut. With the coming of night, it would be on the prowl, circling the creek as it watched for any unsuspecting prey. Defenseless. Nonthreatening. Like himself.

Bear tugged at his bonds in the earth. His hands were tied in front, and he tugged and pulled until his muscles ached more than they did, but the earth was packed tightly around him. Ragg had not dug just a hole, he had dug his grave. Already weak, the thought of this depressed Bear further, and that plus the exertion and the heat and the mosquitoes and his body craving water caused him to collapse into sleep, his head slumped forward.

When he awoke again, it was almost night. A full moon, shattered into fragments by the trees, spilled pieces of silver upon the surface of the creek. Night had transformed the towering trees into dark totems rising up from the earth. Twenty yards distant, as the creek curved to the right, he saw a raccoon approach the water's edge with a crawfish it had caught and started washing it in the water as coons always did. In spite of his pain, Bear could not help but smile, thinking how wonderful animals were in the way they did things. As he watched, the moon broke free of the trees, and the silence was shattered by a deafening bellow as the gator came up out of the water. It made a lunge for the coon who miraculously leapt straight up in the air, landing on all fours and darting away before the huge jaws could open and close again.

Bear licked his lips still tasting the dried blood. It was a bull gator, all right. Big. Bigger than he had ever seen. He had never doubted it was here, and now it was here with *him*, though he did not think the gator had seen him. He knew he'd be hard to spot, the gator not looking for a head sticking out of the ground. It would not be expecting such a prey. He watched it swim slowly out into the center of the inlet, only the tip of the broad, blunt snout breaking the water for air. It swam in a circle, then suddenly went under water in a sleek dive without even leaving a ripple. It had seen something: a snake, a fish—who knew? Prey. Food. A victim.

Like him.

O great Father in the sky, he thought. Give me the wisdom to know what to do. Make my heart as brave as the mother bear who defends her cubs, Holy Spirit. I know that tonight I am to be tested, and I must live and go back to tell the truth so that the liar who is my enemy can be punished for his evil ways.

Bear closed his eyes tightly, determined if death was coming, he would remember only the best moments of his life, starting with his childhood. He could see the face of Miss Angela Slaton, the woman who came to the reservation to teach school. All the kids called her Miss Angel because she was so kind to them and because she learned to speak their language in a way that astounded the elders of the tribe.

And Pastor Hahn, who would come on Sunday to teach them about the Bible and who, with his mother's permission, had baptized him secretly in a creek, for his father would have been furious had he found out. It was not that he was against it all that much but that in the eyes of others, he was surrendering to the white eyes. His mother had made the preacher promise he would never tell another living soul. Bear remembered that crisp October morning, when the preacher led him into the water step by step and how it felt circling about his feet.

The water about his feet. . . .

Suddenly, he became aware that there *was* water. He could feel its presence around his ankles. The water table was so high and the ground so soft it had made it easy for Ragg to dig the hole. But it also meant a possible way out of this. He moved his feet again—they were not tied—and as they moved, the water seeped in around them. What if, he thought. What if he kept working his feet back and forth, up and down, making room for the water to rise? Would it continue to rise and as it did, soften the earth, so that he could generate more and more motion, his body working like a pump?

An hour later, after flexing the muscles in his feet and thighs over and over, he could feel the water continuing to rise, and he experienced a little more freedom of movement. Gradually, the water reached mid-calf, and as he kept on, the ground seemed to have a little more give to it. After a while, he was exhausted and had to rest.

Then he began again. It was not much, but it was all he could do. A Cherokee warrior did not give up. Bear tried to keep his head still, keeping an eye out for the gator which was nowhere to be seen. Perhaps it had swam up creek deeper into the swamp in search of larger prey. Time passed. The water was up to his hip now, and now he could rotate his body from side to side, but only barely.

He kept on. He gulped in the night air, his body craving water and food, but he told himself he was not thirsty. He was not hungry. He called on the great Spirit to feed him strength. Then he decided he would sing to give him strength. His favorite hymn on the reservation had been *Amazing Grace,* the first one the missionaries taught them. He sang the first verse under his breath, the words coming out in fragments, remembering how his mother had sung him to sleep with it when he was a small boy.

Ooh Nay Thla Nah, Hee OO Way Gee
E Gah Gwoo Yah Hay EE
Naw Gwoo Joe Sah, We You Low Say,
E Gah Gwoo Yah Ho Nah

His mind began to wander, and for some reason he recalled a story his grandfather had told him—of a brave caught out on the plains in a terrible blizzard. He had gathered fresh buffalo dung into a large pile, then crawled under it. The warmth had gotten him through the night and he survived the blizzard.

Great Spirit, am I crazy? Tell me.

Suddenly, he saw a movement to his left, turned his eyes and seeing the cottonmouth moccasin only three feet away from him, the thick black body making an evil S curve as it wriggled along the ground. Before he could check it, a shout escaped from his throat. The snake retreated into the water, taking no notice. But something else did.

From its new vantage point, some 20 yards out, the alligator had observed this. It knew the sound. It was the sound the man-things made, and instinct prompted it to swim over there, clamber out of the water, drag the prey into the depths and drown it. But it remembered what had happened before with the other man-thing, and its brain processed the information clumsily, struggling with exactly what it was it saw. Unsure, it decided to adopt its favorite tactic of watch and wait. It lay suspended in the water, almost motionless. The half-lidded eyes fixed on the spot. Its brain told it the hunting time had come.

By now, Bear was sweating profusely from the effort, but he could feel the water continuing to rise around his waist. He could feel it on his hands, and now he could rotate his upper body with more freedom. To the right. Then to the left. Then back again. Twisting his torso to make more room in the hole back and forth, to one side then the other, as space grew around him, the water continuing to rise as the soft earth gave way. He had no idea of how much time had passed.

He grunted from the exertion.

The gator heard the sound. It swam within 40 feet and hovered motionless in the water, watching, its eyes piercing the darkness. A water snake swam past, and the gator lunged for it, the mammoth jaws closing on it with a great click, swallowing the snake live in an instant, but it was only a morsel for its gigantic appetite and made its hunger even more ravenous. Bear heard the sound, knew what it was, but he could see only dimly in the moonlight. He knew the gator was out there in the creek, and he knew sooner or later it would come for him.

He kept wiggling, working his body.

Twisting back and forth.

Pushing down with his feet.

Jamming his fists against the earth.

But he knew he would first have to get his hands and arms free in order to give him the leverage he needed to pull himself out of the hole.

He pushed again. Pressed his fists down with all his strength.

His breath began coming in great noisy gulps of air. In the dark stillness, the gator heard this and swam closer to investigate. This time it would approach the prey very carefully. The ancient hunger to seize something in its jaws, taste the blood and feel the bones cracking and splitting overrode any other urge within it. It knew it was stronger than the man-thing and did not fear it. It remembered the taste of the flesh that it liked so much. Then suddenly, the alligator saw that the man-thing had crawled out of its hole like a large, thick snake covered with mud and now lay on top of the earth.

It did not understand this. This change in tactics made it pause for a moment, sifting through the new data, translating it into a command from its brain. Its thought processes were slow and clumsy. The gator swam in closer, certain its prey could not see it. It was 20 feet from the bank. It paused. The hunger came at it again.

Bear gulped in the night air, paused for a second, then crawled toward his pack going for his knife to cut himself free, but just as his hands fell on the pack, he heard the sound from the creek.

The gator had decided. It would take its prey now. Its body came out of the water preparing to charge for the killing rush, the powerful short legs ready to propel it forward as the jaws were beginning to open.

Bear heard it, smelled it behind him. There was no time to hunt for the knife. With his hands still tied, he pulled his father's .44 from the pack, grasped the familiar wood in a perfect shooter's grip, his thumb pulling back the hammer, his body spinning like a bottle on the slippery earth, and he turned in time to see the alligator's jaws open as it rushed toward him out of the water, its armored hide wet and glistening in the moonlight. He pointed the barrel into the fearsome jaws that opened to clamp their death grip on his legs, pulled the trigger and kept on pulling, hearing the roar of the gator and the sound of the gun, each bullet snapping the gator's head back until the final round blasted through the cartilage at the roof of the mouth and entered its brain where there was no protecting ring of bone.

The alligator gave a final surge and then fell dead upon Bear's own body, its enormous jaws resting on his thighs, the thick, dark red blood oozing out between the rows of teeth and trickling onto the Indian's legs.

The echoes of the gun died away, and the loudest thing he heard was the sound of his breathing. Slowly, he worked himself loose from under the weight, found his knife and cut his bonds. Then brandishing the gun in one hand and the knife in the other, he stood up in the half moonlight, throwing his head back and yelled with all his strength so that the great Father would hear him. It was the same cry of victory that his father had yelled and *his* father, and his father before *him*. The sound echoed through the swamp for over a mile. No human being was there to hear it, but the animals and birds heard it and did not know what it was. They had never heard a sound like it before, and they would never hear one again.

Bear stood still for a moment, looked up at the moon, then fell to his knees exhausted, and with the battle over, hunger and thirst assailed him. He pulled the canteen to his mouth and sipped at it slowly, knowing if he gulped the water down, he would vomit. Then he began to munch on an apple, though his mouth was tender and bleeding from the beating, but he did not care. He was sitting up within a yard or so of the gator and visually took its measurements, thinking it had to be at least 12 feet, maybe more. "You were strong and smart, alligator," he said. "But you did not have the Holy Spirit protecting you, and that is the difference between us. One of us had to die, and I am glad it was you. You will not be killing the creatures of this swamp any longer, and for that, I give thanks to my heavenly Father."

When he finished eating and had drunk his fill, Bear took the knife and prying open the gator's jaws, dug out two of the largest teeth, then put them in his pocket. Now he would rest so he would be strong in the morning.

When he awoke, the smell of death was all around him, and he realized he was covered with mud and blood. He leapt to his feet, stripped down to his skin and plunged into the creek, splashing and washing himself from head to toe, laughing and frolicking as though he were a boy again. Diving under the water again and again until a few rays of the new day's sun found their way through the trees and fell upon his face, flooding him with the blessing of warmth and light.

He sensed a new strength within him. He felt . . . reborn.

Bear emerged from the creek, standing there on the bank, his hard, lean, wet brown body naked to the morning, shaking the water droplets out of his hair, then lifted up his arms and began the Cherokee war dance, his head bobbing up and down, chanting the same words that his ancestors had chanted for thousands of years. He had killed one enemy. Now he would go after the more dangerous one.

The white eyes.

29

7:10 PM, Monday, the sixth . . .

When the convulsions started, the physician and his nurse heard Deborah's cries and came on a dead run from opposite directions, almost colliding in the narrow hallway. Jesse hollered to Lucy, "Get me three cc's of phenobarb I-V. Stat!"

With her usual efficiency, she had the syringe ready for him in a matter of seconds, along with the alcohol-soaked cotton. He found a vein and inserted the needle in a deft, rapid thrust. A moment later, Lucy was back with a bucket of ice water and towels, and the two of them stood on either side of their patient, applying these to his face and neck.

Within the span of two minutes, the convulsions had lessened and finally, Joshua lay there still, except for the even rise and fall of his chest. His mother sat on one side of the bed, Jesse and Lucy on the other. Jesse took one of the iced towels and pressed it to his own forehead. He had not been surprised at the convulsions, but amazed that when they came, they had not been longer in duration. After fifteen minutes or so, with his permission, Lucy retired for the evening, exhausted by the events of the day. Deborah and Jesse sat there by the bed in silence. She looked at her son, whose body seemed even smaller and more fragile than she had remembered. Though a bandage covered up the bruise on his forehead, she could still picture it in her mind and felt her son's pain.

"Deborah . . ." Jesse paused and took a deep breath. "Listen to me, please. By morning, if he's not better enough to suit me, I'm calling an ambulance and we'll take him up to Duke.

Your son's neurological functions are not all I'd like them to be, but at this stage of the game, that doesn't mean much. The next six to eight hours are critical, and by morning, we'll know."

"Is there nothing more you can do, doctor?"

He shook his head slowly. His body felt heavy. His feet seemed to be growing into the floor. He thought to himself that this was worse than when he had interned and pulled the midnight ER shift. "No, I'm afraid not, Deborah. He seems to be resting quietly now, and the best thing I can do now is to leave you with your son. You know where I am if you need me. Just holler out, and I'll . . . both Lucy and I will be here. Okay?"

She nodded slowly, her mouth set in a grim line, the eyes flat. He touched her shoulder gently, gave a slight squeeze, then left the room, turning off the overhead light and leaving just a small lamp burning on the bedside table. When he was gone, she moved even closer to Joshua and lay her head on the bed beside his arm. She could no longer keep the words bottled up within her, and as they left her mouth, she barely recognized her voice. . . .

"Oh, Joshua . . . I'm so sorry. If I hadn't gone to Rocky Mount for the interview, this wouldn't have happened, and I blame myself. I thought getting that job was the most important thing in the world for us, and I realize now it was nothing . . . just nothing. Oh, son, if I could give my life for you, I would. Anything to make you well again."

She stroked his arm, then touched his cheek with the back of her hand. Then she leaned back in the chair, her thoughts wandering through the corridors and dreams of her childhood. Memories crowded in, and she promised herself she would not succumb to sleep, but would remain awake for her son, and for a while she managed to do that, but finally with one long deep breath, her system shut down, seeking the rest it demanded.

When she awoke, she glanced at her wrist, but remembered that when Lucy came for her, she had been in such a panic, she had left her watch on the top of the vanity. The light from the lamp cast a warm glow on her son's face, and she sat there watching the rise and fall of his chest. His lips twitched slightly, but just once, and there seemed to be a momentary pause in his breathing. Then he emitted a tiny sigh, and the regular breathing resumed. The fan overhead turned slowly, and she could feel the air touching her face, gliding across her arms.

She walked over to stand at the window. Outside, the cicadas had quieted down, and the night seemed vast and endless, as though it had surrounded the house and they were an island in the impenetrable darkness. She began to pace back and forth in the tiny room and suddenly became a little girl again, listening to her father's yelling and cursing, her mother's screaming and the sound of his open hand on her face and finally, his fists on her body, the sounds coming through the paper thin wall that separated their bedroom from hers.

She saw all of it now as though it were a series of images projected on the wall: the sights, the smells, the sounds, and without realizing what she was doing, she fell to her knees by the side of the bed and the hurt and the anger and fear all came pouring out of her mixed in a moment of surrender . . . *I don't even know what to call You . . . God . . . Lord . . . so You have to understand, this is very hard for me to do. I never liked You very much. Even when I went to church with Momma . . . I always thought that if You loved me, You would have given me a better father instead of the one I had . . . so Lord, I held that against You. And I . . . I hated church. Yes, all of it. The people weren't there on account of You, Lord. At least, most of them weren't. They were there because . . . maybe they thought by going they would have the right to ask You for things. The preacher was always saying to us that if we told You what we wanted, You would give it to us, but I know now that isn't the way it works.*

What I wanted was that stupid job in Rocky Mount, but what I needed was to stay here with my son . . . and now what I need is for him to be well, but I don't have any right to ask You this, Lord. I've never prayed like this in my whole life. God, I haven't been a bad person, have I? I don't think so. I've tried to do the

best I could with Joshua . . . I'm sorry I resented Charity's spend-
ing all that time with him . . . because I'm jealous of the way
Joshua trusts her and loves her and the way she loves him.

Lord, make me like Charity. I need this if I'm going to be a
better mother and teach my son the right things. Whatever it is that
she has, Lord, I want all of it I can get. Maybe Charity can teach
me. All I ask is this one thing . . . that my son be made well and
whole again . . . I want nothing for myself. Nothing. . . .

Deborah was a little girl again, very small, and her mother
was combing and brushing her hair, the way she used to love for
her to do. She could feel her mother's hands pulling the brush
through her hair with long, even strokes in the morning. She
opened her eyes. She was sitting forward in the chair, her upper
body slumped on the bed. Joshua's hand was stroking her hair,
and she heard the small voice, "Mom . . . Mom?"

She raised up with a start and looked at him.

"Joshua! Are you? . . . "

He smiled at her. "Mom . . . Charity was right. God delivered me! And Mom . . . I'm hungry."

"Thank You, Lord." The words came as a whisper.

She stood up feeling giddy. "Doctor? Doctor Reardon! He's
awake. Joshua is okay. He's. . . . "

Before she could finish, Reardon and Lucy were by her side,
an inexpressible joy welling up within her, transforming itself
into tears. Within minutes, the sun was up, and Lucy made a
quick breakfast, then brought the tray to the bed, and Deborah
fed her son who sat propped up against the pillow, gulping down
the cereal, the pancakes, the juice and the milk. Between mouthfuls, he told her and Reardon the story of what had happened.
He would pause for a moment and then say . . . "I remember
Chief Ragg doing this," or "I remember when Bear did that."

Jesse and Deborah listened in amazement, not able to say a
word. Jesse was lost in thought. If what the boy said was true,
then . . . my God, what in the world had happened in that swamp?
A blow such as he received could do this to the mind, twisting
facts until reality blended with fantasy, and the patient couldn't
tell where one ended and the other began. He'd seen it enough

before to know. He moved closer to Joshua.

"Son, how old are you?"

Joshua frowned. "How old am I? I'm eleven going on twelve."

"When's your birthday?"

"October tenth."

"What was your teacher's name last year?"

"Mrs. Sanders."

Jesse looked at Deborah. She nodded.

"How much is nine times seven?"

He paused slightly. "Sixty-three."

Joshua looked up at his mother. "Mom, why is Doctor Reardon asking me all these questions? And where is Bear?"

"Well, right now, we're not quite sure."

"Is he all right?"

Deborah said, "Joshua, honey, don't worry about Standing Bear right now. You need to get better."

At that, Lucy came back into the room, whispered something in Reardon's ear, and he asked Deborah to excuse him, the two of them leaving the room.

"But Mom," Joshua continued, "Bear is my friend, and he knows what Chief Ragg did. He's a bad man. He. . . . "

"Joshua Grayson, that is no way to talk about the man who saved you. He carried you out of that swamp on his back. If it weren't for him, you might not even be here."

Joshua would have none of this, and he balled up his fists and pounded the mattress, his eyes becoming wet.

"Mom, I *know* what happened. Don't you believe me? You're my mother, and you're *supposed* to believe me. Well, aren't you?"

Deborah could remember having said that to her own mother when she told her about her father wanting to touch her and the way he looked at her. She felt the shame rise within and flushed. She drew near her son and looked into his eyes and said, "Joshua, I believe you. It's just that . . . I don't understand what all this means, but I know you're my son and you don't tell lies, so somehow we're going to figure all this out. Okay?"

He was silent. "We're blood brothers, you know. Me and Bear, and if he was here, he could tell you the same story, and then you'd really know."

Jesse burst back into the room, his face flushed with excitement.

"He's here! He's come back. Lucy heard something at the back door, and she found him there collapsed against the door."

He couldn't speak and motioned for her to follow him. For a sick boy, Joshua showed amazing agility in getting out of bed, and though his mother protested, he followed her through the hall to the examining room where the four of them stood around the treatment table looking down at Standing Bear. When she saw him, Deborah drew in her breath sharply. Joshua's eyes widened, and he moved in to stand next to his friend whose face was bruised and covered with insect bites. Suddenly, Bear's eyes opened, he blinked rapidly, then his gaze focused on Joshua, and he stuck out his hand and pulled the boy to him.

"My brother," he said, his voice breaking. "It's good to see you. Hey, us Indians gotta stick together, you know." And then the ex-Marine and grandson of a Cherokee chieftain passed out.

30

10:04 AM, Tuesday, the seventh . . .

"So, Chief, tell us the part again about when this character BB was going after Joshua, uh, what's his last name?"

"Grayson."

"Yeah, Grayson. That's it. How about picking up where BB was trying to steal the kid." The *Observer* reporter, a short, round man with a red face and a cigarette dangling from his lips, was sitting on the edge of the desk, scribbling furiously in his notepad. There were two other men in the room, one from the *Raleigh Times* and the other from the *Norfolk Ledger Dispatch*. Ragg leaned back in his chair, lit up a fresh cigar and told the story again, adding a bit more to his heroics—how he had gone up against a half-man, half-monster and managed to wrest the boy from his grasp.

"And then, Joshua ran off into the swamp, right, chief?"

"Yep, I reckon he was scared to death. Who wouldn't be! I tried to get off a shot at BB, but he was faster than greased lightning, and he ran off in the opposite direction. Standing Bear went after him, and I yelled for him to come back, but that was one determined young man. Then after I'd found Joshua unconscious with his skull near about caved in, I heard yelling and screaming from out there in the dark, and then things got real quiet. Well, you know, fellas . . . there was no way I was gonna leave the boy and go out there hunting for trouble. We'd already had enough of that for one night, so I decided to wait for first light then try to find my way back. I knew the boy was bad off, but trying to get out of the Gut in the dark would have been asking for it. There's cottonmouths near about every step you take, and that BB, he can track you like a bloodhound, but when he comes after you, he's more like a gator."

"And let me get this straight, Chief," said the man from the *Observer.* "You carried Joshua out of the swamp on your back?"

"Well, yeah, I knew I had to get him to a doctor, so I tied his wrists and slung him over my back. It was slow going, and I didn't know it at the time, but with carrying the boy and all, I must have strayed off course, but that was okay since I ran right into Deer Lick Road. And that's where that farmer found us, because I don't remember much after that until I woke up in the doctor's office."

All the reporters were scribbling furiously in their little note-books, exchanging glances with one another and nodding their heads. What a story this would make. They all said it was a shame they couldn't get any pictures of BB—dead or alive. Their readers would love it.

The phone had been ringing during the interview, and Ragg had told Peele to handle all his calls, but noticed he had stepped out to the bathroom. When the phone rang again, Ragg said, "Boys, I'm gonna have to take these calls now. I've still got a police force to run, so go ahead and finish up with your picture taking, and then, if you have any more questions, just call me. Okay?"

The reporters nodded, a few last flashbulbs went off, and then they left the office in a group, eager to get back and file their stories. By now, pieces of the story had been heard by probably half the townspeople, and people were matching up their pieces with what others had heard in an attempt to patch together the entire story, but everyone agreed on one thing: Curt Ragg was the man of the hour. Of the day. A real, honest to goodness hero, and Sweetwater ought to be proud to have him as their chief of police. A few people asked about Standing Bear, but no one seemed very concerned. The Indian had never really been welcome in Sweetwater, and some of the regulars drinking their mid-morning Cokes at Clark's Drugstore said as far as they were concerned, it was good riddance to bad rubbish.

Back at the department, the phone kept on ringing, people calling from everywhere, including the nuthouse doctor. Ragg had told him he was sorry as he could be, but BB was dead and that was all there was to it. He wished *he* had gotten to kill him, instead of Doc Reardon's nigger. At that, he snapped his fingers and picked up the phone to find out about the Grayson kid.

Jesse had already attended to Bear's wounds, amazed that he had come through the experience as well as he did. He seemed a bit steadier now and more in control, but Jesse knew that once the high was over and the body was no longer in a condition of stress, it would shut itself down for the rest it needed. He had Lucy prepare a good, hot meal, and while Bear wolfed down the food, Jesse had him relate his account of the story. The man's powers of recall were amazing, and he told his story to Jesse with the door closed while Lucy, Deborah and Joshua were out in the kitchen. He was astounded as Bear played out the details of what he remembered, then managed to piece the rest together.

Even before he finished, Jesse realized that Joshua's and Bear's stories matched, the boy's version ending where Bear's began: what Ragg had done to him, leaving him for dead in the Gut. He pondered this for a moment, then went to fetch the others and asked Bear to tell them about the alligator. The Indian took his time, going into some detail, and when he finished, the others sat there numbed by his ordeal.

"And," he said, "I got something here . . . wait a minute, "it's in my pants pockets. Lucy, would you bring them to me, please?"

Lucy did as he requested, her nose wrinkling at the stench of the discarded clothing. She handed the pants to Bear who reached into the right-hand pocket, felt around, then withdrew the two huge teeth and holding them out in his open palm, motioned for Joshua to take them. When the boy held the teeth in his own small hand, they looked even larger. His only response was a long, muted "Wow!"

Reardon then gave Bear a mild sedative, ushered everyone out of the room, and within minutes his new patient was sound asleep. Joshua had convinced his mother he had to stay in the room with Bear, *to watch out for him, you know, Mom, just in case,* and she relented after realizing he would not take no for an answer. Jesse agreed, smiling to himself.

They heard the phone, and Lucy picked it up, listened for a second or two, then made a face and handed it to Jesse.

"It's for you, Doctor," said Lucy. "It's him . . . Ragg."

"Uh huh. Okay, let me take it in the study." As he walked into the room, Jesse said to himself: *Lord, I'm about to do some powerful lying here, and I just wanted You to know this before I got started.*

"Doc . . . Hey, doctor, this is the chief. How's the little feller doing?"

"Well, Chief, I'd say about as well as can be expected at this point."

"He come around yet?"

"No. He tried to say some things and tell us what happened, but he's still in the coma, and frankly, all we got were bits and pieces. From the way he spoke, it's clear to me his memory is badly scrambled."

"Poor kid. You mean, like delirious?"

"Yes. I can't really make head or tails of anything he says."

"That's a shame—it really is. Well, I'm just glad I got him back in one piece. You don't think there's gonna be any long-term damage, do you?"

"You know, Chief, I'm not sure. But if he doesn't start showing some improvement, I've advised his mother that we should take him up to Duke for testing in the morning."

"Duke, huh? Well, my heart really goes out to Miz Grayson. You'll be sure and let me know if anything comes up, won't you?"

"You can count on me, Chief."

They said their good-byes, and after Jesse hung up, he told Lucy he would be out back in the garden. He wanted to think for a while, and he needed some time alone. She nodded, knowing better than to quiz him further. Sitting on the bench under the chinaberry tree, Jesse chewed at his lip and kept nodding his head slowly, occasionally making little grunts. After 30 minutes or so, he clapped his palms on his knees, stood up and went straight into his study, looked up a number, then reached for the phone. After talking without interruption for four or five minutes, he listened intently for a similar period of time. Then he said, "Okay, but remember what I told you. Ragg does not know Bear is alive and back here, and he thinks Joshua's memory is all haywire. . . . A good time? Oh, let's say four. He should be pretty much rested by then and feeling like talking to you."

He set down the receiver, nodding to himself, then heard Lucy calling him and went into the examining room. One thing about patients. They kept on getting sick no matter what else was going on in the world: atomic bombs, BB, Ragg, whatever. Sick people needed to be seen, that's all there was to it.

Just before five, two men arrived, parking in the back as Jesse asked them to do, and Lucy showed them into the study. Sheriff Handy was the taller of the two, wearing freshly starched khakis with a large pistol on his belt. The other was two inches shorter with a pleasant face, glasses and wearing a seersucker suit and a red tie. His name was Wheeler Munson, the county prosecutor. When they were all seated in the study, Jesse started from the top and told them exactly what he had witnessed, without relating either of the stories he had heard. They sipped from the glasses Lucy had poured for them.

"That nurse of yours makes the best lemonade in the county, Jesse," said Wheeler.

"Mmm," added Wade in agreement, then put down his glass. "Now, fellas, we got some serious business to attend to, and I reckon I'm as eager as Wheeler here to get to the bottom of it. Jesse, when can we talk to Standing Bear?"

"Right now. He's had a good nap, and he's waiting on the sun porch."

They walked down the large hall by the kitchen and pantry, then made a right and found themselves in a room filled with plants, shrubs and flowers, all Lucy's handiwork. There, seated in a wicker chair by the window was Bear. Munson recoiled slightly when he saw his face, but Handy gave no notice, since in his career he had seen far worse.

"Standing Bear," said Wade. "We haven't met personally, but I'm Sheriff Wade Handy, and this here is Wheeler Munson, the county prosecutor. From what we hear, you've been through quite an ordeal. Doctor Reardon filled us in on just a little of it, but we want you to start at the beginning and tell us the whole story."

"How far back do you want me to go?" said Bear.

Munson and Handy exchanged glances. The lawyer answered. "Far back as you need to, okay?"

Bear nodded. He told them about the incident when he was two, what had happened between Ragg and his mother. He touched upon the war, his wounds and his decorations, both men listening solemnly and nodding. Then he related Ragg's stopping him for the bogus taillight charge, and everything that happened in jail, including the scene with BB and Carver. Then he told them exactly what he had told the others earlier in the day. When he finished, Jesse refilled his glass from the pitcher.

Wheeler let out his breath. He had been taking notes in a notebook as fast as he could, and now he started tapping the pencil against his teeth. "Boy, I've heard some stories in my lifetime, but this here takes the cake."

Handy nodded. "Bear, we're much obliged for your telling us all this. I know you ain't exactly feeling great. You can go on back to your room now. Not that we're trying to get rid of you, but. . . ."

"But you're trying to get rid of me. I know." Bear managed a slight smile. The sheriff smiled back.

When he was gone, Wheeler said, "Jesse, now we need to talk to the boy. Is it all right?"

"Sure. I've already discussed this with his mother, and she doesn't mind."

Wade said, "The thing is, we'd like to talk to him with nobody else in the room."

"I figured you would, so I ran that by her, too, and it's okay." He gestured to Lucy who was standing in the hall at the doorway, and his nurse left and a moment later, returned with Joshua in tow. A half hour later, the two men left the sun porch and found Jesse who was in his study with Lucy going over some reports from the lab. Lucy could tell by the looks on their faces that they needed some privacy, and she excused herself, closing the door as she left.

Munson spoke first. "Jesse, I can tell you right now, neither of us have any doubt that both Bear and the boy are telling the truth, and we don't think a jury would either. Lot of people around town like Ragg, but to tell the truth, just as many don't like him. Far as the town knows, he's a big hero, but we know different. Now the problem is, we want to avoid a trial if at all possible, because that would spare Joshua and his mother a lot of grief. Course, this thing may never *get* to trial, if Ragg confesses once he realizes we got the goods on him."

Handy stood up and stretched and taking a handkerchief from his pocket, blew his nose loudly, then again. "Hay fever," he said by way of apology. "It usually comes just before Labor Day, but this year, it's starting a little early."

"Remind me when you leave, and I'll give you something for that," said Jesse.

"Okay, now let me tell y'all what this comes down to," said Munson. "Abuse of power by a local law enforcement official is not a county offense, it's state, and it's serious. That means I need to call Raleigh, fill them in on the facts, they'll get a judge to issue an arrest warrant and then they'll send somebody down here to serve it, take Ragg back, and he'll face a grand jury up there. I can't speak to the charges, but I would say he's got enough to put him away for some time, the most serious part being assault and battery with intent to kill."

Munson took off his glasses and rubbed the bridge of his nose, then put them back on. "Now, when it gets to that part, it's his word against Standing Bear's, but based upon what we've heard from both Bear and the boy, I think the grand jury would return a true bill. And if it went to trial, Ty Baines, the fellow who would be arguing for the state, is tough as nails, and if I know him at all, he'll go for attempted murder. Now, I don't know who Ragg would get to defend him. He has no money, and the state has to appoint someone, but whoever they get, when that guy hears the whole story, his heart ain't gonna be in it, I can tell you that." He paused and dug in his ear briefly with his finger. "Plus, there's that part about what Ragg did to the boy back in the spring."

Jesse's face was a question mark.

Munson's eyebrows rose. "You don't know?"

The doctor gave a quick shake of his head, wondering what they could be talking about.

"Wade, you tell him."

The sheriff related the incident in the bathroom at city hall. Jesse was stunned. He felt the revulsion rise within him, along with the bile. "The boy told you that?"

"Yep. And didn't bat an eyelash either. You know, when I heard that I wanted to go downtown right then and work Ragg over with my bare hands, but now, y'all didn't hear me say that."

"Does his mother know?" asked Jesse.

The sheriff shook his head.

Jesse took a deep breath, started to say something, then changed his mind. There weren't any words that would work.

"Jesse, can I use your phone?" asked Munson. "It may be too late, but let me see if I can get hold of somebody up at state and get this thing rolling."

He sat down at the rolltop desk, took a little book from his coat pocket and after getting the operator, gave her a name and number. Jesse and Handy strolled down the hall, then back into the sun porch. They looked out back and there was Deborah, her son and Bear sitting under the huge oak. Even from this distance, the bruises on his face were clearly visible. Wade knew if this thing went to trial, they'd need to get some photographs made and fast, before the bruises healed. He made a mental note. After a time, Munson came out to find them.

"Okay, I've spoken with Judge Tillman, and he understands enough of the situation to take action. He's gonna issue a warrant and have his chief deputy and another man down here tomorrow morning at nine o'clock sharp to serve it on him."

"Tillman? That wouldn't be *Rollie* Tillman, would it?" asked Jesse.

The man nodded.

"Well, I'll be. I played high school football against him in the playoffs, but that was back when gas was a nickel a gallon." Then, as though shifting gears abruptly, he said, "And. . . ?"

"And . . . they'll take him into custody, handcuff him, then take him on back up to Raleigh. Most of the proceedings will take place up there."

"So that may be the last we'll see of him?"

"Well, I didn't say that, Jesse. I mean, the law is one thing and justice is another. He *could* get off with a light sentence." Munson saw how Jesse reacted to this, and quickly added, "I said *could* now."

"But how . . . ?"

"Jesse, you know a lot about how the body works and all that kind of stuff. And you know when a man's sick, sometime you can't tell exactly what it is and how it's gonna turn out?"

"Sure."

"Well, it's kinda the same way with the law and the courts. I mean, at the most they'd give Ragg five to seven, and he could be out in two for good behavior, walking around free as a bird. The fact that he was a policeman for all those years would carry weight with some people. Of course, you and I both know that what he did was wrong, and the Lord knows it too, but unfortunately, God doesn't sit on the parole board."

Jesse started to say something, but just shook his head. Handy cursed under his breath. Munson let out a long sigh, his shoulders slumping. The silence lasted for only a moment, though it seemed much longer.

Finally, Munson stood up and stretched.

"Okay, Jesse, we're gonna get on down the road. I've told everybody not to talk about this to a living soul, and they understand. Same goes for everybody here, okay?"

Jesse nodded.

The two men started out the door and were almost to their car, when Jesse saw them pause momentarily, the two of them no more than 18 inches apart, one talking, the other listening intently. After several minutes, they turned on their heels and came back to the house.

"Jesse," said Handy. "Wheeler here has come up with a plan. It makes sense to me, but Bear and Joshua and his mother would have to agree to go along with it. It could shortcut this whole thing if we do it right. Plus eliminate the need for the boy testifying or anything like that."

"Well, let's go run it by all of them."

After hearing what they had to say, all parties agreed, and instructions were given for tomorrow morning. The men shook hands and once more started out to the car. Then Jesse hollered for them to hold up, ran into the dispensary, then back out to where they stood, the look on the sheriff's face saying oh, oh, what now?

"Here." He gave the vial to Handy. "For your hay fever . . . three times a day."

The sheriff smiled, they shook hands and left. Jesse had a last-minute chat with Deborah who had decided that she and Joshua would go back to the cottage. Then he frowned momentarily.

"Listen, I know you're eager to get home, but if Charity should see you, she's going to want to know everything, and it would be pretty hard to pledge her to silence. In fact, I'm not at all sure she'd understand, and it might cause her some undue stress, something she doesn't need right now, in spite of her miraculous recovery. Deborah, why don't you and Joshua stay here for another night—just to be safe? You can call Charity and tell her that I decided Joshua was not well enough to leave, but don't frighten her. Tell her he's in no real danger. That should satisfy her. Better yet, you probably want to fetch Joshua some clean clothes, and that'll give you a chance to talk with her. I don't think she'll be wanting to come over here, but if she brings it up, tell her we've all had a long day, and that I suggested—no, *insisted*, that we all go to bed early and get a good night's rest. You know, doctor's orders." He said this last with a wink.

Deborah nodded. Lucy said she'd drive her home and wait for her.

Joshua was beside himself with joy. They were going to stay the night. He made a beeline for Bear where he sat on the sun porch, and Deborah could hear the words coming out of him a mile a minute.

"Bear, Bear! We're gonna spend the night here. Now tell me all about the gator again. Remember, you promised!"

31

9:00 AM, Wednesday, the eighth . . .

Ragg had been in the office since a little before eight, still getting calls from well wishers and a few newspaper folks from all the way down to Wilmington and over to Greensboro. Naturally, he was glad to talk to them, and in the midst of all this, promptly at nine o'clock, a tall, heavyset man walked into his office, came over to his desk and said, "Mornin'. I'm looking for Curtis L. Ragg." Ragg didn't know what it was, but something about the man bothered him.

"You're talking to him, but it's *Chief* Ragg, if it's all the same to you." He leaned back in the swivel chair. "Now state your business, bub."

"Chief, I'm Harley Gurganus, assigned to the state coroner's office. The people over at Dorothea Dix need some papers signed with regard to a person known as 'BB Rainey.' It's my understanding that he was killed by a person who was acting in self-defense, and since, according to Dr. Maynard's records, your department arrested this individual and actually had him in custody, I have some release forms that need to be signed. Just a formality." Gurganus lay a sheaf of forms on the desk in front of Ragg, who glanced at them with a look of disdain.

"Well, now, ain't that something? Release forms, huh? I'll tell you what, Gurganus. I'm taking care of official business right now for the town of Sweetwater, on account of that's what they pay me to do, and I'll get to you when I've got time."

"Oh, I understand that, Chief, and I got no problem waiting. Say, by the way, what all did happen out there with BB?

I'm just curious, you know. They don't tell us very much up there in Raleigh. There was some talk about an Indian missing, but I didn't get the full story."

Ragg hitched up his belt and holster rig, his chin jutting forward. "Standing Bear was—*is* his name. That poor Indian may be out there in the swamp, alive, leastways, I hope he is, and I mean to go looking for him first thing in the morning 'cuz that's my job. But if he *ain't* alive, then he was killed by this feller, BB, who got himself killed by a nigger named Goodboy Found, and if you doubt any of this, just call Sheriff Wade Handy. You got that, cap?"

"Chief, don't take no offense or anything. Like I said, it's just curiosity on my part."

Ragg hitched up his pants again. "Yeah, well you know what they say about curiosity and the cat."

"Oh yes'sir, I surely do. Anyway, if there's a room I could wait in that has a phone, I'd love to call my sister. She lives just over the river toward Windsor."

Ragg gestured down the hall. "Sure. There's a phone in the town council room just up the hall, first door on your right. But don't you be calling long distance or anything, you hear?"

"No sir, Chief. I wouldn't do anything like that."

Ragg nodded, picking up what he thought was a softer tone in the man's voice and got back to reading a newspaper story that had already broken in the *News and Observer.* He took an ancient pair of scissors and cut out the article, opened a folder and put it with the other articles, then thought better of it and rummaged around for some thumbtacks and put the story on the bulletin board.

It wasn't until ten minutes later that he remembered about Gurganus and wondered what had happened to him. Ragg didn't like strangers coming into his office acting like they were somebody, using his phone and stuff like that. He got up from the chair and walked down the hall to the meeting room and opened the door, expecting to find his unwelcome visitor talking on the phone.

Instead, he found himself staring into the smiling faces of Standing Bear and Joshua Grayson, seated together on the other side of the table. His face telegraphed his shock before the words even left his mouth.

"What the—you're supposed to be dead! You couldn't have gotten away unless—"

"Whoa now, hoss," said Gurganus, who stepped out from behind the door where he had been patiently waiting. "Chief Ragg, you're under arrest for attempted murder and for making lewd advances to a minor. I'll have your gun, please."

Gurganus stood well over six feet and held out his huge hand, beckoning for the chief of police to hand over his service revolver. Unable to speak, Ragg kept shaking his head slowly, still not believing what he was seeing and hearing. He spun around and started to reach for his gun when he saw another man come out of the small closet. In his hand he held a blue steel .38 with a six-inch barrel in a grip that was as unwavering as his hard blue eyes.

"Officer Ragg, I'm Chief State Deputy Frank Willis. Sir, I am ordering you in the presence of witnesses to unholster your gun, nice and slow, and drop it on the floor. Then place your hands behind you, so I can handcuff you."

Ragg started to unholster his gun, then with a roar sprang toward Bear, wanting to get his hands on his enemy's throat. He was screaming obscenities at the top of his voice, but he had barely moved a step when a pair of giant arms seized his arms and twisted them behind him as easily as if they were pipe cleaners. Within seconds, he was handcuffed and his gun was in their possession. Ragg was yelling and screaming at the top of his voice, and Gurganus motioned for Bear and Joshua to leave the room. A string of curses followed them as they left, but as soon as the door closed, the man with the blacksmith hands turned around and said tonelessly, "Chief, this kind of behavior ain't going to help your case one bit."

Ragg turned his stream of invective toward his captor, and in a sudden, almost effortless motion, Gurganus slapped the policeman directly across his face, the *crack* sounding like a ball being hit by a bat. Ragg's ears were ringing, and he exploded out of the chair trying to bite or kick, and in the attempt tripped and fell sprawling on the polished oak floor.

Gurganus picked him up as though he were handling a tenpound sack of potatoes and slammed him down in the chair.

"Chief, we can do this the hard way or the easy way. Which one's it gonna be?"

32

9:47 AM, Wednesday, the eighth . . .

When Bear and Joshua returned to Reardon's office, they found not only Deborah waiting, but also Sheriff Handy and Wheeler Munson. Deborah's nerves had been on edge the whole time, despite the assurances that had been made; and when she saw her son get out of the car, she ran out to envelop him in a huge hug. Once inside, they related what had happened at the police station.

"Well," said Handy, "y'all did just great. Harley Gurganus called me a few minutes ago and said it couldn't have gone any better. Ragg's words were a confession heard by witnesses and would stand up in any court in the land. In fact, on the basis of that alone, I don't see how he could plead anyway *but* guilty. But if he does decide to make the state go through the motions of a trial, if I know Judge Tillman, he will bury him under the jail."

"Where is Ragg now?" asked Jesse.

"He's in a pair of handcuffs in the back seat of a car, and they're on their way to Raleigh," said Munson, "so there's nothing more to worry about."

"For anybody," Handy added, giving Deborah a reassuring glance.

The sheriff turned to Joshua and stuck out his big hand. "Son, I'm right proud of you. I know that wasn't easy to do, but all this is over now, and you and your ma can get on with your life."

"Thank you, sir." Joshua looked up at Bear, took his hand and exchanged grins.

Deborah said, "I want to thank all of you for the help you've given me, and . . . Bear . . ." she paused. "Without you, my son might not be here with me." She started to hug him, but thought better of it and offered her hand.

Bear took it and gave a polite shake. Then he turned to the two men. "Well, I don't know about you fellas, but I want to get on home and forget about all this for a while," said Bear. "It's only been two days, but I feel like I've lost a week."

"I'd be glad to drop you off," said Handy. Bear accepted, and they left, Munson leaving in his own car. Deborah and Joshua also left, declining the offer of a ride, preferring to walk back to their cottage. Deborah was sure that now it was all over, Charity would want to know everything, and the sheriff had told her she could be quite open with her. It didn't matter anymore.

* * * * *

Jesse sat at the table and picked at the chicken pot pie that Lucy made for him, managing to down a wedge of tomato from the salad but ignoring the pecan pie completely. That was Lucy's first clue that something was on his mind. When the doctor didn't eat lunch, something was up, and when he didn't eat her pecan pie, then something was eating on *him*. She stood there by the table, arms akimbo.

"All right, doctor, what is it?"

"Excuse me?" He looked up, feigning ignorance.

"Oh, please, doctor. I know something is working in that mind of yours. You didn't touch your lunch, and besides, you don't think after all this time, I can't hear those gears grinding away in that brain of yours."

He laughed and spread out his hands. "Okay, Lucy, you got me. I just uh . . . need some time alone after all this. A few things I need to catch up on, you know, personal business. Just tell our patients we've closed down the office for the afternoon, and they'll have to come back in the morning."

"But doctor," said Lucy, "people are gonna be disappointed to hear that."

"Well, I guess they'll just have to be disappointed then."

"Now, Doctor Reardon, you listen to me. There's a. . . . "

"No," he shot back. "You listen to *me*, my wonderful, faithful nurse and everything else. I've been serving this town and county right here in this office six, sometimes seven days a week, ten hours a day at the least, sometimes more, and I haven't had a vacation in so long I'm not even sure I know what the word means anymore, and if I want to take part, mind you now, I said *part* of an afternoon off, in light of everything that has been happening, I think I have that much coming to me. Now, Nurse Melton, what was it you wanted to say?"

"Doctor. . . ." This was followed by a breath and a long pause. "Doctor, I think you're exactly right, and I will pass on the message to our patients." She tossed him a smile with a shrug of her shoulders, then disappeared into her kitchen—safe territory. Jesse got into the Olds, pulled out onto the street and headed down toward Main, then turned west. As he drove, he heard a noise under the hood that hadn't been there last week and drummed his fingers on the steering wheel, a frown on his face. Then it occurred to him that with the war about to end, Detroit would start making new cars again, and he would just up and buy one. It wasn't as though he didn't deserve it.

But right now, thought Jesse, there were other things far more important. After another minute or so, he pulled up in front of the tiny house, having made sure of the address before he left. It barely qualified to be called a house. It looked to be no more than 500 square feet, the clapboard warped in places, the paint peeling off in huge scraps. There was a '37 Ford parked out front that had seen better days. When the door opened, Bear greeted him with a look of surprise.

"Well, doctor, I didn't expect to see you this soon."

"Is this a bad time?" asked Jesse. "I could come back."

"No, no. Come on in, but I gotta warn you. It's awful hot in here."

"I've got an idea. Why don't we take a little drive over to the park? You know, we could sit and talk a while. That is, if you feel up to it."

Bear shrugged his shoulders. "Sure, why not?" He saw Reardon eyeing the house. "Yeah, I know. It's kinda rough, but it's all I can afford for eight dollars a month, and it's not worth that."

Jesse smiled in acknowledgement and waved his hand as if to say that it didn't matter to him.

"Hey, those pills you gave me keep the pain down," said Bear, "and I'm getting my strength back pretty fast. In a couple more days, I ought to be my old self again."

Jesse ran his fingertips over Bear's face, the marks of the beating lessening from what they had been. "Yes, you seem to be healing fast."

"My grandfather used to say red skin is tough skin." Bear managed a wry smile.

Jesse clapped the young man on the shoulder and led him toward the car. Within a few minutes, they had reached the park and were seated on a green wooden bench near the park's only statue. A huge oak towered over them, its shade a welcome relief from the blazing mid-afternoon sun. Bear was silent—waiting for the words he knew would come. The doctor had something important on his mind, or he wouldn't have taken off from his practice in the middle of the day.

Jesse started by telling Bear that the statue was of his grandfather and told him the story of how the Yankee gunboat had sailed up the river and the battle that had taken place. Bear listened intently, nodding all the while.

"Doctor Reardon, I know what war is, and it must have been a lot tougher back then. They had real grit to fight for their land and what they thought was right, even though we both know slavery was wrong. I guess deep down inside, they knew this, too. Don't you think?"

Jesse rubbed his chin. "Oh, they knew it was wrong all right. It's just that the South was so proud, we couldn't admit it. Grandaddy did, though, because Granny saved his letters and gave them to me when I graduated college. He said in one that it wasn't so much he liked slavery, but that he loved the South more—the land, the people . . . all that it meant to him."

Bear was silent, waiting for the rest that he knew would come.

"Bear . . . you've done not only Deborah and Joshua a great favor, but you've done the town a great service as well." He paused and laced his fingers together. "You see, I've known— well, a *lot* of people have known for a long time what kind of man Ragg was. I suppose we just looked the other way. You know how it is. We get busy with our lives, our families, our careers, this and that, and it's easier to just ignore things, figuring that if you do, they'll either fix themselves or go away. In this case, I think God stepped in and took a hand. I really do." He paused, crossed his legs and draped his arms over the back of the bench. "The longer I live, the more I believe that God loves us more than we can ever know. What do you think, Bear?"

"Doctor Reardon, I think—"

"Please, drop the doctor. Jesse will do fine."

Bear smiled, nodding. "Anyway . . . Jesse, the great Spirit of God walks among us and when we deny it, then the evil one takes possession of us. Just like with Ragg."

"Bear, were you ever baptized?"

Bear told Jesse the story of what happened to him as a child. The physician seemed pleased at this. The two men talked for the better part of an hour, sharing their lives with one another. Bear told Jesse about what he had seen when he was a little boy and was surprised to find out that Jesse already knew.

"You knew all this? I don't understand."

Jesse hesitated, looking out across the park and then uncrossing his legs. "Your mom . . . Ragg made her pregnant, and she didn't dare let your father know, or he would have killed Ragg on the spot. So she tried a homemade tribal remedy for abortion, but there were complications, and she came to me. At first she wasn't going to tell me, but she finally did."

Bear held his head in his hands, looking down at his shoes. The Indian shook his head slowly from side to side and muttered something under his breath that Jesse did not understand.

"I guess my father found out what Ragg had done, and that's why he went after him."

Jesse paused for a moment, looking at the brave, young man seated beside him. He looked and behaved much older than his 21 years, and there was a quality in his face Jesse couldn't define. It was like rough sawn wood that had been weathered by the elements. There was nothing mean or nasty in this man. Just hard and resolute. Now, he groped for the words that were still bound to the pain he held in his heart. "You know, Bear, I had a son once, and in a lot of ways you remind me of him. Stephen had his own mind and when he made it up, nothing could stop him. He was brave, independent and a man of principle."

"What happened to him?" asked Bear.

"He was in college when Pearl Harbor came, and he joined the Air Corps the very next day. He was a copilot on a B-24 when they ran into some heavy flak and went down over Hamburg. There was nothing to send home. I got a flag and his posthumous medals, but none of that meant anything. I still miss him."

Not knowing what else to do, Bear put his arm around the older man's shoulders and held him tightly for a long moment. Jesse started once to tell Bear what he had on his mind, stumbled, then started again and managed to get it all out. The younger man listened to him carefully, mulled it over and finally they came to an agreement and shook hands.

"Well," said Jesse, "I better be getting back before Lucy decides to fire me. And she might just do that." He laughed.

Bear said, "Yeah, I had a platoon sergeant in the corps who reminds me a lot of her." The two of them shared the laugh and walked back to the car, each lost in his thoughts. When they returned to the house, before Bear got out, Jesse put his hand on the man's arm to stay him.

"How do you get by—I mean, what do you live on?"

"Oh, I get $37 a month from this shrapnel in my leg, and I do a few little carpentering jobs, you know, this and that." Bear shrugged.

Jesse nodded, shook his friend's hand, then drove home lost in thought. He had lost a son and Bear had lost his father. Somehow, thinking about this did not depress him but actually lifted his spirits, and he felt better about things than he had in a long time. Ragg raped Bear's mother, Naomi, and killed his father, then years later Ragg has his life saved by Bear, then turns around and tries to murder him. It reminded him of what Lucius Tanner, a former handyman used to say: *Doctor Jesse, I don't understand all I know about this.* Neither do I, thought Jesse. Neither do I. He sighed deeply, now more resolved than ever as to the course of action he would take in the morning. When he arrived home, there were patients stacked up waiting, yet in spite of this, he walked in whistling with a new bounce in his step. Lucy observed all this but asked no questions. That was Lucy.

Early that evening, Deborah fed Joshua a good supper, then made him take a long hot bath. Her son seemed to have snapped back from his ordeal. The once dark purple bruise was already beginning to fade, and Joshua said his head only hurt a little bit now. The concussion had been slight, Reardon said, and with his youth, her son would be up to snuff in another day or so. Joshua went out on the porch in his pajamas and was eating a bowl of homemade peach ice cream. He had just had his bath, and he was still excited and told his mother for the third time about what had happened when Ragg came into the room where he and Bear were waiting. She listened as though she were hearing it for the first time, proud of her son. She knew he was no longer a little boy.

"Mom, do you think Buddy will ever come back?"

"I don't know, Joshua. I really can't say." She hesitated. "Were you scared while you were out there?"

"Yes ma'am . . . a little. Well, sometimes a lot. But I prayed like Charity taught me and when I did I wasn't scared anymore. Even when I saw BB for the first time and thought he might find me. And you know, just before I heard Chief Ragg yell, I was praying that somebody would come to rescue me, and then it wasn't five minutes before Bear came running right up to me. Boy, God really knows how to take care of us, doesn't He?"

Deborah was silent, rocking back and forth. Then she answered him. "Yes, son, He does," then gave a start. Standing Bear seemed to appear out of the darkness and stepped up on the porch.

"I just wanted to check on my little brother," he said.

"Wow, Bear. I didn't even hear you!" said Joshua.

"You white eyes have to watch us redskins," he said.

Bear laughed and tousled the boys hair, still wet from the bath. Deborah said, "Joshua, why don't you fix Bear a dish of Charity's fresh peach ice cream. I'm sure he'd love some."

Before Bear could say no, Joshua vanished through the screen door. Anything for his blood brother.

"Bear," she said, "what about the bomb we dropped? What do you think will happen?"

"I think it means that the time for killing is coming to an end," he said. "The Japanese are tough fighters, and they'll hold out until they realize they don't have a chance, and then they'll surrender."

"Soon?"

"Maybe." At that moment, Joshua came out with the ice cream. Bear spooned it up with gusto, and Deborah watched her son looking at his friend, hanging on his every word, almost like a big brother. It made her feel good to see them together. She knew something wonderful, something miraculous had happened in the swamp, and sitting there on the swing, looking at her son, who was far braver than she thought, she looked up through the willow tree at the moon and thought surely she was going to cry. She bit her lip hard to keep back the tears.

"Joshua, it's bedtime, and young man, I don't want to hear a peep out of you."

Joshua opened his mouth as if to protest, and Bear put his finger to his mouth, shaking his head. "Little brother, you better do what she says. Following the chief's orders is something all braves have to learn to do." He winked at the boy. Deborah was stunned as Joshua promptly said good night, then trooped into the house. She said, "I'll come in shortly and tuck you in, honey."

Bear put down his bowl on the porch, stood and laid his hand upon her forearm. "Your son . . . he is very brave. He will grow up to be a fine man. I can tell. In our tribe, he would be greatly honored for what he has come through and the way he conducted himself."

She was stunned by his words and the quiet way he spoke and did not know how to respond.

"Standing Bear, I . . . we owe you so much. You brought my son back to me, and he's all I have. I know I can never repay you, but I will never forget what you did for us."

"I have already received my payment," said Bear. "In the Cherokee nation, if a person saves another person's life, that person becomes a brother to the person whose life he has saved. And it is a vow that can never be broken."

"Then . . . you're Joshua's big brother. Yes?"

Bear nodded slowly.

"I like that," she said. "He always wanted a brother, and now he's got one."

"I wanted one, too," he said. Without waiting for an answer, he said good night, then walked out into the night, beyond the willows until he was gone. Joshua lay in bed, watching through the window. He couldn't hear what they were saying, but he saw Bear walk up the hill in the direction of the house then melt into the darkness as silently as he had come. His mother came in and bent down to kiss him, then sat on the edge of the bed.

"Honey, you really believe in God, don't you?"

"Uh huh. I talked to Him, Mom, and I know He heard me. I know it!"

"Yes son, I believe you. I. . . . " She started to add something but checked herself and bent over to give him another hug, then walked out, leaving the door open a few inches so the hall light could shine in.

Joshua said, "It's all right, Mom. You can close the door all the way. I'm not scared of the dark anymore."

She smiled to herself and closed the door then went into her room where she lay down on the bed. She felt strangely light, her body limp. An indescribable wave of emotion began to well up within her. She had lost a husband and, she had thought, a son. Then Joshua was returned to her in a way she could barely comprehend.

Deborah did not know how God could plan things. How could He know? Without Standing Bear, her son would be gone forever. She had witnessed it. She knew it was real. Thoughts and images began to spin in her head, and overwhelmed by them and not knowing what to believe, she buried her head in her pillow and put her fist in her mouth to stifle the sound of her crying. She did not want Joshua to think she was unhappy. They were tears of joy, but then, why couldn't she know God in the way her son did? What was wrong with her? What was missing? Deborah finally surrendered to sleep, falling into a darkness where no dreams dared enter.

33

6:45 AM, Thursday, the ninth . . .

They called it Second Thursday.

It had been a tradition in Sweetwater for longer than anyone could remember. On the second Thursday of every month, the City Council would meet at 6:45 in the back room of George's Cafe, otherwise known as the Greek's. Anyone who had something to say, strictly off the record, that is, could show up, have biscuits and coffee with the group and get it off his chest.

As Jesse walked in the door, Herb Johnson was just calling the meeting to order. He looked up to see one of the town's most respected and best loved citizens, then raised his eyebrows in a look of mild surprise. Jesse sat down in one of the maple captain's chairs and drew it up to the table.

Greetings were exchanged, nods and handshakes, then the mayor said, "Well, Doctor, this is a surprise. Not that we haven't had enough of these in the past few days, mind you."

Jesse nodded. "Mister Mayor, I found myself with nothing to do, and it being such a beautiful day, I thought I might just pay y'all a friendly visit."

"Well, I'm sure we're all delighted to have you here, aren't we boys?"

A chorus of grunts and nods answered his question, then the men went back to eating.

"You have a complaint, Jesse?"

"No, not really."

"No complaints?" Herb adopted a tone of mock astonishment. "Trash collection? Street light out? Barking dog? Sewer stopped up?" In his eight years as mayor, Herb had heard them all.

"No sir, Herb. I'm a satisfied citizen."

"I'm sure we're all glad to hear that." Herb looked around at the other four members of council, and they all nodded in unison, their mouths full of George's ham biscuits.

"Well, I had just called the meeting to order, and our first priority was to fill the vacancies on our police force. Gentlemen, we all know what happened to Officer Carver, and more recently, the uh . . . deplorable circumstances regarding Chief—former Chief Ragg."

A few throats were cleared, Bill Woolard lit a cigar, this adding to the smoke from the cigarettes. Jesse saw the rising cloud of noxious fumes and was glad he was sitting on the other side of the large table.

"Anyway," continued Herb, "do I have any suggestions or recommendations from council?"

"Well, whatever we do, we need to do fast." The voice came from Will Sams, who ran the local butcher shop. "We have only one policeman now, that Peele boy, and for a town of this size, that's crazy. I mean, he's not even what you could call a trained officer, and if something happened to him, we'd *really* be in a pickle."

"I'm well aware of that, Will," shot back Herb. "And what I can do, if y'all agree, is call up to Raleigh and ask if they have any applications there. You see we need to be real choosy about the man we hire. With the war about to end, or so the newspapers say, Sweetwater's going to start growing again, businesses coming in, a factory or two, then people moving in looking for work, and that's all the more reason we need to find the right man for the job."

The mayor's words elicited a minor chorus of assents. The waitress came in, replenished their coffee, then slipped out silently.

"So, if there is no more discussion, I'll . . . yes, doctor?" Herb saw Reardon's hand go up.

"May I speak?"

"Well, certainly, Doctor. I'm sure we'd all be interested in what you have to say."

"I have someone in mind for the job whom I'd like to recommend."

Herb smiled blankly. "And who might that be, Jesse?"

"Standing Bear."

A chorus of throat clearing ensued, this followed by some muttered profanity, barely audible.

"Gentlemen, gentlemen," said Herb. "I'm as surprised by this as you are, but then, as I said, it's been a week of nothing *but* surprises." He turned to face Reardon. "Jesse . . . Standing Bear is . . . well, you know, he's . . . an Indian." He said the last word as though he had just tasted something unpleasant in his biscuit.

"That's right, he's an Indian *and* a United States citizen," said Jesse. "Grandson of a Cherokee chieftain. He's also a veteran of three years in the Marine Corps and holds a Silver Star for bravery and a Purple Heart with two Oak Leaf Clusters. He served his country in war, and I think he would like to serve it in peace. He's brave. He's honest and he's fair-minded. He was left to die in the Gut by Ragg, and it was only through this man's enormous courage and strength of character that he managed to escape and come back to tell us the truth. I know his head and his heart as well, and I also know that in time, he would make a good chief of police. Perhaps even a great one."

"But he's not even a Christian," said Herb, his lips forming a frown.

"Yes, he is," said Jesse. "And he's been baptized."

"Then why doesn't he go to church?"

"Apparently because none of his Christian brothers and sisters have invited him." Jesse threw the group a withering glance. No one met his eyes.

"Yes, I uh. . . ." Herb was groping now. "Jesse, did Bear ask you to come here?"

"No, he did not. As a matter of fact, it was only after a long conversation and my urging that he gave me permission to come and talk to y'all."

"Well, that's commendable," said Herb, "but Jesse, he's so young and besides, he has no real experience in law enforcement."

"What experience did Ragg have?" countered the doctor. "Ragg was twenty-one when he quit driving a truck and joined the force for one simple reason: he couldn't keep any other job he'd had. We liked him because Chief Harrell was getting too old and weak for the job. Plus, Ragg was mean and nasty enough to keep the few bad apples in line and crack their heads whether they needed it or not. We must have liked that because we never called his hand on the things he did over the years, and every man in this room knows I am speaking the gospel truth." Jesse paused, taking a sip of his coffee and thinking it wasn't nearly as good as Lucy's.

"Doctor Reardon," said Herb, adopting a cooler, sterner tone to his voice. "You've come here as an interested citizen, and we appreciate that and welcome your comments. But you are acting in no official capacity, and as you know, this is not an official meeting. Therefore, on behalf of council, let me thank you for your interest in this young man and for sharing your thoughts with us." Herb liked to keep trouble down before it ever had a chance to start. He knew that's why the people elected him mayor.

If there was one thing Jesse liked less than being patronized, he had never encountered it. He took a deep breath and let it out slowly before trusting himself to speak. "You are denying him the position?"

Herb took a quick visual poll of the other four, and said, "Jesse, I'm afraid we are. Strictly off the record, of course."

"Well, I'm afraid that leaves me no other choice. Strictly off the record, of course." He said this with a straight face, meeting Herb's puzzled stare.

"I'm afraid I don't understand, Doctor," said the mayor.

"I'm going to call a press conference and provide the news-papers with a list of two wrongful deaths in the past, deaths that occurred directly as a result of questionable and irregular police procedure on the part of Curtis Ragg. Deaths, I might add, that should have been investigated and looked into but were not, which means, I am informed by people whose business it is to know these things, that this council could be named in a lawsuit should the state or the families decide to. . . . "

"Now just hold on, Jesse." The mayor stood up. "You can't. . . . "

"Plus. . . . "

"Jesse, I've heard about. . . . "

"Plus!" The word landed like a grenade on the table. The mayor sat down, and the rest of council sat up and took notice.

"Plus . . . I've decided that I'm tired of practicing medicine. I'm ready to take down my shingle and retire."

Now it was Buck Pender who spoke up. "Jesse Reardon, for God's sakes, man, you can't retire. You're the best doctor this town's got, and we all depend on you."

"You've got James Wilson and. . . . "

"That drunk!" snorted Buck. "I wouldn't let him treat my hogs. If that man's a doctor, I'm a Baptist preacher." This drew a few snickers from the group.

"What about Vince Barnwell?" countered Jesse.

Will Sams set down his coffee cup so hard, it splashed out onto the table. "Aw, c'mon, Jesse. Vince has only got one lung and a bad heart along with it. He can barely keep up with the patients in that little hospital of his, and you know it."

Others started to chime in, voicing their dismay, if not dis-pleasure, when Herb finally silenced them with his hand.

"Doctor Reardon." He paused and chewed his upper lip. Suddenly, the air in the room seemed close. "You can't close your practice. You just can't. It would . . . well . . . the first question families or companies ask before moving into a town is 'Do y'all have a good doctor?' And the other thing. How about all those people who pull up in front of your office first thing in the morning and find out you're not practicing any-more. How will you explain it to them?"

"I won't."

"I don't follow you," said the mayor. They'll want to know why. So what will you tell them?"

"I'll tell them to come see you," said Jesse, quietly and deliberately, and one by one, he returned the glances of the five men whose eyes were now fixed on him.

Herb took a long breath, thinking suddenly he had had one cup of coffee too many. His stomach was churning furiously. "Jesse, I gotta say something. Your family has been in this town since 1840. Three generations of doctors, all fine men." He cleared his throat. "And if you do this . . . well, if you'll pardon me for saying so, it's blackmail." The minute the word left his lips, Herb regretted it.

Reardon's brows turned downward, his eyes narrowing slightly. "Blackmail, is it?" He snorted. "This town has had a bigot and a bully for a chief of police far too long, and you, me—all of us are guilty for letting it happen. But I've already said that. What I *haven't* said and I'm going to say now is that I know all of you in this room. I've treated you for everything under the sun. I've looked down your throat and up your behinds. I've seen your wives with their clothes off, delivered their babies, and I know things about most of you that I've kept secret, and I don't have to spell that out, do I? I've taken out your appendix, your gallstones, your kids' tonsils, and anything else that needed to come out, I've sat up all night with your children, I've nursed them through near death with whooping cough or pneumonia. I've set their broken bones and whatever else they had wrong, and during that time I've managed to learn something about humanity, gentlemen. And what I've learned tells me that we need a fresh, clean start in Sweetwater, and this is as good a time as any to begin." He cleared his throat, clasped his hands together and rested them on the table.

The silence was broken only by the click of somebody's Zippo lighting a cigarette. Buck Pender let out a long whistle under his breath, and that seemed to serve as a signal.

Herb glanced nervously at the men around the table. Then he cleared his throat and said, "Do I hear a motion that Standing Bear . . . uh, what's his last name?"

"That *is* his last name."

"Oh. Well, what's his first name, then?"

"John."

"Okay. Well, do I hear a motion that John Standing Bear be appointed to the post of Chief of the Sweetwater Police Department?"

Nothing moved in the room but the overhead fan circling lazily and causing the tobacco smoke to break up.

"Gentlemen," said Herb wearily, "there is a motion before Council."

"Wait a minute," said Hank Garland, who usually said nothing at these meetings. "This isn't an official council meeting."

"It is now," said Herb. "I just made it one. Now, do I hear a motion or not?"

Buck Pender stubbed out his cigar in the ashtray and said, "I so move."

"Do I hear a second?" asked the mayor.

Will Sams said, "I second it."

"All in favor say aye."

"Aye," said the four as one voice.

"Then, John Standing Bear is now our new Chief of Police of the town of Sweetwater. I'll make the formal announcement tomorrow morning when I swear him in." Herb cleared his throat and ground out his cigarette with great care in the big green ashtray. "Doctor Reardon, if you would, I'd appreciate your relaying this to him. Would you please have him at council chambers at nine o'clock?" There was a cool, crisp tone to the mayor's voice.

Jesse nodded by way of thanks and got up to leave.

"Jesse, one more thing," said Herb. "Can I see you sometime soon? My stomach is acting up again." The former coolness of his tone had been miraculously transformed into a plea.

"Sure, Herb," said Reardon. "Come on by at seven-thirty and beat the rush. Lucy might even serve you a good cup of coffee and one of her blueberry muffins."

Once the door had closed behind Reardon, Elvin Leggett said, "Well, I'll be . . . Doc's got a lot more starch in him than I ever thought."

"Yeah," said the mayor. "The other thing is, he was right in everything he said about Ragg, and we all know it."

They all looked down at their hands, no one wanting to meet anyone else's glance.

"Well, boys," said Herb. "It looks like we got ourselves a new Chief of Police, and I'm gonna get behind him in every way, and I expect each of you to do the same. In fact, I'm counting on it, unless you want James Wilson treating your hemorrhoids." He pounded the gavel once. "This meeting stands adjourned!"

They walked outside onto the sidewalk and felt the sun on their faces.

"It's gonna be another scorcher," said Buck. One or two others started to agree when from a block away in the city hall tower, the fire siren started its low guttural wail, starting to increase in pitch and volume until it was almost deafening.

"Good Lord, what is it now?" shouted Sams.

George Stephanis, the owner of the restaurant, exploded through the screen door, his eyes wide with excitement.

"You gotta hear it! Come inside, come inside! President Truman's on the radio again! We just dropped another one of those bombs!"

34

7:00 AM, Thursday, the ninth . . .

Cliff Barnes couldn't believe it when he got the call.

He had been driving a taxi, Sweetwater's one and only, for 14 years, and in all that time he had never gotten one call from that Trace lady. And then on Wednesday afternoon, she had called him and told him she wanted to be picked up at 7:00 in the morning. Then she had said, not 6:59 and not 7:01, and she wanted to make sure he understood. He had told her he'd be right on time, and that had been it.

As the taxi drove her downtown, Charity's nose wrinkling at the strong smell of tobacco in the back seat, her mind touched upon recent events. She had known nothing but joy now that Joshua was safely home, and she had thanked the Lord many times for it, delighting in the fact that her prayers and the prayers of others had been heard. There was no doubt in her heart. She had heard the news about the bomb being dropped on Monday, but to her the war was something dreadful and distant, but not a part of her everyday life. She was much more familiar with the *other* war that never made the headlines at all: the one that people fought with The Enemy every day. People that you never, ever suspected of being in trouble or struggling until you heard they had done something foolish or cruel or destructive that meant Satan had them in his grasp. And by then, often it was too late. For every Curtis Ragg that was exposed, there were a dozen others in the devil's hire whom God's avenging sword would bring to justice in His time.

There was a handful of shopkeepers hosing down their side-walks and putting wares out in front of the stores when she alighted from the taxi at the office building on 104 Main. They couldn't believe it. Charity Trace had come downtown. Why that woman hadn't set foot on Main Street in over ten years or more. Everybody knew that Charity would always call in her grocery order to Ward's Superette, and the colored boy would bring them out on his bike. Same for whatever she needed from the drugstore and anyone else. But it was her, sure enough, and instantly, tongues began to wag, but no one could figure it out. They attributed it to the bombs, the heat and all the other excite-ment that had been going on lately. This rare excursion of Char-ity was just one more thing to be added to the list.

When Cliff helped her from the taxi, she told him to wait right there, that she would only be ten minutes or so, and then he could take her right on back home. Cliff said, "Yes ma'am," doffed his hat, and climbed back in the car, wondering what in the world was so important for her to be downtown at this hour. When her business was concluded, she came back out, he held the door for her, and a few minutes later, he had deposited her safely back home.

Once inside, Charity began to stroll through the house slowly walking from one room to the other. She touched this vase, that table, paused in front of a framed photograph, a painting, then some dried flowers. The house had been the home of the Whitley's for well over a hundred years. Charity paused to look at a portrait that had been done of Caleb on his fiftieth birthday. My man, she thought, with his patrician nose, the high fore-head, the clear, blue eyes that could search the very soul of a congregation and a voice that would set their hearts on fire.

"Charity, can I come in?"

She turned, pressing these thoughts from her. "Yes Joshua, you *may* come in."

"Yes ma'am. *May* I come in?"

"Get in here, young'un, and let me give you a hug. Are you glad to be home?"

"Oh, yes ma'am."

"Would you like . . . ?"

"Yes ma'am!" She didn't have to finish the question.

"Now," she said, when he was seated at the table with the biscuit in front of him. "I know you talked to God out there in Devil's Gut, and Joshua Grayson, I want you to tell me everything He said, and everything you said to Him."

Between mouthfuls, Joshua managed to give a good account of his adventure, and he tried to remember what he had said to God when he had prayed. Charity hung on his every word, pausing now and then to ask him to repeat something, then poured herself another cup of coffee.

"And you talked to God, and He talked to you, didn't He?"

"Yes ma'am." Joshua took a swallow of milk to wash down the biscuit. "Charity, when I prayed, it was right then that I heard somebody yell, and then it wasn't five minutes before Bear showed up. He was the angel God sent, wasn't he?"

"Yes, child, he was. Praise the Lord," she said, her face beaming.

Joshua went on with his story, about the sheriff and the two men from Raleigh who came down to arrest Ragg, and he and Bear waiting there in the council room and. . . .

The wail of the siren began as it had on Monday morning, echoing over the rooftops and down the streets, from one end of town to the other, and Charity made a face and put her hands over her ears. "Oh, what a dreadful sound," she said, shaking her head in distaste.

Seconds later, Deborah came flying into the kitchen, all out of breath.

"We dropped another bomb, on a place called Naga-something and the Japanese, well they . . . the man on the radio said that President Truman expects them to surrender real soon."

If the first bomb upset business as usual in Sweetwater, the second shut it down entirely, and it was a rerun of Monday morning, only more so. In the midst of the excitement, the mayor forgot all about Standing Bear until late in the afternoon, then remembered to call Francis Manning at the newspaper and ask him to be at City Hall promptly at nine on Friday morning and to bring a camera. The day wore down into evening, and as dark fell, it brought a brief shower that managed to cool things off. In their little cottage, Deborah and Joshua sat at home glued to the Philco, and when the announcer said that surrender was imminent, the boy asked his mother what "imminent" meant, and she said, it meant soon, and he said, like when I ask you can I go swimming, and you say soon. Is that what it means, huh, Mom?" Deborah looked at her son, laughed and said, "Yes, dear, that's exactly what it means."

The phone rang. It was Eugene Corey. He wanted Joshua to come over. His dad was shooting fireworks in their back yard.

"Can I go, Mom, huh? Can I?"

She started to resist but then asked herself: Deborah, when will you learn? The war is going to be over soon. Your son has survived being lost in Devil's Gut, a mad man, an evil cop and Lord only knows what else, and here you are worried about his riding his bike two blocks to a friend's house. She shook her head and laughed.

"Yes, go ahead," she said, "but be home by nine o'clock. No later."

"Aw, Mom, everybody's gonna be there. Can't I stay till ten?"

He put on the longest face he could find and looked down at his worn sneakers. Deborah said, "Nine-thirty."

"Deal," said Joshua, paused to kiss her as he dashed out through the door. Suddenly the house felt very empty, and she decided she would visit Charity. Deborah knew the older woman did not go to bed for another hour or so, and she might enjoy the company.

"Charity, it's me." She knocked on the screen door.

"Come in, dear. It's late, but I'm still putting up beans. Say, listen girl. You're not still thinking about moving to Rocky Mount are you, and taking that job?"

Deborah smiled. That was Charity. Right to the point. She wanted to be more like that, and she made a silent resolve she would work on it.

"Why do you ask?"

"Oh, no special reason. I just thought maybe in light of what happened and all, that you might feel a little better about staying on here."

"Charity, I still have to have a job," said Deborah. She could hear the sound of cicadas in the giant oaks that ringed the house, their leaves still dripping from the rain.

"Yes, I reckon you do. Have you prayed on this?"

"Oh, Charity, you're not supposed to pray about things like that." She saw her friend give her a long searching look. "Well, are you?"

"Child, absolutely! If not, what's prayer for? I pray about everything in my life. From the time I get up until the time I go to bed. Big things, little things, in-between things, it doesn't make any difference. If I'm in it, then the Lord's in it *with* me, and that's that."

"So I should pray about that tonight?" Deborah smiled at Charity.

"Why certainly. Whether or not He decides to answer it, it's always good to talk to Him. You know, tell Him what's really on your heart."

"Is that what you do when you talk to God?"

"Of course I do. Deborah Grayson, I've been doing that since I was a little girl. How do you think I've managed to live this long?" Charity was going to tell her about her visions, but she decided not to. In time and with God's help, Deborah would find these things out for herself.

"Well," said Deborah. "I think I'll go on home and wait for Joshua. Is there anything I can get for you, Charity?"

"No, dear. I'm just fine. I'm going to sit here by the window and enjoy this delightful breeze. It was so hot today, and now, praise the Lord, that shower has cooled things off. We don't get many August nights like this, and I want to enjoy this one."

"See you in the morning," said Deborah and she gave a half turn, then kissed Charity on her cheek.

"God willing," came the response. Deborah thought she had never seen such love in one person's smile, and she paused, then knelt and gave Charity a warm hug. "That one's for me *and* Joshua." Just as she closed the screen door, she heard Charity's soft voice humming behind her, and the sound brought a smile to her face.

She walked down the path by the willows to the cottage, busied herself with a few chores in the kitchen, and before she knew it, her son came home bursting to tell her everything he'd done. He had gotten to hold a Roman candle, but he was careful and Billy's father helped him. She listened, nodding, smiling, then when he ran out of breath, mentioned the word bath, saw the usual frown, but he tromped into his room dutifully, shed his clothes and within a minute was splashing in the tub, talking out loud as though someone were in there with him. What an imagination her son had. After she had tucked him into bed and heard his prayers, she retired to her room.

In the hundred-year-old house just up the hill, Charity sat in the chair, the shadows playing tricks with her in the dimly lit room. Then she heard it. The familiar tread in the hall. She looked up to see her man.

"Honey, the Lord sent me to tell you it was time."

"Oh, glory. You mean I can go home with you at last?"

"Yes . . . at last, my sweetheart."

"Oh, Caleb, I've waited so long for you. All this time and no one to hold me. To love me the way you used to do. And now we'll be together for all eternity."

He knelt by her chair, taking her hand in his and brought it to his lips, smiling at her. Then he leaned over, his mouth joining with hers, and all the years of yearning and emptiness were erased by one, long, lingering kiss.

Oh, glory, she thought.

In that instant, the Lord came for her, and Charity was transformed into pure light that filled every room in the house with a radiance that outshone a thousand sunrises. Then, as suddenly as it had come, the light vanished, and a century of memories rushed from the house like a mighty river overflowing its bank, flooding the summer night with witness and wonder.

35

7:31 AM, Friday, the tenth . . .

Deborah was up much earlier than usual and awoke feeling wonderfully alive and vibrant, better than she'd felt in a long time. She told herself it was too nice a morning to waste inside and after peeking in on Joshua and seeing he was still asleep, decided she would go visit Charity who would be in her garden.

But she was not.

She walked up on the back porch, peered in through the screen door, but could see nothing.

"Charity?"

She went inside into the kitchen. The familiar smell of fresh baked biscuits, coffee and fried streak o'lean was missing. There were no dishes laid out on the blue and white checkered cloth.

"Charity, are you in here?"

Deborah walked into the living room to find her in her favorite chair by the window. She was sitting perfectly upright, the Bible lying on the floor by her feet. At first, Deborah turned to tiptoe out, thinking Charity might have dozed off, one of the aftereffects of the stroke. Then, something made her turn and call out her name. Then again. Charity did not respond. Deborah rushed to her side and saw that she was not breathing, though her eyes were wide open as though she were looking at someone. Her hand trembling, Deborah picked up the phone.

"Dr. Reardon? Yes, this is Deborah. It's . . . Charity. I think you'd better come over." In barely five minutes, he was there, this time without his black bag. He touched Charity's neck, looked into her eyes, then closed them and sat down heavily in the blue wingback chair, letting out his breath in a long sigh.

"She was a great lady, Deborah. A great fighter." He paused, looking out the window. "It's too late now, of course, but I wish I had spent more time with her. She could have taught me so much."

He sighed, shook his head, then went to the phone and called for an ambulance. There would be the usual paperwork, the death certificate, cause of death . . . he paused, reflecting on the phrase that he had seen and read a thousand times in his life. *Cause of death.* How is it, he thought, we are always concerned about the cause of *death*, but never about the cause of *life?* He mused upon that until the ambulance drivers came, loaded the body onto a gurney and left for Edgewood Mortuary.

After the ambulance pulled away, the man and the woman sat there in silence. Deborah wondered if Joshua was up yet, but figured the minute he was and found her missing, he would come to find her. What would she tell him, and how would he handle this? He had known death before, but then, he was so much younger then. The last six months had been a lifetime for both of them. Yes, she would be strong for her son, and he would be strong for her.

"You're thinking?" said Reardon.

"What?"

"I meant it as an observation, not a question."

"Oh. I was thinking about Joshua, and how to go about explaining all this to him."

"Deborah, your son understands a good bit more than you think he does. In fact, I'm sure of it. We tend to underestimate the awareness level of children and overestimate the wisdom of grown-ups—like us." He laughed, then his face suddenly adopted a serious cast, and he looked straight at her.

"Deborah, do you type?"

The question caught her completely off guard. "Type? Well, yes."

"Light bookkeeping."

"Yes. They were both my best subjects in high school. My typing might be a little rusty, but. . . . "

"How are you at managing time?"

"Martin . . . he always said that was one of my strong points."

"Well, then . . . that's settled."

"Doctor Reardon, I'm afraid I don't understand."

"Deborah, I want you to come work for me."

Before she could respond, he went on.

"The practice keeps getting busier every day, and I need someone to help me with managing the office, paperwork, records and such. That kind of stuff is not Lucy's strong point, and anyway, she has all she can handle right now. She's excellent with the patients, and I don't want to take her away from that. Now let me see, where was I? Oh, yes. The job pays 25 . . . no, 30 dollars a week, lunch by Lucy, plus two weeks vacation if you can get it, but don't count on it."

Deborah sat there bewildered. What was going on here? What about the job in Rocky Mount, which paid five dollars less, by the way? What about a place to live? She and Joshua couldn't stay here in the cottage. How would she like working with Doctor Reardon? What if they didn't get along? What about Lucy?

"I know what you're thinking," said Jesse, "but don't worry . . . you and I will get along fine," he said, "and you'll love working with Lucy. Why don't you plan on coming in this afternoon so that Lucy and I can show you the ropes and get you settled in. Then Monday morning, we'll start in earnest."

"Doctor Reardon, I haven't even said yes."

"Sure you have. It's written all over your face. Now you go check on that wonderful son of yours, break the news to him about Charity, and I'll see you at one o'clock. Okay?"

"I don't really know what to say."

"When in doubt, always say thank you. My mother taught me that."

She realized her mouth was open. "Thank you . . . Doctor."

"Please . . . it's Jesse. Uh, as long as there are no patients around."

"Yes. Well, thank you . . . Jesse."

Jesse glanced at his watch. He had to be at City Hall in ten minutes for the swearing in ceremony, and he went out the screen door with a wave of his hand and a smile. Deborah walked down the back steps, down the path by the willow tree, into the little house that had been home for her and Joshua since Martin's death, went into the bedroom and gently tugged at her son.

"Honey, get up now. I have some bad news . . . and, well, something else that we need to discuss."

The boy opened his eyes and yawned, then reached out for her.

"Mom, what is it?"

"We're not moving, Joshua. Sweetwater is going to be our home."

He sat straight up in bed and kissed her on the cheek with a loud smack. "Mom, wow! What changed your mind?"

She told him about the job. Then after he had calmed down somewhat, she told him about Charity. Gently, easily, holding onto him as she did. He blinked hard, and she knew he was going to cry in spite of himself. The tears began streaming down his face, his small body shaking in her arms.

"But why, Mom? Why did Charity have to die? Just when everything was working out great. Why, Mom?"

"Joshua . . . Charity told me once that God would call her home when her work was finished here, and I think it finally was. In fact, I know it. Honey, I know a lot more now about God and about myself than I did a week ago."

He nodded. "Me, too. It's not like I'm a little kid anymore."

"Well, you'll always be my little boy, even when you're all grown up and taller than I am and married. . . . "

"Married?" Joshua made a face. "Mom, I don't ever want to leave you."

She started to respond, when the phone rang. Deborah said, "Let me get that, and you get out of bed and get dressed, okay? We have a busy day in front of us."

She walked into the small parlor and picked up the receiver.

"Hello."

"Um, Mrs. Grayson, I know it's kinda early, but I just heard about Charity. Oh, I'm sorry . . . this is Hack Benbow, her attorney. Ma'am, can you stop by the office this morning? We need to have a little talk."

"Is something wrong?"

"Well, I'd rather wait and discuss that with you when you get here. Is ten o'clock okay? We're right next to Clark's Drugstore."

"All right. Certainly, then. Ten o'clock."

She arrived ten minutes early, a little on edge, fearing the worst. With Charity gone, he was going to tell her that she and Joshua would have to move out and find another place to live.

The lawyer came out of his office and offered his hand. "Miz Grayson, I'm Hack. Won't you please come in?" He seemed a nice enough man to her, wearing a light blue suit with a yellow tie and no smile. That put her on edge.

"Well," he said. "Charity's death was a great shock to all of us, and I'm sure to you and your son, Joshua. You must have been very close to her."

"We are . . . were."

"Well, let me fill you in on some things," he said, tenting his fingers, his face taking on a serious cast. "Just two days ago, Charity called me and asked me to do something for her, and I could go into a lot of legal language, but to put it simply, Miz Grayson, she has left you her house."

Deborah drew in her breath sharply, the lawyer taking no notice as his eyes scanned the document lying in front of him.

"Of course, it's free and clear with no mortgage, and the taxes and insurance are paid up for the coming year."

Deborah's heart raced. The house? Hers and Joshua's? She tried to contain herself, not knowing whether to laugh or shout or cry.

The lawyer continued, glancing down at the document in front of him. "Now, as to the matter of Joshua. Charity had a little money set aside . . . just over $1600, and she wanted this put into a trust fund to be made available for your son's college education when that time comes."

He said a lot more, but Deborah heard very little. She signed some papers, he spoke again, she signed still more papers and left there in a daze. Once home, she called for her son, then getting no answer, checked the noteboard.

Mom. I am over at Jerry's. I love you. I love Charity, too, and I am sorry she's gone, but I'm glad she got to go home to be with Caleb. . . . Joshua.

She walked outside, then on a whim, went over to the garden and stood there between the rows of growing things. I can handle this, she thought. I'll have to learn, that's all.

"Charity, don't you worry," she said aloud, walking up and down between the rows. "I'll tend this garden just like you were here by my side. You have my promise. Oh, how I love you, Charity. And Lord, I am learning to love You, too, but give me time. Give me time."

She knew she was going to cry in spite of having told herself she would not. To help settle herself, she walked up to the big house which was now hers but which, she knew in her heart, would always be Charity's . . . through the back door and into the kitchen, the way she had come so many times . . . into the large living room or what Charity had called the parlor, then upstairs into Charity's bedroom . . . then downstairs and back into the kitchen where she sat down at the table, letting her hands glide along the polished, weathered oak.

"Mom?"

"Yes, Joshua, I'm in here."

Her son came bounding in, letting the screen door slam behind him.

"Mom, will you . . . ?"

She held up her hand. "Joshua, you are not to let the screen door slam. Remember what Charity said?"

"Aw, Mom, sure. But Charity's dead."

There was a moment of silence, with Deborah slowly shaking her head from side to side. "No son, she is not." Her son's face betrayed his bewilderment, and Deborah explained about the house and the money, as he sat there, his mouth half open.

"Joshua Grayson, as long as we live in this house, Charity will be with us, and I can tell you she is very much alive." His face turned into a question mark. She motioned for him to approach her, and when he was standing beside her, she touched his heart with her finger and put his hand upon her chest.

"Right here," said Deborah. "This is Charity's room for as long as we will live here, do you understand?"

Joshua swallowed visibly then stammered out his answer. "Yes ma'am."

"Good. Now what was it you wanted to ask me?"

He chewed on his upper lip for a second. "Mom . . . um, can you learn how to make ham biscuits as good as Charity? Huh, Mom?"

Deborah let out a long sigh, standing up. "Son, no promises, but I'm gonna give it my best, okay?"

He nodded, then quite unexpectedly, moved closer to her and gave her a fierce hug which she returned, and mother and son stood there in the kitchen each wanting to cry, each afraid it would sadden the other, both mourning the loss of their friend, yet rejoicing in the fact that no matter what happened, Charity would be with them as family. Now and forever.

36

6:14 PM, Tuesday, the fourteenth . . .

It was as though Charity's funeral on Saturday had set the pace for the rest of the weekend. The heat had grown even more unbearable, slowing the pace of life in Sweetwater to a crawl. The land baked while the flat grey fields, now shorn of their tobacco and corn, lay shimmering under the relentless sun. Cotton was yet to come. People simmered and sweated and stewed, hunched over in front of radios listening to the newscasts, while sipping ice water and pressing the frosted glasses against their brows. Why wouldn't the Japanese surrender? What were they waiting for?

Jesse pondered these very same questions as he listened to the commentaries on the radio each night. Some said that Hirohito would surrender only with conditions, but that MacArthur had advised Truman to hold out for *unconditional* surrender. Jesse had gone to Charity's funeral on Saturday, having been told by Hack Benbow that her will had named the people she wanted invited, which included himself, Lucy, Deborah, Joshua, Standing Bear and Hack. She had lived alone the last 20 years of her life, choosing not to join a church or become involved in social functions and clubs, all of which had made her something of a recluse. It wasn't that people in Sweetwater didn't like her or respect her. Most folks respected Charity Trace mightily—they just didn't understand her. Nor, reflected Jesse, did they really know her. She was more of a Christian than half of those that sat in the front pews and sang the loudest, and they knew it, too.

The memorial was held at the funeral home, Charity having requested in her will that there be no sermon or services as such, but that any of her friends could stand up and say a few words if the Holy Spirit so moved them. Both Deborah and Joshua spoke briefly, before tears overcame them. Those attending had driven the short distance to the cemetery where she was laid to rest beside Caleb. There were hugs amidst tears, then the small group had dispersed, Jesse driving Deborah and Joshua back home.

Sunday was ushered in with the sound of church bells, the late morning air filled with well-ordered hymns from white churches and the sounds of joy pulsating from the colored churches in Black Bottom.

Monday was a new day, as though the atomic bombs had never even been dropped. Four hundred superfortresses bombed Japan, and still, no word. Then on Tuesday, the emperor's voice was heard on the radio, translated into English. Japan had accepted the unconditional surrender, though, the announcers said, Hirohito never said the actual word. No one cared. All that mattered was that the war was over. Within minutes, bedlam broke out, the day echoing what had happened when the first bomb was dropped almost a week earlier.

The town's new chief of police generated almost as much interest as did the surrender. People quoted the article in the *News and Observer* saying that Standing Bear was the first Indian chief of police in America as well as the youngest and the most highly decorated. The writer managed to get a quote from Herb Johnson in which the mayor said that, "America had a duty to show the world that the war had not been fought in vain and that all citizens of this great country deserved a fair chance to make a contribution to society, and furthermore, he was proud of Sweetwater's town council for having had the courage to make such a bold decision." Jesse read the article, let out a *hmph,* then chuckled.

During the day, hundreds of people streamed into Sweetwater from the county, and together with the townsfolk, formed a broad river of humanity flowing up and down Main Street, all laughing and singing, hugging each other and waving flags. The high school band turned out again, playing until they wilted in the heat. The word was circulated that there would be a victory celebration in Reardon Park this evening with lemonade and fireworks, and the usual speeches by the mayor and, of course, Colonel Dan Weston, the head of the American Legion, who had lost an arm in the first war in the battle of Belleau Wood.

Standing Bear stood in his office, listening to the sound of the band from the park. In a few minutes, he would walk down there, just in time for the speeches and then the fireworks which were due to start as soon as it got dark. He'd been urged by both Jesse and Mayor Johnson to make himself highly visible during the day and to be sure to wear all his medals, and he had done so, feeling sad at first when he took them out of the cigar box, then a bit better when he had pinned them on and looked at himself in the mirror.

The crowds, though large, had been very well behaved, and about the worst he encountered was seeing some half pints being sneaked out of back pockets, but he looked the other way, as long as they stayed in line. There had been only two drunks that got a little too loud, one of them looking at Bear and making some crack about if he was a chief where were his feathers, and Bear had laughed it off. But big Bobbie Eller who worked at the ice plant and who was the strongest white man in Sweetwater and who had parachuted into Normandy on D-Day with the 82nd and gotten shot up while singlehandedly wiping out a German machine gun nest, did *not* let it go.

He was wearing his medals, like Bear, and when the man made the remark, Bobbie turned and picked the man up off the ground so all could see, holding him in a grip like a vise and told him and everyone within earshot that by God, Sweetwater was proud of their chief of police and anybody that didn't like it would have to answer to him, big Bobbie. There had been a moment of awkward silence, then a huge rousing cheer came up from the crowd. Bobbie then put down the man and almost in the same movement, hoisted Bear up onto his shoulders for all to see, and hollered out "Geronimo!" the word that paratroopers sang out when they jumped from planes. The crowd cheered, and Bobbie hollered it again, and the crowd cheered even louder. Then the ex-paratrooper set Bear down on the sidewalk. Bear wished that his mother and father had been here to see this, also knowing that if the crowd had cheered for another second, he wouldn't have been able to hold back his tears even though Indians were not supposed to cry.

Someone hollered out, "Hey, Chief, where's your gun?" and he had replied, "I don't need one," and smiled at the man, and the man had smiled back and made an okay sign with his thumb and forefinger and those people watching flashed him a big grin. He'd carried a rifle a long time in combat, and he had killed people with it, some from 100 yards away, and some with his assault knife in hand-to-hand combat. One Japanese soldier had been hardly more than a boy and Bear had plunged the knife into him, watching him drop his empty rifle and fall to the ground, his life spilling out of him. Bear knew it was only by the Great Father's hand being upon him that he had managed to come home alive and in one piece.

But what he liked most of all was that never having had a brother of his own, he now had one in Joshua. He'd heard that Charity had left the boy and his mother the house, and maybe, thought Bear, he could move out of his shack and rent the cottage. That might be nice—to be that close to his brother. After all, he had promised Deborah that he'd look after him.

One other promise he made himself: the colored people in Sweetwater were going to get a fair shake from now on, and he wanted them to know the law was not their enemy. Naturally, the Klan would come after him when they heard about this, but he had faced far tougher enemies than the Kluxers, and if it came to a showdown, he would be ready for them.

A few random firecrackers boomed in the distance, as a prelude to the main event, and he cradled his head in his hands and closed his eyes for a moment. As he did, he recalled the names of some of the men he had fought alongside of on the coral reefs red with blood, the beaches strewn with bodies. He forced these images from his mind now and turned to the business at hand. Parker Peele was his new assistant who had been part time before the events of the past several days, and he had been delighted when Bear invited him to go full time. Peele had soldiered with Patton in the eighth army, and he and Bear had struck up an instant friendship.

"Parker, you hold down the fort, while I go on up to the park for the celebration. Anything happens, you come and get me, okay?"

"Yes sir, Chief."

The phone jangled just as Bear headed for the door. Peele answered it, listened for a brief moment, then gave it to Bear. "It's Harley Gurganus from up at Raleigh," he said.

"What's up, Harley?"

"Chief, first of all, congratulations and all that. I'm really proud of you, son, and I know you'll do a fine job."

"Well, thanks, but you didn't call just to tell me that, did you?"

"No, Chief, I surely didn't. It's about Ragg."

"What about him?"

"He's flown like a bird."

Bear felt the floor move beneath him. "What? How did it happen?"

"They were holding him at county, waiting arraignment, and when the news came of the surrender, they decided to let everybody out in the main yard and let them go hog-wild—you know, to let off some steam. While this was going on, that boy slipped out of here, and nobody knows how. Shoot—the guards, inmates—everybody was having too good a time to be paying any attention. He's slick, that one. I'll give him that much."

"Harley, you think he'll come back here?"

"No, he'd be crazy to. If I were in his shoes, I'd light out for as far away from this state as I could get, but then I ain't him, and I don't know what winds his watch."

"Well, when did he escape?"

"We're not sure since the way things have been today, but my guess is around sometime after lunch."

"Harley, I sure wish you had called me sooner."

"I knew you were going to say that. Thing is, I found out not more than two hours ago when they did a count. I tried to get through to you, but long distance couldn't get a circuit open until now. It's been crazy."

"Yeah, I know. Same here. Well, thanks for telling me, but I really don't expect him to come back here. I don't like the man at all, but I can tell you this, he's no fool. I found that out in the Gut."

"I hear you, Chief. Well, y'all take care now, and let me know if anything happens or if I can be of help."

"Ten four, Harley."

Bear hung up and relayed the gist of the conversation to Peele, confirming what his assistant had pieced together from what he'd just heard.

"What now, Chief?"

Bear didn't answer—he was already on the phone to Deborah. She had told him at the funeral that Sunday afternoon, she and Joshua would move their few possessions into the big house, that she wanted to get settled before her first full week of work began. He let the phone ring four times, until it occurred to him she and Joshua were probably at the park, along with just about everybody else in town. He'd go find her and tell her the news.

But Deborah was not *at* the park.

The day had been so hectic at the office, with there being more than the usual number of patients, including heart attacks, strokes, fainting, heat exhaustion and a few bloody noses. One man shot himself in the foot during the day's madness, and another lost the tip of his finger from a highly explosive firecracker called a cherry bomb. She had arrived home much later than usual, wanting only to fix Joshua his supper, then relax and unwind in a leisurely hot bath. While he waited for her to prepare his supper, he kept begging her to let him go to the celebration by himself since she had told him she was too tired for that. After some hesitation, she gave in, making him promise that he'd come straight home after the fireworks were over. Joshua promised he would, and he told her not to worry — that he'd be there with all his friends.

It was eight o'clock when she finally washed the dishes and climbed into the tub. The phone rang. She started to get out to answer it, then realized it was probably another reporter, like all the others who had been trying to get to her all day. She turned up the radio on the little footstool by the tub, letting the music drown out the phone. She sank down into the water, feeling her body start to unwind. She knew that Bear was there to keep an eye on things, and Ragg was safely behind bars, so there was nothing to worry about, was there?

37

1:36 PM, Tuesday, the fourteenth . . .

Ragg had known from the start that he could not stay locked up. An ex-cop who had gone bad wouldn't last very long inside, and when you threw in the thing with the boy—which sooner or later would get out—he'd be looking at some real hard time. Nothing he couldn't get through, of course, but it wouldn't be a picnic. Realizing this, he waited his time, hoping for a diversion, and then the news of the surrender broke. He could not believe his good luck. The prisoners started shouting and yelling, the guards letting everybody out into the main yard. Ragg had stayed in the kitchen, where he washed dishes, hoping that somebody would make a delivery this afternoon.

Sure enough, the Merita bread truck showed up, and Ragg offered to help the man unload, since there was no one else around. When they were through, the driver told Ragg to close the doors, and as he walked around to the front of the truck, Ragg leaped inside the back and closed the door behind him. By the time they reached the main gate, he had concealed himself as best he could behind a stack of cartons in the corner. He held his breath as the truck pulled to a stop for inspection at the main gate. He looked at the rear door, knowing that any second, it would be flung open and a guard would poke his head in. Outside, however, caught up in the excitement of the day, the two guards were passing a bottle back and forth and waved the truck on through with shouts and cheers.

The driver pulled out onto the tar and gravel road leading to the main highway, and after they had rounded a curve, Ragg knew they were no longer visible from the guard tower. He crept along the floor and unlocked thc latch on the right rear door, until it was swinging back and forth with a loud banging noise. Then he flattened himself against the other door and waited, hoping. Hearing the noise, the driver, whose name was Homer Darden, cursed, realizing that the prisoner who had helped him unload had failed to lock the door properly. It didn't surprise him. Anyone dumb enough to get caught didn't have sense to lock a door right. Darden pulled over, leaving the motor idling and went around to latch the door. Just as his face appeared in the doorway, Ragg landed on top of him with his full weight, knocking him to the dirt, then delivered a flurry of blows to the head in quick succession, until he was satisfied the man was unconscious.

Ragg knew he had only seconds, and that's all it took for him to hoist the driver into the truck and close the door so they couldn't be seen from the road. Then he yanked off the tan uniform shirt and trousers and shucked his prison shirt, ripping it into three lengths. In another minute he had the man's arms tied behind his back, his ankles secured and a gag around his mouth so he couldn't cry out when he came to. Now wearing the tan uniform including the cap, Ragg drove to the highway, taking a right away from town until he found a dirt road that looked deserted. He followed this for a mile or so while it wound through a patch of piney woods then braked to a halt in a swirl of dust. He opened the back door, pulled the driver out and had started to drag him into the woods when he suddenly stopped and went back to get the torn shirt. A few minutes later, he had found a place that was hidden from the road and propped Darden up against a tree. Ragg paused for a moment, a bit winded from the exertion and the heat, then using what was left of the shirt, tied the man securely to the tree. As he turned to leave, Darden gave out with a moan. Ragg spun on his heel and slammed him with his fist just above the ear. This was no time to take chances. Eventually someone was bound to find him, but in any case, he felt nothing for the driver. In this world, you had to play the hand you were dealt.

It wasn't until he climbed back into the truck that he realized the rest of his good fortune. Delivery men collected their receipts in cash, and in the small metal box, he found just over $80 dollars in small bills and change. It was all he would need—for now. He put on the cap again, along with a pair of sunglasses he found and looked in the rearview mirror, pleased with the image that looked back at him. No one would ever recognize him, and by the time they got out his picture, which he knew would take every bit of three days, he'd be long gone.

Ragg drove in silence for a while thinking about the plan. The more he thought, the more he liked it, and the more he liked it, the more he laughed to himself. Finally he was laughing out loud while pounding on the steering wheel and shouting over the sound of the straining engine.

"Yessirreebob. Ol' Ragg's gotta long haul to make this afternoon. Got to make a delivery all the way down to little old Sweetwater, and nobody knows it but me."

When he reached Tarboro, he found a hardware store and bought some rope, a knife, a roll of tape and talked the man into selling him a brand-new .38 and a box of bullets for just 12 bucks. Ragg told him it was a birthday present for his brother. It took him until five to reach Sweetwater since the roads were jammed with traffic, and the truck wouldn't go much faster than 45 mph. Once in town, he drove right down Main Street, recognizing a good many of the faces in the milling crowd on the sidewalk. No one paid any attention to the driver of a Merita bread truck. He could see workmen putting up the platform in the park and figured they were planning a celebration tonight: speeches, lemonade, band concert, fireworks—the usual. So much the better, he thought.

Ragg parked in the back lot behind the stores on Main Street and sat there for a few minutes knowing that once the company missed the truck, they'd call the police and the highway patrol would start getting news of it. No need taking a chance. He had to dump it since it would be easy to spot. There were plenty of cars to choose from in the lot, people having come into town from all over to join in the fun. They probably wouldn't come looking for their car until late, and by then, half of them would be drunk, milling around in the dark and probably thinking they forgot where they parked. Tomorrow half of the grown-ups in North Carolina would either be drunk or fighting a hangover and not much use for anything. Ragg got out and walked around, checking one car, then another until he found one with the keys under the floor mat. A black '40 Ford, too. There were a blue zillion of them on the road. From the toolbox in the truck, he took a screwdriver and switched plates with another car. That would make it even more confusing, when the owner of the car reported it stolen. That was the best part of having been in police work, thought Ragg. You knew just what they were thinking and oh my, what a big help that was.

Ragg had only one regret—that he hadn't killed Bear when he had the chance. The Indian's luck was about to run out, though, and Ragg knew that today was the day. Bear had robbed him of his fame and his job and his pride and his freedom. He owed the Indian, and pay day was here. He pulled away from the center of town and drove down river hill, turned off to the left and parked in a spot he had used before. Nobody would be there this time of day—they were all downtown—and he would catch a little nap before dark. He would need all his energy later.

When he awoke, the sun was setting, and he knew it would be dark in a few minutes. After glancing around, he stepped outside the car to empty his bladder. Then he drove up from the river, turning onto Reynold's Avenue, passing by the sign that read Jesse M. Reardon, M.D. Through the bay window, he could see him sitting in his study. Ragg tipped his hat and smiled. He'd have need of ol' doc later on. Everybody had a part to play, and Ragg was going to see they got the chance to do just that.

Darkness fell over Sweetwater, and this made Ragg feel even better. He was home at last and all set to go fishing. Now, all he needed was the right bait, and he knew just where to find it.

38

9:12 PM, Tuesday, the fourteenth . . .

The speeches had been made.

The band had played itself out.

All that was left were the fireworks.

After that, most folks would be ready to go on home and call it a day—and a night. The usual number of rowdies who had drunk more than their fill were still whooping it up, but Bear let them be. He had found Joshua not long after he arrived and asked about his mother. The boy had told him that she had been too tired to come and had told him she was going to get into the bathtub and not get out until she was good and ready. That explained why she hadn't come to the phone, thought Bear.

"Little brother, after the fireworks are over, I'm gonna take you home. Meet me here at my car, okay? Joshua at first looked puzzled, but seeing the look on his friend's face, agreed and then ran off to join his friends. Finally, the last skyrocket went streaking up into the sky, exploding in a shower of sparks. Elizabeth Roberson, the song leader from the Methodist Church, led the crowd in *God Bless America*, and it was over.

Bear didn't have to go looking for the boy. Joshua came running up to him, breathless. "Wow, Bear, did you see that last skyrocket?"

"Yep. Now c'mon, little brother. I have to get you home."

Bear grabbed the bike and tossed it in the back of the Ford and within several minutes, they pulled up in front of the house. Joshua told Bear they were all moved in now, and that he'd have to come to see them, maybe have supper. "My mom's really a good cook, you know."

Bear nodded and took the bike out for Joshua and let the boy wheel it up to the front porch. Before the door could even open, Deborah appeared in a long robe, wearing a look of surprise.

"Chief, you're not arresting my son, are you?"

"Not hardly," said Bear. "I couldn't do that to my blood brother. I just thought it'd be better if I brought him home myself."

"Oh, well, that was thoughtful of you. Any special reason?"

"As a matter of fact, there is. Can I come in?"

"Sure."

Within several minutes, he relayed to her what Gurganus had told him. Both mother and son were shocked at the news.

"Oh, Bear, you don't think he'd come back here, do you? After all that has happened. Wouldn't that be kind of foolish?" Deborah had sat down in Charity's favorite chair and gathered the folds of the robe about her legs.

"You're right, it would be. And I don't really think that's what he's going to do, but I still wanted you to know. Listen, if it'll make you feel any better I'll stay outside in my car until morning. You know—kinda keep an eye on things. By then, maybe they will have picked him up somewhere, and we can all rest easy."

"Oh, there's no need to do that," said Deborah. "You belong back at the station, especially tonight. I bet the phone will be ringing off the hook."

"Yeah, we've already had our hands full this evening. Just a few boys that had too much to drink, and there'll be more of it as the night wears on. Listen . . . will you two be all right staying here by yourselves?" There was a note of genuine concern in his voice that touched Deborah.

"Sure we will. Hey, I have a brave here to take care of me." She put her arm around Joshua and he blushed slightly.

"All right, but do this for me. You sleep upstairs, don't you?"

She nodded.

"Well, I'd feel a whole lot better if you'd lock all the doors and the downstairs windows. And if you hear the slightest noise, you call me, okay?"

"I promise," said Deborah.

Bear nodded and was gone. When he left, Deborah started up the stairs, then remembered what he had said. She went around the house and locked every window and both doors. Then she went back up to her room, thinking how fortunate she was to have someone like Bear to protect her and look after her son. He was right, though. There was no need to take chances.

An hour earlier, when night had fallen in earnest, Ragg had driven the car down the narrow dirt road between the tobacco field and the woods and parked it out of sight. He stood in a clump of trees for a moment, and not detecting any movement downstairs, walked up to the back of the house and let himself in. The screen door off the back porch had been unlocked, just like all the other screen doors in town. He knew about these things. He'd done it so many times before and gotten away with it.

He entered the house cautiously, listening for a moment, then heard her singing. He climbed the stairs, then went down the hall to the door that was closed. He could hear her splashing in the water, enjoying her bath. Standing there with his ear to the door, he'd been tempted to walk right in on her and have a little fun, but this was the wrong time to fool around. He had serious business to attend to, and in less than a minute, he had found the perfect hiding place downstairs in a small closet just off the hall. He closed the door behind him, then scrunched down in the back, draping an old bedspread over him, just in case.

Time passed.

He heard Bear and Joshua come home.

He heard Bear tell her the news of his escape.

He heard Bear remind her to lock up.

He heard Bear leave.

And at that point, it was all Ragg could do to keep from laughing out loud. Yeah, you lock up, little lady, and everything will be just fine. You have Bear's word on it. Ragg remained motionless in the back of the closet, ears cocked to pick up the slightest sound. From time to time, he licked his lips like some ravenous creature waiting to spring out of the musty darkness. He was less than human. He had become a great two-legged rat.

39

11:10 PM, Tuesday, the fourteenth . . .

Deborah's body would not respond. Her mouth felt gummy and it was hard to breathe. She was lying on her side and felt something tight on her wrists. She opened her eyes, blinked hard at the light, her mind refusing to accept what she saw.

Joshua was sitting in a large armchair in the corner of the room, his hands tied behind him, a piece of tape over his mouth. He started to struggle, and she could hear him trying to speak, but she didn't need any words. His eyes telegraphed his fear. Her hands were tied in front, and she had tape over her mouth, and she could not believe it: there he sat on the side of her bed smiling at her.

Ragg!

"Now, don't go getting yourself all worked up, Miz Grayson. I didn't come here to hurt you or the boy, so put your mind at rest. But now, I *do* need your help with something, and if you'll be patient with me, I'll tell you what to do, okay?"

He saw her looking at the gun.

"Don't you worry none about this. Why, if I'd a wanted to hurt y'all, I would have done it long before now. So just calm down and relax. Like I said, nobody's gonna get hurt."

She felt the initial fear start to subside, but in its place anger began to boil within her. She watched as he picked up the phone and dialed a number. The phone beside Jesse's bed rang once, then again. He was not surprised to get a call, for that was part of being a doctor in a small town. It came with the territory.

"Doctor Reardon, speaking."

"Well, doc, this here is your old buddy, Ragg."

"Ragg? What are you—I don't understand." Jesse shook the sleep from his eyes.

"Well, doc, there's not a whole lot you *need* to understand, but I want you to listen real careful like, okay? And try not to get ahead of me. Just let me tell you what I'd like you to do. But first, I want you to talk to a friend of yours."

Ragg removed the tape from her mouth and put the receiver to her lips just long enough so she could do what he thought she would.

"Jesse, it's him. He's got a gun! He's got us tied up and. . . ."

"All right, doc, you get the picture. So here's what I want you to do. Don't you go calling our chief of police or nothing like that 'cuz if I see him pulling up outside before it's time, I might lose my temper and then I couldn't be held responsible. Kinda like old BB. Poor boy didn't know what he was doing."

"Just what is it you want me to do?"

"That's better, doc. What I want you to do is to get up whatever cash you got in the house and bring it over here. Now we both know you take in a lot of money and you must have some of it laying around. Right?"

"Well, I only have. . . ."

"Doc, this is like Truth or Consequences. You don't tell the truth, you got to pay the consequences. So you just bring what you have 'cause a traveling man like me, he needs all the help he can get. When you get here, I'll decide whether or not you pass the test. Now you listen to me, doc. I want you over here in ten minutes with the money. So get moving."

It took just over eight minutes for Jesse to throw on some clothes and grab the stack of loose bills he kept in the lock box in his study. He thought about calling Bear, but knew he couldn't take the chance. In the state of mind Ragg was in, the man could do anything—and probably would. When he arrived at the house, he walked up the wide steps in front and let himself in. The lights were on, but the shades down, and there in the parlor were Deborah and Joshua both trussed up, their mouths taped. Ragg stood there, motioning with the gun for him to come in and close the door.

"Good to see you, doc. Nice to know you're still making house calls. Now if you'll just give me that money, ol' Ragg here will do his part."

Jesse handed over the packet of bills. Ragg thumbed through the one's, five's, ten's. There was just over $100. "Doc, you done real good," said Ragg.

He made Reardon sit in the chair and tie his own ankles securely with the rope. Ragg tied the physician's hands and taped his mouth, then sat down by the small table with the phone.

"Y'all listen to this, now, 'cause this is the good part."

He called the station, the number he knew so well, and when Bear answered, Ragg spoke in a very plain and matter-of-fact voice. He told Bear that he was at Deborah's house, and they were having a little family get-together, with Doc, too, and he wondered if maybe Bear wouldn't mind dropping in. He removed the tape just slightly from Jesse's mouth and said, "Here's doc to verify what I just said."

"Bear, it's all true. I—" Ragg jerked the phone away and pulled the tape back into place.

"Now, Bear, before you get all steamed up, I want to explain the rules to you. Peele is probably out making rounds, and you're holding down the desk, but if he should come back in before you leave, you don't tell him where you're going. Two: you don't make any phone calls. Three: you come right over, you get out of the car in front where I can see you, take off your shirt, turn your pockets inside out. Then drop your pants and turn around nice and slow so I can make sure you're clean. Don't be shy. I want to see skin, boy. And you better be here in ten minutes 'cause I'm counting."

"Ragg, if you hurt anybody, I'll. . . ."

But Ragg had already jerked the phone wires out of the baseboard. Bear slammed down the phone and tried to collect his thoughts. Ragg had worked with criminals so long he had learned their ways, and that made him doubly dangerous. But Bear knew he couldn't do anything now. The longer he waited, the worse it might be. He grabbed the .44 and the Smith and put them in the front seat, even though he knew he could never get either of them into the house the way Ragg would be watching him.

Ten minutes later, having obeyed Ragg's instructions to the letter, Bear joined the others in the living room. Ragg motioned him to stand in front of the others where he could keep the gun pointed directly at him. Ragg knew better than to get close to Bear to tie him up. That would be dangerous. The Indian's eyes were blazing, and Ragg could feel the rage building within him. Let him rage, he thought. There wasn't anything he could do about it.

"Now, y'all just stay put. The *chief* and I are going to go out on the back porch and have a little powwow. I can see you through the windows, so don't anybody try anything funny. And Bear, don't think about yelling or anything. You make one sound, and the boy here will get one in the shoulder. Sure would mess up a good pitching arm."

So saying, Ragg motioned Bear through the back door with his gun. The small porch was flanked by a huge spruce tree on each side. Both men were illuminated faintly by the light coming from the living room. They stood about eight feet apart. Every minute or so, the sound of firecrackers would be heard, punctuated by a cherry bomb that sounded like a blast from a howitzer. It was a good night to work, thought Ragg. People would keep on celebrating, and it provided the perfect cover.

"Well, Tonto, you surely have caused me a peck of trouble. Made me lose my job, get put in jail, I don't know what all. Oh, I know what you're thinking—I can't get away with this. Well, let me tell you how easy it is. I got a car no one knows about and a license plate you can't trace, and I'll be gone from here in the next ten minutes with doc's money. I'll drive somewhere, but you don't know where, until I find a bus station, and then I'll catch a bus to somewhere else, and then maybe a train. Keep putting the miles between us. See, right now, people aren't gonna be worried about some small town ex-police chief on the lam.

They're still gonna be celebrating for the next couple of days, and by that time, this old boy'll be gone with the wind."

Ragg looked up at him, then grinned.

"Dadgum, I knew I left something out." He laughed out loud. "I'm taking the boy with me."

Bear sucked in his breath sharply.

"Oh, just as a keepsake, you know. In the morning, I'll leave him somewhere in the woods off the road, but he'll be all right. Trust me. But if anybody tries to follow me, all bets are off. You understand? I won't be responsible for what happens to him. He's a right good-looking little kid, too." Ragg smiled his crooked smile.

"And don't worry, this time, I won't be coming back again, but before I go, I did want to leave you with a souvenir. Say, which leg was it you got hurt in the war?"

"My left one," said Bear, his mind feverishly trying to find an answer. He knew Ragg meant what he said and was over the edge.

"Well, I guess that leaves us the right one, don't it? Now, like I said, I wouldn't kill you because I could get the chair, but they don't electrocute a man for shooting somebody in the knee-cap. Even if they catch me, when I finish my stretch, I'll be in pretty good shape, but you'll still be hobbling around on one leg using a cane. I swear, Tonto, it looks like your policing days are over before they even got started good. And don't you worry about anybody hearing the shot, since it'll sound like just another cherry bomb. But it's not all bad, boy, because when I shoot you, you're only gonna feel pain for a little bit. You see, I'm gonna finish that whipping I gave you in the Gut. Fact is, when you wake up, you're not even going to know your right name."

Bear didn't think he could beat Ragg's trigger finger, but that didn't matter. He had been wounded twice before and survived. What mattered was that his little brother would not—*must not* fall into the hands of this piece of garbage that tried to pass for a man. He could not allow that to happen. His rush just might throw off Ragg's aim, and if he could get to him, he would take him down, wounded or not. It was not the best of hands, but there were no more cards left in the deck, and he had to play it out.

He took a deep breath and measured the distance between them. It was down to seconds now. Ragg saw the hatred blazing in his enemy's eyes, and he knew he would do this thing now and that he would delight in it and savor the memory for years to come. He cocked the .38 and pointed it down at Bear's right knee while smiling his crooked smile.

The gunfire was the loudest sound the three people in the house had ever heard, and they stared wide-eyed through the open windows, horrified at the scene they had just witnessed, knowing that the image had been burned into their minds forever.

40

11:46 PM, Tuesday, the fourteenth . . .

Lucy sobbed uncontrollably as Jesse held her close to him, stroking her back to stop the trembling. "It's all right," he said. "It's all right."

The others watched. Finally, when she had calmed down and the shaking had stopped, she managed to get the words out.

"I was listening in on the extension. Maybe that's wrong, doctor, but I always do it when a call comes at night. You never know who's going to be on the other end of the line. And anyway, the Lord sent me to look after you, and that's what I'm doing."

Jesse nodded, waiting patiently, realizing how dear she was to him.

"There was no way I was going to let you come on down here alone and face that piece of no-good trash. Lord only knows what he had on his mind, but I knew it was of the devil. So I took the twelve-gauge from where you *thought* you had it hidden in your coat closet in the study. When you keep house for a man, you find out where everything is. Knowing you, I figured it'd be unloaded, but that's all right. I knew where you kept the shells, too, and I put in a number four. Well, before you even got into your car, I was ready to go, and the minute you left, I lit out running as fast as I could. When I got here and saw the shades down in front, I went around back. Then I lay low behind that big spruce where nobody could see me, thinking I was going to have to go inside the house, when all of a sudden, Ragg and Bear came out on the porch."

She paused, taking a long drink from the glass of water that Deborah had gotten her.

"I swear before God, doctor, I never intended to kill him. But then, when I heard him saying what he was going to do to Chief Bear and then, taking Joshua with him—I thought, Lord, we got rid of him once and he came back, and one day Satan might just do this all over again. That was a chance I couldn't take 'cause I love y'all so much."

Her voice dropped to a whisper as she put down the water and clasped her hands in her lap.

"My brothers taught me how to shoot when I was growing up, and I knew I only had one chance, it being a single shot. And that's how it all happened." She shook her head slowly from side to side and dabbed at her eyes.

Each person relived the moment. Those inside remember seeing Ragg being literally hurled off the porch by the force of the blast. Bear remembered staring directly into Ragg's face, waiting for the bullet that would shatter his kneecap, and in the next instant, the man's chest had exploded, Ragg registering total disbelief in the second before he died.

"Lucy," said Bear, "I owe you one."

"Aw, Chief, I'll just mark it down on the books and hope I don't ever have to collect it. The good Lord will mark it down in His, too."

Jesse felt obliged to speak up. "Lucy, all these years, I've been wondering why I hired you, and tonight God gave me the reason I never knew."

"Yes, sir, that's the way the Master works. We serve a mighty God."

"That we do," responded Jesse. He had long since called the ambulance. Whit Sewell had come promptly and Bear explained what had happened while they stood near the body. Whit just shaking his head and saying, "Jumpin' Jehosaphat, would you look at that?" After he left, the five of them sat quietly in the living room, and then Deborah abruptly rose from her chair and went into the kitchen.

"Mom, what are you doing?" said Joshua.

"I'm going to try my hand at making some of Charity's ham biscuits, that's what." She managed a laugh.

"And I'm going to give you a hand," said Lucy. "I'll fry up the ham."

"And I'm going to eat all you can make," said Joshua.

"First," said Deborah, "you're going to set the table for our guests."

An hour later they were still sitting there having polished off nearly two dozen biscuits, Joshua admitting they were almost as good as Charity's. *Almost*, thought Deborah. What a son she had. Between mouthfuls, she warned Lucy that when the news broke, now it would be *her* all those reporters would want to talk to.

"Let 'em come," said Lucy. "I'll run 'em off just like I did that other one. I ain't got time to mess around with people like that."

"But Lucy," said Jesse. "You'll be famous, don't you know that?" He said this with a twinkle in his eye.

"Doctor, let me tell you something. I know what the good book says about killing, but then you know, King David was seven times a rascal and a scoundrel, but still, he was a man after God's own heart. So I'm praying the Lord will forgive me, and maybe I will be a *woman* after his own heart."

Jesse came over to her and hugged her fiercely, holding back the tears. "Lucy Melton, I think you will *definitely* be that."

Lucy threw back her head and shouted, "Glory!"

Later, when they were all talked out, Jesse and Lucy went on home, then Bear went to the door after giving Joshua a big hug. Deborah walked up to him and stood there, not knowing what she was supposed to do, but her arms made the decision for her. She hugged the man, saying nothing, then thrust him from her, looking directly into his eyes.

"How about you coming for supper tomorrow night?" she said.

"Yay," shouted Joshua. "See, I told you."

His mother frowned. "Told him what?"

"Just that . . . you know—you were a good cook."

"Oh," she said.

Bear looked at the both of them, then nodded.

"Make it seven," said Deborah. "I'm a working woman now."

"Seven it is." Then he was out the door.

Fifteen minutes later, her son was safely tucked in bed for the second time. She realized how much she loved him, and how blessed they both were. Only a week ago, Sweetwater had seemed a dreadful place, and then all this had happened. It was her son, though, who astounded her. He was changed forever. He had left a part of his boyhood behind him, and she knew he would never be that little boy again. She studied his face carefully, the small lamp reflecting in his eyes like tiny candles.

"Joshua, do you know how much I love you? Do you really know?"

His eyes misted over. "Sure, Mom. You tell me all the time."

"Well, I'll just have to keep on telling you then, won't I?"

"I guess so." He looked straight into her eyes. "Mom, Buddy's probably not coming back, is he?"

"I don't know, Joshua. It's been a while, so. . . ."

"Mom, can I get another dog? A big one? Like one of those K-9 dogs they have in the Marines? Bear said he'd show me how to train him and everything. And he could protect me if anything happened. Okay?"

She started to give her usual response . . . *we'll see* . . . but suddenly changed her mind. "Why not? I'll get the word out to our patients that my son is looking for a dog."

"A *big* dog."

"Yes, a big dog." She managed to hide her smile.

"Oh, Mom, you're the best mother in the whole world."

"Do you really think so?"

"I *know* so, and nobody better try to tell me different." He yawned. "Mom?"

"Yes, Joshua?"

"I have to go to sleep now. I already prayed once, but I want to pray again. Do you want to hear me?"

"Son, I wouldn't miss it for the world."

Dear God, thank You for taking care of me in the Gut and for sending Bear to rescue me 'cause he's my blood brother now . . . and God, You take good care of Charity now that she's in heaven. I'm happy she's finally with Caleb 'cause I know she loves him an awful lot. And God, I'm sorry that Ragg got killed, but he was a bad man, and Lucy is sorry she did it . . . but not too sorry.

Take good care of my daddy, too. I used to worry about him, but I don't anymore . . . and God, thank You for giving my mom her new job and our new house . . . and Lord, I would talk to You some more, but I'm getting real sleepy so I have to go to bed now. Amen.

"That was wonderful, Joshua. I'll see you in the morning, okay?" She bent down and kissed him, his eyes already closed. Leaving the door open, she entered the living room and went over to the open window. A slight breeze made the curtains billow into the room. The radio had said the unprecedented 14-day heat wave was breaking with cooler air coming in from the northwest.

Deborah sat in Charity's chair and felt the night air glide across her face like the touch of silk. Without warning, a trickle of tears began to course down her cheeks, her lips tasting salt, her heart exploding with joy. In spite of the late hour, the exhaustion and fatigue she experienced earlier were gone. In their place, she felt a new strength and resolve growing deep within.

Deborah ran her palms over the arms of the chair, brushing the fabric that had known the touch of Charity's hands. As she stared into the night beyond the window, the face of the woman she had learned to trust and love came into view. Deborah's soul resounded with the laughter of joy. The laughter of total release. The peace she had been seeking so long had come to her. A deep, sure calm that touched every part of her being.

She knew that everyone who had come into her life—Bear, Charity, Jesse, Lucy—were angels. Each of them had to have been sent to her. Everything that happened had to have been planned. There could be no other explanation. Oh, Charity, she thought. You were right all the time. Deborah knew at this very moment that no matter what came or what God would ask of her, she would walk with Him for the rest of her life.

It was more than just surrender.

She *belonged* to Him.

She looked up now and saw Charity's hand reaching out to her. She took it, fell on her knees by the chair, and one by one, her words became a prayer as leaves and limbs become a tree. The night blossomed into song all about her, and God saw it and knew that it was good.

The Blessing for Going Forth

Like Abraham, I have been a sojourner, driven before the wind in many a land. In a hundred-year-old house, this story first saw north Georgia light and flowed onto the page like quicksilver.

Time ran like a river by my orchard of prayers, the fruits of the spirit ripening in the sun. When my strength would ebb, the Holy Spirit, *Ruach HaKodesh,* would send the ancient voltage coursing through me that I might not falter but press on to the prize.

Lord, I know that for every hurting Deborah and lost Joshua, You send us a Charity and Standing Bear. Their kin and kind are salt and light, their presence a sermon beyond words.

Bless this book to the nourishment of all who are hungry. May it be like those other stories once told around desert campfires, when You wrestled with Jacob and named him Israel.

O, Lord, may we one day soon be witness to another match this mighty.

Ron Levin
March 1996

If you enjoyed *Devil's Gut,* I invite you to read
my first book, *The Long Journey Home*
(ISBN 0-9640720-0-9). In the event you are not
able to purchase it through your local bookstore,
you may order direct. Copies are ten dollars,
including postage. Please mail your order as
follows:

Ron Levin, Director, My Father's Business
4303 Old Greenville Highway
Liberty, SC 29657

Baruch Hashem Adonai!
Blessed Is the Name of the Lord